The Jennings

by

S. M. R. Cooper

This is a work of fiction. All characters, organizations, and events portrayed in this novel are either products of the author's imagination or are used fictitiously.

A CooperWolf Book

"real life beyond imagination"

This work is dedicated to my parents

For teaching me how to love

How to work hard

And how to rescue myself

Acknowledgements

Thanks to all the people who took the time to give me feedback about the Jennings, their romance, and their adventures. And, as always, many thanks to Patrick and to TheChannel 2600 for helping me with the technical support.

CHAPTER ONE

Christopher Jennings sat back in the carriage. "I say, Rem," he began, his voice sounding a bit weary. "Are you planning on touring London all night?"

"I am, my boy!" Lord Remington said jovially, clapping his friend on the shoulder. "I have much to celebrate, after all!" He had earlier that day become engaged to the honourable Miss Letitia Godwin, who had accepted his proposal not half an hour after he had won a significant bet on a horse race. "Three thousand, by gad!" he chortled, taking a drink from his flask before tucking it away in his pocket. "And the prettiest girl in London, to boot!" He paused, and snickered, and clapped Jennings on the shoulder again. "Except I think you might disagree!" he said, grinning.

Jennings lifted one eyebrow. "Why ever would I suggest your fair bride-to-be was anything but the loveliest creature on earth?" he said somewhat defensively. "In fact," he added, his eyes twinkling. "I could not at first understand why such a pretty girl would become so attached to *you*."

"Oh, I see how it is!" Remington laughed. He leaned forward and said confidentially, "I wondered that myself, at first, you know. But there she is, smiling at me exactly as though I've won her heart." He shook his head in apparent disbelief. "I'm a lucky chap, ain't I, Jennings?"

"You are," Jennings agreed. "But she is lucky too, Rem ... assuming you live through the night. I don't know how you keep on like this, going from one place to the next so far into the wee hours. I'm so knackered I can hardly stand!"

Remington expressed some disappointment. "Never say you're giving up, Jennings! We've still got hours to spend at Timothy's!"

"Timothy's!" Jennings exclaimed. "I thought we were going to Sir Montague's card-party!"

"We are!" Remington said. "But *after that* it's on to Timothy's!"

"Oh, no, no, no!" Jennings said, waving his hands to fend off any argument on the matter. "I will go with you to Montague's, but then you must take me home." He laughed. "I do not know what is in your flask," he added. "But it gives you far more energy than I can summon!"

"Hollands," Remington said, patting the pocket where he had slipped his flask. He surveyed his friend through narrowed eyelids. "You *are* looking a bit worn, my boy," he allowed. He grinned then, and his eyes held a knowing gleam. "You wasted your energies at Lady Morton's," he said. "Dancing with that girl."

Jennings looked slightly embarrassed. So that's why you thought I would disagree," he said. "About Letitia."

"Indeed!" Remington agreed. "For your eyes are all on – what was her name? – Miss Carlisle, and I think not even the delightfully perfect Letitia will compare for you now." He smiled. "But that's all right for me, I suppose, isn't it? I'll have my Letitia, and you will have Miss Carlisle."

"Have Miss Carlisle?" Jennings said. "We have barely been introduced! I only danced one dance with her!"

"If we had not been already promised to Lady Halworth's supper, you would be dancing with her still!" Remington said, adding with a touch of sentimentality, "But I could not bear the thought of celebrating my engagement without my closest friend!"

Jennings smiled. "And I would not be anywhere else," he assured him. "Except my bed," he added regretfully. "I will be no use to you at all in an hour. I will go with you to Montague's party, and then – I am terribly afraid – I will be obliged to bid you good night."

"Very well," Remington relented, hanging his head like a lectured schoolboy. Suddenly he looked up again, beaming with renewed excitement. "But you will join us tomorrow for lunch?" he asked. "Letitia and me? I'm to call on her at one o'clock."

"I promise I'll be there," Jennings said, chuckling. "Shall I meet you at your house, or shall you come to fetch me?"

"I will come to fetch you, I think," Remington said after a moment's consideration. "Since I do not entirely know where I might end up!" He laughed. "Who knows what might happen after Timothys?"

Jennings shook his head. "You are insane, my boy!" he said, grinning. "I hope the fair Letitia knows what she is getting herself into!"

"Oh," Remington breathed in mock seriousness. "I certainly hope she does *not*! Or she will bolt, I am sure of it!" He laughed again, and then gestured out the window of the carriage. "It's Montague's," he said. "Say," he added with a sly wink. "Perhaps Miss Carlisle's father will be here – I believe he is the very-gruff-and-grouchy Sir James Carlisle – and you might ask for his daughter's hand in marriage."

"Of course," Jennings responded drily, rolling his eyes. "It could not possibly be too soon for such a course of action on my part, simply because Miss Carlisle – I am quite convinced – does not remember my name."

* * *

Lady Morton's house was still ablaze with light as her guests continued to drink and to dance far into the wee hours of the morning. Most of the doors to both the upper balcony and the garden were propped open, allowing lively music to pour out into the warm night air, and groups of guests milled in and out of these doors, gathering on the balcony to look out over the neighbouring park or strolling in twos and threes among the carefully tended shrubbery of the garden. Some couples, as the night wore on, moved to the very back of the garden, taking advantage of the ample vegetation to conceal them from public view, but for the most part the guests remained close to the house, refilling their wine glasses at every opportunity and engaging one another in increasingly boisterous conversation.

Miss Elizabeth Carlisle stood at the edge of the balcony, leaning against the stone parapet and gazing out over the park. How strange it looked at night, she mused, with the moonlight glinting off benches and statues and casting stark shadows among the trees. Even at nearly one in the morning, she could see people moving in the park.

She had only come to the party to humour her stepmother, the exquisite Mrs. Charlotte Carlisle, who had told her some days ago, with a tone of some irritation, that a young lady must not sequester herself into an unnecessary spinsterhood. Elizabeth had tried to protest, but Mrs. Carlisle would hear no refusals, and all but forced Elizabeth to accompany her to Lady Morton's party.

"It's no good being shy, my dear," she counseled her

stepdaughter. If Elizabeth felt it ironic to have the world explained to her by a woman barely ten years her elder, she did not reveal it, nor did she bother to point out that it was not shyness that prompted her to stay home but rather a deep dislike for insipid conversation and frippery people. She had rather docilely followed Miss Carlisle, and had been fortunate enough to find a few of her friends with whom to pass the time, but the gentlemen seemed disinclined to converse with her or to ask her to dance. I suppose, she thought, that I am already a spinster, and not any sort of beauty compared to these more glamorous ladies in their elaborate gowns. It did not occur to her that her appearance was in fact very appealing, and her manner quite pleasing, but the rather dark specter of her father – even though he was absent from this particular gathering – stood always beside her, frightening away prospective suitors with his cold rudeness and domineering nature. Who would want such a man for a father-in-law? And so more than one gentleman looked at Elizabeth out of the corner of his eye, admiring her beauty and her ever-present smile, only to shrug his shoulders in resignation and move on to someone whose father was more amenable.

But late in the evening, she encountered a less skittish gentleman. He had spent some time in a cluster of young men, one of whom had apparently become recently engaged, and while he did not appear to be drinking as determinedly as his friends, he certainly seemed to be ensconced in their conversation. He spared no attention for the party going on around him, even as more than one lady sneaked glances at this handsome, affable man and wished that he would ask her to dance. But when Elizabeth moved toward the balcony in search of fresh air, he turned from his cronies and held the door for her as though he had been awaiting her for some time.

"Thank you, sir," she said warmly, and went out onto the balcony.

He did not follow her outside, but when she returned several minutes later, he came over to her and made a small bow. "Forgive my intrusion, miss," he began solicitously. "I hope you will not find me too forward, but I was wondering if you would care to dance?"

Elizabeth's cheeks coloured slightly, and gave a smile rather more self-conscious than usual. "I – I would be delighted, sir," she said, accepting his proffered arm and going with him onto the dance floor.

"Please allow me," he said as they joined the other dancers. "To introduce myself: I am Christopher Jennings. My friend there –" He nodded his head toward the group of gentlemen with whom he had been spending the evening. "Is a great friend of Lady Morton's."

"It is a pleasure to make your acquaintance, sir," Elizabeth said, relaxing more into her normal self in the face of Mr. Jennings' broad genial smile and easy-going manner. "I am Elizabeth Carlisle."

They chatted easily about innocuous things during the dance, and afterward, he gallantly escorted her off the dance floor, where her stepmother was waiting for her with a delighted grin spread almost indecorously across her face.

"I certainly hope I might see you again, Miss Carlisle," Mr. Jennings said, bowing again. He turned and bowed also to Mrs. Carlisle, and turned then to rejoin his party.

"My dear, how wonderful!" Mrs. Carlisle said when he had gone. "He is quite the thing! Why, half the ladies in the room have been casting eyes at him! – and he gives them not a glance, but *you* he asks to dance!" She clapped her hands together in glee and gave a tinkling little laugh. "Perhaps there is hope for you yet, my dear!"

Elizabeth tried to ignore her embarrassment at her stepmother's well-meant but rather indelicate behaviour. "We only had one dance," she said gently. "I doubt he even remembers my name."

It was not much later that Mr. Jennings and his friends left Lady Morton's, and Elizabeth wandered through the party, speaking occasionally to this friend or that, completely unaware that Mr. Jennings had any regard for her whatsoever. It seemed unlikely, after all, given that he was one perhaps seven gentlemen in the last two years who had bothered to dance with her or even to acknowledge her existence. Being a practical person, however, Elizabeth was quite contented to have enjoyed her dance with Mr. Jennings, and if she felt any futility in wishing to see him again, she did not let it dampen her spirits. In fact, she seemed to be much more cheerful now than when she had come to Lady Morton's some hours ago.

She stood for some time on the balcony, her attention seemingly on the park below but her mind quite somewhere else. Eventually she realized that she was now alone, that all of the other party-goers had either gone down into the garden or back to the dancing. It had become chilly too, and Elizabeth decided to seek out her stepmother and ask to go home; she could stare out a window just as easily form the comfort and warmth of her own bedchamber.

Pushing away from the parapet, she walked across the wide balcony toward the doors that opened onto the ballroom.

Suddenly a powerful hand grabbed her from behind, wrapping strong fingers around her throat before she could cry out. With a swiftness that did not seem possible, Elizabeth was pulled off her feet and into the air, flying over the stone railing and into the darkness as her arms and legs flailed helplessly against her abductor.

* * *

Christopher Jennings climbed wearily up the stairs to his front door. He had instructed the servants not to wait up for him, and so the entry hall was quite dark; rubbing his bleary eyes in hopes of navigating the darkness more easily, he made his slow way up the stairs toward his room.

As he neared the door to his bedchamber, he was assailed by all-too-familiar feeling. Chills ran up his spine and down his arms, and a heavy foreboding settled over his heart – the slate had something to say to him, and it was likely not good.

Finding a sudden burst of energy, he bounded up the last few stairs and down the narrow hall to his room. The door had been left open, and he saw that his housekeeper had stoked up a fire for him that still smoldered, giving off a flickering red light that showed him the way to his writing desk. There, in the large center drawer, was a square wooden box, its lid adorned with elegant carvings depicting a cheerful garden scene. It was a very old box, its edges smoothed down by years of handling, and Jennings' hand reached out for it with a reverence that contrasted sharply with his apparent urgency.

He carefully opened the lid, revealing an irregularly shaped piece of slate. As he gazed upon it, a picture formed unbidden in his mind of Miss Carlisle, and of the park that bordered Lady Morton's house, yet the only words written upon the slate were: "Save her."

"Good God," he murmured, and, turning abruptly on his heel, he raced headlong back down the stairs and out into the cold night.

* * *

The claws that carried her, flailing, off of the balcony now wrapped around her waist as she was dragged down onto the grassy ground of the park. She was pulled violently through bushes that tore at her skin and her clothing, and, although her hands scraped at the dirt and clutched at clumps of grass, she was powerless against her attacker's incredible strength. She tried to scream, but one giant claw, still curled around her throat, now squeezed until her vision turned black and she feared she would lose consciousness.

A second massive claw ripped down her shoulder and back, tearing the fabric of her gown as though it were paper and cutting a trench into her side. The movement cause the other claw to loosen its hold on her throat, and she gasped a desperate breath in and tried again to scream. The claw clamped down, digging into the flesh of her neck, and shoved her face into the dirt. Her gown was completely torn from her as the second claw raked down her legs, and, as she struggled to breathe through the grass and soil clogging her nose and mouth, she felt the agonizing stab of her attacker sinking large fangs into her hip. Blood spurted from her, and this, coupled with the lack of air, made her lightheaded and weak; she found that her arms and legs were increasingly heavy, and that she could barely move any part of her.

Abruptly the claws released her, and air rushed into her grateful lungs. Before she could react to this unexpected reprieve, her attacker dealt her a stunning blow to the stomach, sending her tumbling under a bush. The pain was overwhelming, but what mattered to her more was that her breath was entirely forced from her. She curled up, her arms around her stomach, but this afforded her no protection as the blows came again – one after the other, in her stomach, her face, her legs, her back. She still lay under the bush, its sharp branches stabbing into her while unrelenting claws scratched and punched her. Her blood poured out of her, and then finally all consciousness, and she lay pale and still.

The claw reached out once more, slowly, and delicately scooped up the chain that Elizabeth wore around her neck. With a sudden yank, the claw tore through the chain, taking it – and the ring suspended from it – off into the night.

* * *

Jennings hurried as quickly as decorum allowed, back to Lady Morton's and into the ballroom still lively with dancing. His sharp eyes, no longer befuddled by the weariness that had assailed him half an hour ago, easily found Lady Morton, standing beside Mrs. Carlisle and speaking quietly about something that made both women laugh.

"Lady Morton," he announced himself, coming to stand before her. He could hardly explain to them that an antique slate had given him special knowledge of events, but he had prepared a plausible excuse for seeking out Miss Carlisle; he hoped that Mrs. Carlisle would help rather than hinder his efforts. "I realized when I arrived home that a piece of jewelry had snagged on my cuff and I had inadvertently stolen it from the lady with whom I was dancing." He looked at Mrs. Carlisle and made a slight bow. "I believe it is Miss

Carlisle's, ma'am, if you might help me find her so that I can return her property to her."

Mrs. Carlisle's eyes darted briefly toward the balcony door. She smiled warmly – perhaps too warmly – and extended her hand. "I am most happy to deliver it, sir."

Mr. Jennings looked down for a moment and then back at Mrs. Carlisle, smiling a bit self-consciously as he explained, "I was hoping – forgive me, ma'am – I was hoping to be able to deliver it to her myself." *Please allow this*, he thought with well-concealed apprehension – he had no actual jewelry to show.

Now both women smiled broadly at him. "How kind of you!" Lady Morton said, her eyes lighting up with the thought of a budding romance between this very personable man and one of her favourite friends, sprouting up here at her own party. Mrs. Carlisle placed her outstretched hand on Mr. Jennings' arm and said, "I quite understand, sir! I am sure Elizabeth will be very gratified … to have her jewelry back!" She lifted an eyebrow knowingly and angled her head once more toward the balcony door. "She is on the balcony, I believe, sir, enjoying the night air."

Jennings nodded gratefully and made quick bows to the women. Acutely aware of their scrutiny, he hoped his expression remained one of self-conscious embarrassment rather than of the dread that was swiftly overtaking his heart. Once on the balcony, he saw that only two people were there – a man in deep blue standing very close to a blonde woman in a green gown – neither of whom looked as though they were aware of much outside of their conversation.

"Where could she be?" he mused under his breath. He glanced over the parapet into the garden, where many couples and groups of friends milled about; none of them was the lovely girl with whom he had danced some hours before. He could hardly start bellowing her name out, but he felt a growing sense of urgency, as though seconds rather than minutes would make the difference in Miss Carlisle's fate. Closing his eyes, he took a deep breath and silently asked the now-distant slate where he should look.

In his mind's eye he saw again the image of the park, with all of its trees and shadows – and now a darker shadow beneath it, broken and unmoving, and what looked to be a pool of blood.

His eyes flew open, and, wasting no time, he dashed down the staircase that led from the balcony to the gardens, moving past party-goers who were largely far too engrossed in their conversations – or too inebriated – to take notice of him at all. He pushed his way through Lady Morton's carefully shaped shrubs to the low stone wall that bordered her grounds, and debated whether he should call out. Perhaps not, he decided; if Miss Carlisle was not there, he would only create a scene, which would do neither of them any good.

He looked over his shoulder – no one was watching that he could determine – and hoisted himself over the wall. Landing with a soft thump on the park lawn, he tried to see through the foliage with only the light from Lady Morton's house and a faint moon to help him.

"Wherever have they gone off to?" he heard Lady Morton's voice, coming down from the balcony.

"It's not like Lizzie to wander off," Mrs. Carlisle answered.

Jennings looked for a second in their direction, but then returned his attention to the dark ground, stepping carefully through the twisting branches and moving them aside with tentative hands. "Miss

Carlisle," he whispered. "Are you here?"

"They must be in the garden somewhere," he heard Lady Morton saying, even as his foot came in contact with something that was neither ground nor branch.

Looking down, he saw with alarm a slender, bloodstained wrist. "Oh, God!" he cried out, pulling his foot back and immediately crouching down. There beside him, almost hidden beneath a bush, was the body of a woman, her clothes torn nearly off of her, and every inch of her covered with dirt and blood. Her skin, where he could see it, was as pale as death, and her eyes, half-closed, were glazed and sightless. She did not appear to be breathing.

"Lady Morton!" he shouted. "Lady Morton!" He put his head on Miss Carlisle's chest; she was in fact not breathing, but, although her skin was ice cold to his touch, he thought he could detect the smallest tremor, the tiniest beating of her heart.

Lady Morton and Mrs. Carlisle had already descended to the gardens; at Mr. Jennings' cries, Lady Morton bounded in a most unladylike manner to the wall, over which she could see Mr. Jennings kneeling beside a still and crumpled form. Next to her, Mrs. Carlisle – and another guest, Mrs. Driscoll, who had come to the wall to see what was happening – gave shrieks of dismay, and Mrs. Driscoll fainted, landing in her husband's arms even as he himself blanched upon seeing Miss Carlisle's body.

"Temple!" Lady Morton yelled over her shoulder to her butler. "Temple, help!"

Jennings ignored all this noise, instead focusing on the woman who lay apparently dead before him. Not knowing what else to do, he chafed her arms and the sides of her face. "Miss Carlisle," he called to her, his voice barely above a cracked whisper. "Elizabeth." He leaned over her, his silent prayers filling the space between them almost as physical objects. "Elizabeth."

Overshadowed by the hushed murmurs of concerned partygoers and Mrs. Carlisle's despairing sobs, into the stillness that now sat heavy over the gloomy park, came a breath - a stifled, gasping breath. And then another, and another. Elizabeth's hand twitched, and then her bruised and battered body shuddered.

Her eyes opened, just for an instant, and she saw Jennings' kind face staring down at her. "Help me!" she choked out with the last of her strength, and then she fell into unconsciousness.

CHAPTER TWO

Christopher Jennings slowly mounted the staircase to Lady Morton's second floor, to the room where Elizabeth had been recuperating for three days.

"She is much improved," Lady Morton had told him when he arrived. "She is able to eat and to converse for short times." Her expression darkened as she continued, "Dr. Pemberly was quite aghast at the extent of her injuries. He spent nearly three hours cleaning and stitching that monstrous cut on her side, and she bore it so stoically!" Her eyes filled with tears at the memory. "But he was here again this morning, and he expressed great relief and hope at how she has mended so far." She smiled then, and, putting a kind hand on Mr. Jennings' arm, she guided him toward the stairs. "She will be quite happy to see you, I'm sure," she said warmly. "She is all gratitude."

Jennings managed a small smile in return, but inside he was consumed with guilt. If only he had returned home to the slate sooner; if only he had run faster! If only he had thought to look in the park before returning to the house. If only ... well, it did him no good to dwell on such thoughts, since he had done the best he could, but his steps were heavy as he approached the door to Elizabeth's room, and his hand when he raised it to knock was shaking quite badly.

"Come in," a woman's voice said in answer to his tentative knock. The voice was much stronger than he expected to hear, and when he opened the door he discovered that it belonged not to Elizabeth, but to her stepmother, who stood by the side of the bed looking down on Elizabeth with undisguised concern and affection.

15

When Jennings entered, both women turned to look at him, Elizabeth inclining her head slightly on the pillow and peering out through eyes that, even after three days, were still swollen and bruised almost to the point of being closed over.

"Mr. Jennings!" Charlotte Carlisle said brightly, gesturing at her stepdaughter with a small wave of her hand. "You see she is doing much better!"

Jennings surveyed the girl lying in the bed, dwarfed rather pitifully by a mountain of pillows and blankets. Her arms were wrapped in lengths of bandage, and there were cuts and bruises all over her face and neck. Her hair, tousled around her pale face, had been cut haphazardly in a few places, since the blood that had caked onto it proved too difficult to wash away. She lay still, and when she moved at all it was with extreme care. If this was "doing much better", then he was indeed surprised that she had survived the attack at all.

"Miss Carlisle," he said softly, his voice threatening to break with his stifled emotions. "I am so, so very sorry!"

Elizabeth attempted to open her eyes a little wider; Mr. Jennings stood solicitously beside her bed, looking down on her with such tenderness and concern that her heart was quite touched, and she felt tears of gratitude stinging her eyelids. "Mr. Jennings," she whispered haltingly, her throat still ravaged. Her hand lifted slightly off the bed and reached toward him, and he quickly bent and took the hand in his own.

"When I realized," he said, and cleared his throat. "When I saw that you needed help, I ran as quickly as I could to you. I –" He cleared his throat again, and looked down, unable to meet her gaze, and his jaw stiffened as he struggled with his feelings. "I should have been faster."

Her fingers squeezed his as much as they were able. "No!" she said, her face showing the forcefulness that her voice could not manage. Her brows drew together, and tears slid down her cheeks. "You saved my life!"

Jennings did not know what to say, or how to argue the merits of asking Elizabeth to blame him as thoroughly as he blamed himself. He stood in silence, still looking down at her and holding her hand, wanting to wipe away her tears and to erase all of her hurting.

Mrs. Carlisle spoke into this silence, her expression and tone at once pleasant and yet guarded, as though she felt obliged to share unhappy tidings. "It is quite fortunate you were there, Mr. Jennings," she said, smiling at him. "Almost miraculous that you knew she would be in the park."

Jennings lowered his eyes, bowing his head and replying diffidently, "I had a feeling, ma'am. I – I can't explain it."

"Because," Mrs. Carlisle continued as though he had not spoken. "As Lizzie's father asked me just this morning – what on earth was she doing in the park at such an hour?" She gave a nervous sort of laugh, and reached out and took Elizabeth's other hand in hers. "I tried to explain to him what you explained to me, Lizzie – I really did – but you know how he is." She gazed at Elizabeth with an almost desperate pleading in her eyes. "How am I supposed to explain to him, when he does not wish to listen?" She seemed ready to burst into tears, and her elegant hand, wrapped tightly around Elizabeth's, shook slightly.

Elizabeth well understood her stepmother's dilemma: Sir James

Carlisle was not an easy man to talk to about anything, certainly not about things that fell outside the common. How was his wife to press him on this matter – that had created an extraordinary amount of gossip in the town – when she could not even successfully debate with him on changing what he ate for breakfast? And, of course, it could not be expected that Charlotte would take sides against her own husband, for several reasons not the least of which was Sir James' great ire were she to do so.

"Do not distress yourself, Charlotte," Elizabeth murmured. "I understand." She turned her face away from her stepmother and went on in an even smaller voice, "I know my own father."

Mrs. Carlisle gave way then to a sob, quickly stifled behind the lace handkerchief she held in her free hand. "He began to question me!" she said, her eyes glistening. "Asking me why I was not with you. I did stand firm on that, I can assure you! – it is perfectly permissible to walk onto the balcony unattended, in full view of everyone!" She paused, composed herself and forced a new smile. "But he would not entertain any other word that I said," she added, shaking her head. "When I said that something had carried you off the balcony, he – he said that it was total nonsense." She blinked away the tears that still threatened to spill over. "He said it was preposterous," she said, shaking her head again. "But if he would but come here and see you, dearest! – he would know that only some great monstrous creature could have inflicted these injuries upon you!"

Mr. Jennings listened to this wordlessly, feeling increasing confusion, but at this last he felt compelled to interrupt. "Surely, ma'am," he said, looking at Mrs. Carlisle with a puzzled frown. "Her father has come to see her?"

Impossibly, Elizabeth suddenly looked even more pitiful, and she sank low into the pillows and closed her eyes. Her stepmother's smile faltered for a moment, and she answered with resigned sadness, "Indeed no, sir. He is ... sure ... that whatever the nature of the attack, it would not have occurred if she had not run off unaccompanied."

A sound like an angry sob came from Elizabeth's tortured throat, and she opened her eyes again to stare at Mrs. Carlisle. "I did not do that!" she protested weakly, and, as this pronouncement was made with the last remnant of her strength, she gave way to a fit of coughing that shook her battered body and caused her to grimace in pain. "I ... did ... not!" she gasped in between coughs.

"Lizzie!" Mrs. Carlisle cried, leaning over her stepdaughter and gently stroking the side of her face. "You mustn't do this to yourself! You know I believe you, and that Lady Morton believes you! Anyone who has ever met you would believe you!"

"I believe you," Mr. Jennings said quietly. He had released her hand when she began coughing, but, now that the fit was subsiding, he impulsively took her hand again.

"You see?" Mrs. Carlisle said triumphantly, smiling in earnest. "You are not abandoned, dearest, whatever notions your father may get into his head!" She looked out of the corner of her eye at Mr. Jennings. "Sir James is ... old-fashioned," she explained delicately. "He does not favour women to be unaccompanied – even on a balcony where everyone might see them – but he did allow that such behaviour did not violate propriety. He will not, however, no matter what I say to him, believe that any sort of creature or person could have spirited Lizzie away from the balcony unseen. He feels that she has fabricated such a tale in order to protect the identity of someone he assumes is Lizzie's clandestine lover."

Sir James' interpretation of events seemed to Jennings to be, at the least, ridiculous, and decidedly unfair. Good Lord, it was his own daughter! – even if she had in fact been in the park with someone, did she then deserve such a horrible fate as she had suffered? Hoping he was successfully hiding his disapproval of her husband, Jennings asked Mrs. Carlisle, "Does he think, then, that this supposed lover attacked Miss Carlisle?"

"I do not know for certain what he thinks about that," Mrs. Carlisle admitted sadly. "But I believe that he feels Lizzie's lover should be the one who takes care of her now." She sobbed again, and squeezed Lizzie's hand. "He feels that her behaviour – he thinks she went into the park on her own, you see – he feels that she has brought about her own ruin, and that this person he imagines she went to meet should take equal blame."

Jennings did not know what to say to this. He gazed down at Miss Carlisle with great compassion and worry writ plainly on his face. For her part, if she had attended to any of their conversation she gave no sign, and the tears that hovered at the corners of her eyes were accompanied by neither sound nor any change in her expression. "How can I fault him?" she said finally, her voice hoarse. "He judges all the same; why should I be any different?"

Mrs. Carlisle abandoned all attempts not to weep openly. "Because you are blameless, dearest!" she cried, still wiping at her eyes with her handkerchief. "You should not be judged!"

Jennings' jaw tightened as he watched Miss Carlisle's bruised

20

and woebegone face: clearly she had no hope that her father would alter his opinion, and the life that now lay before her was perhaps even more frightening in its uncertainty than all that she had already endured.

* * *

Lady Morton came to Elizabeth's room late in the afternoon. She was evidently incensed beyond the point of articulating thoughts, and she stood for a moment with her hands clasped almost desperately in front of her, and silently struggled to control her agitated breathing.

"My dear," she said, when she at last found her tongue. "A trunk has been delivered here for you, from your home."

Elizabeth looked at Lady Morton with curiosity. "I believe," she said, pausing frequently to catch her breath. "That my stepmother was sending some of my things, since I will likely be here for some days." Realization struck her, and she added, "Is that upsetting to you, ma'am? If it is, I readily understand, and am more than happy to arrange to be brought ho–"

Lady Morton held up her hand to stop Elizabeth talking. "Dearest girl!" she said with a tone that would not brook argument. "You may stay here as long as you wish! You are certainly in no position to travel even down the hall! – and I will not allow you to have any silly notions of 'arranging' anything!" She shook her head. "Indeed, it is quite the opposite, Elizabeth! It is not your stepmother, but your father who has sent the trunk. And he has sent it with this note." She pulled two folded sheets of paper from her sleeve with a

21

hand that trembled in anger. She opened her mouth to read the note aloud, but then apparently reconsidered, and looked at her young guest with an expression of utmost compassion. "I fear that it will upset you, my dear," she said more quietly. "Perhaps I shall not read it to you?"

Elizabeth lay completely still, a crushing weight on her chest. Although she wanted very much to believe that her father had changed his mind, had somehow found the place in his heart where she ought rightly to be, she could not imagine, on having known him her whole life, that he had written anything in the note but his continued disapproval.

"Do not distress yourself," she said, her voice still hoarse, and now quite forlorn. "I am prepared, I think, to hear whatever is written there." She was not sure that she believed her own words, but it seemed better to know for certain than to wonder what it said.

Lady Morton gazed at her for another moment, her heart breaking for Elizabeth's sake. Then, her voice trembling now more than her hands, she read Sir James' message aloud.

"My dear Lady Morton," it began. "That you have sheltered Elizabeth is a kindness that shows the goodness of your heart, but it also shows, I believe, a tendency to place kindness above Christian duty. Despite my best efforts, Elizabeth has clearly defied all my moral teachings, and has brought her fate upon herself. I would be remiss to forgive her a transgression so easily avoided had she simply followed ordinary feminine modesty; her denial that she went into the park for a clandestine meeting, in the face of all evidence to the contrary, has made the situation even more ridiculous. If you wish her to stay in your care, I can only think that God will reward you for your inordinately giving nature. When she has outworn her welcome, however, do not think to send her here, for I cannot in good conscience allow such a wanton girl into my home. As far as I am concerned, the girl I have raised is dead to me, and this girl you now entertain, whose scandalous behaviour is so far outside what is acceptable, has replaced her without any regard for my feelings or for the honour of our family name. I have sent some things to you for her – at the request of my wife, who has, unfortunately, a weakness of spirit when it comes to her stepdaughter – but for my part, I must assert most strongly that Elizabeth Carlisle is no longer any daughter of mine. I remain, in all other endeavours, your most obedient servant, Sir James Carlisle."

The silence following Lady Morton's reading of the letter was for several seconds broken only by her own breathing, still drawn sharply in and out of her nose as she quivered with disgust for Sir James – a man she had, until today, considered a friend. For her part, Elizabeth did not know what to say or how to feel. Her heart had broken entirely in two upon hearing her father's sentiments delivered so coldly – not even to herself but to Lady Morton! Had she been such a wretched daughter that he could find no affection for her at all? – could he not even oblige himself to come and see her and tell all this to her face? His opinions of what he dismissively referred to as the "weaker sex" were well-known to her – and to anyone of Sir James' acquaintance – but that he would be so single-minded as to give her no benefit of the doubt seemed to Elizabeth to be unfairly cruel. "I have always been honest with him," she murmured, her ragged voice suffused with emotion. I have always been the best daughter, and the most honourable person, that I could be. And he treats me now as though we have never met.

Tears flowed over her cheeks, stinging the scratches and cuts that so harshly decorated her face. What would she do now? Where could she turn? She could hardly stay with Lady Morton forever; even if her ladyship were to suggest it, Elizabeth could not bear the thought of hurting Lady Morton – who would certainly feel the disapprobation by society of her sheltering a ruined girl.

A soft cough from the doorway startled both women, and Lady Morton turned quickly to look behind her. "Oh, Mr. Jennings!" she said. "I did not know you were there, sir!" She smiled and reached out a hand to him. "Do come in, sir! I believe Miss Carlisle would greatly love a visit from a friend!"

"Indeed, ma'am," Mr. Jennings said, stepping into the room. His stern expression suggested that he had heard all that Sir James had written, and that it had caused in him a great and crushing anger, but he ignored that for the moment, and smiled warmly at Elizabeth, holding out to her the bouquet of wild flowers that he had brought. "Flowers for you, Miss Carlisle," he said. "I hope they might bring you at least some measure of cheer, if nothing else."

Elizabeth looked up at the man who had been her saviour, the man who had been all kindness and friendship, who had asked no questions and made no judgments, even though her story – as she readily admitted herself – was improbable. She saw in that instant, as Mr. Jennings stood there offering her flowers, a great truth: not everyone felt as her father did, and to judge herself by her father's standards was unfair. She had always known it, but had hidden it away in favour of pleasing the only man who had been a part of her life. Why had she done that? – when she had disagreed with him in so many things, why had she stayed silent? Why had she considered his views ahead of her own, when his regard for her had always been so ... conditional? Why had she done that? Well, because that is the way it is done, and parents should be honoured ... but should she not have been honoured as well? Looking into Mr. Jennings' eyes, she caught a glimpse of a happier world where her father was wrong. How wonderful, she realized, tears still pouring from her eyes. How wonderful to shrug off undeserved disapproval, and to meet people – like Mr. Jennings and Lady Morton – who believed in her, who cared for her, who liked her.

"You will not believe me, Mr. Jennings," she said. "But your flowers have cheered me more than you can know."

Jennings stepped forward, setting the flowers on the table beside the bed and sitting down carefully on the edge of the bed next to Elizabeth. His countenance had become even more stern, and something in his demeanor suggested that he was pondering a great decision. He took her hand and brought it to his lips, and for a long moment he considered what he wanted to say to her.

He was tormented by the thought of her in the park, struggling for her life while he made his leisurely way home. He had, to some extent, accepted the logical truth – that her injury was not his fault – but he could not shake his lingering feeling of partial culpability. He must, at the very least, improve her situation now, especially since her father had heaped further harm upon her by disowning her in this fashion. This lovely girl who had so recently danced with him, smiling and laughing, captivating him with her guileless charm – she was now brought low by circumstances he had been, even with the slate's timely counsel, entirely unable to prevent, and, if Lady Morton could not take her in as her ward, then Elizabeth would frankly have nowhere to go. Jennings feared that she would end up on the streets, and he found such a notion to be completely, overwhelmingly intolerable.

Well, he decided. There's nothing else for it.

He took a deep breath, summoning his courage as best he could in that brief second, and, still holding her hand in his, began speaking to her.

"Miss Carlisle," he said, watching her rather intently. "I realize that I have only known you a very short time, and that you have no particular insights into my character or manner; I know that what I am about to suggest to you may seem ridiculous to you – and if it seems repugnant to you, I will gladly seek some other solution – but I believe that it would be the best course for you given your circumstances." He coloured slightly, and looked away for a moment, but then brought his compassionate gaze back to hers. "I was not able to stop your attacker, Miss Carlisle," he said. "And I cannot flatter myself that I could prevail upon your father to change his long-held opinions. But I believe I can offer a solution to your current predicament, by giving you a new home."

Behind him, Lady Morton gave a low gasp, but Elizabeth's only response was to look plainly confused. "I – I do not understand, sir," she said. "What do you mean?"

Jennings discovered that he no longer needed courage, and that his next words came very easily to his lips. "Miss Carlisle," he said, smiling gently. "Elizabeth. If you will accept it, I am offering my home to you, that you might become its mistress." When he saw that her expression, though openly incredulous, was not one of disgust or alarm, he took heart and leaned closer to her. "However odd it may seem to you, Miss Carlisle," he said. "I am most humbly asking – if it pleases you to consider it – for your hand in marriage."

CHAPTER THREE

Elizabeth sat for a moment in stunned silence, staring up at Jennings with plain incredulity. "Sir," she said finally when she could find her voice. "You should not joke!"

Jennings smiled and shook his head. "I am quite in earnest, Miss Carlisle," he said placidly. He leaned toward her and added, "Do you see any other way out of your predicament?"

Elizabeth could not, in fact, see any other way out of her predicament, but to foist herself upon a man who had already done so much for her! – whom she had known less than a week, and who would hardly wish to be saddled with a wife he barely knew. She did not even have a dowry to recommend her. No, although the frightened part of her leapt at the chance to solve her problem so easily, she could not accept his offer.

"Mr. Jennings," she began. "I could not possibly importune you in such a way."

He shook his head again. "It does not importune me in the least, Miss Carlisle," he said, his manner easy-going, as though he had asked her to tea rather than for her hand in marriage. "As I said, if it is repugnant to you, we will find some other solution … but I do not immediately see what that solution could be." He glanced briefly toward Lady Morton, who stood behind him as still as a statue, her face frozen in an expression of expectant awe. "Lady Morton would gladly house you for a thousand years," Jennings said. "But you have expressed concern that she would be harmed by opening her doors to you."

"She would be harmed!" Elizabeth averred stringently. "She has daughters whose reputations would be linked with mine!"

Lady Morton seemed inclined to argue with Elizabeth on this point, but Mr. Jennings continued before she could speak. "I suppose it's pointless to attempt to convince you otherwise," he said drily. "And, I suppose, you might be right about it, although I doubt very much that it would be as disastrous as you predict. But since this is your feeling, can we assume, then, that you do not wish to accept a place in Lady Morton's household?"

Elizabeth's eyes filled with tears. "It is precisely because of her incredible kindness and generosity that I could not possibly bear to burden her in even the slightest part."

Jennings, moved by Elizabeth's woebegone countenance, gently squeezed her hand. "Do you think," he asked delicately. "That your father will reconsider his feelings?"

Elizabeth made a sound like a scoff mixed with a sob. "I do not," she said without hesitation.

"I am not vicious," Jennings pointed out, smiling warmly. "I live in extremely comfortable circumstances. We seem able to converse easily with one another. These present a most agreeable foundation for contentment in marriage, do you not think?" He paused for a moment, watched her as she digested all that he had said. "I am most happy to make this offer, Miss Carlisle," he assured her. "If you do not believe it would result in misery for you, then I beg you will not refuse me for any fear of … importuning me, as you say."

Elizabeth did not know what to feel. She could see very well his sincerity, but she questioned how well contented he would be when the unnecessary guilt and notions of responsibility he apparently entertained had faded. He was a very eligible prospect for any young lady, and she was sensible that she would be fortunate to marry him regardless of her situation, but, indeed, that was the problem – he could choose almost any girl he wanted, and to settle on her might be a decision he would quickly come to see as a mistake. She could not bear the thought of causing even a moment's unhappiness to the man who had saved her life.

"Sir," she said. "Mr. Jennings. I – I cannot allow you to take a step so disastrous to your happiness."

Jennings looked surprised. "Why on earth would it be disastrous to my happiness?" he asked. He did not give her time to respond, but instead repeated, "Do you see any other way out of it, Miss Carlisle?"

Thoughts ran through her head of every possible outcome. "I could enter a convent," she offered. "Or become a governess or –"

Jennings' smile broadened as he interrupted her. "Or a scullery-maid or a milliner?"

"Well, yes!" Elizabeth said rather defensively. "I must do something, after all! Why not the same as many other women before me?"

Jennings did not bother to answer her question. "Do you want," he said deliberately. "To be a milliner? Or a governess? Or live in a convent?" He gazed into her eyes with disconcerting directness as he waited for her reply.

She imagined the sort of existence that awaited her should she pursue any of the options she had described. Life in a convent would likely not be rewarding to her, but it would be a much easier life than that of governess or scullery-maid. Added to the drudgery of such professions would be the unavoidable awkwardness of employment under families who would be well aware of her earlier station – families who would be obliged to see her father in society. She envisioned the endless years of tedious and difficult labour that stretched before her, and her heart sank even further than it already had. "No," she admitted, fresh tears filling her eyes. "But what else am I to do?"

Jennings chuckled. "Why, Miss Carlisle," he said brightly, taking her hand and bringing it to his lips. "You can accept my offer, if it does not seem as dreadful as the other choices you mentioned!" He shook his head, and his voice carried the ghost of a laugh. "You would choose these other delightful avenues," he said. "To spare me from – what? – a charming and genteel wife? Someone intelligent and kind-hearted, who will be the loveliest hostess in all England?" Something occurred to him, and he said animatedly, "You'll no doubt wish to throw parties. My house has not seen a party since before my mother passed away!" He noticed then in her eyes the faint look of hope that hid beneath her fears and heartache, and this prompted him to confide to her, "You see, Miss Carlisle, I never dance."

A slight frown drew her brows together for an instant. If he never danced, she wondered, why was he suggesting that they throw parties? "What do you mean?" she asked him. "You danced with me the other night."

"Exactly," he said, kissing her hand once more. "Exactly my point." He continued to stare directly into her eyes, so that she found she could not turn away, and her many concerns began to melt away in the face of his friendly and open demeanour. What had moments before been an impossible course of action now seemed not only possible but perfectly acceptable, and his questions played over and over in her mind as she looked back at him: Do you want to be a governess? Do you see any other way out of your predicament?

Indeed, no, she did not want to be a governess, or a maid, or a ward in Lady Morton's home. If she spoke the whole truth, she did not even want to return to her father's home, where she had been, while tolerably happy, never quite able to relax or to be herself. A life with Mr. Jennings would be one free of the censure and judgments of her father. Good God, she realized with a start. I do want to accept this offer!

"Mr. Jennings," she said, searching his face for his reaction to her next question. "Are you quite – quite – sure about this, sir?"

He laughed again. "I am most decidedly quite sure, Elizabeth. And if you accept my offer," he added. "I will do all I can, every day of my life, to guarantee that you do not regret your decision." His voice betrayed some measure of his emotion, but his calm and affable expression never wavered as he waited for her to speak.

Discovering as she said the words that a great weight had been lifted from her – a weight that had almost been past bearing – Elizabeth managed, through her tears, to croak out her consent. "I do accept your offer, Mr. Jennings."

Lady Morton, no longer able to contain herself, clapped her hands together in delight and laughed her excited approval. "Oh, it is everything one could wish!" she crowed. "I could not be happier for both of you, my dears!" She came forward and gently patted Elizabeth's cheek. "I told you all would be well, dearest," she reminded her guest. "And you could not ask for a better man than Mr. Jennings! Why, I have known him since he was a babe-in-arms!"

Elizabeth, still overcome, could do no more than feebly nod her agreement with Lady Morton's assessment. It seemed, indeed, that there could be no better man on earth than this person who had now rescued her twice. "I – I do not know what to say, Mr. Jennings," she murmured. "Except that I thank you."

"Thank you, Miss Carlisle," Jennings said. "For allowing me to be of service to you."

* * *

Lady Morton intercepted Jennings as he made his way downstairs from Elizabeth's room.

"Mr. Jennings," she said, lightly touching his shoulder. "I don't suppose I could trouble you to walk with me?" She looked around her – as though she feared being overheard – and added, "I would ask your opinion of something that my groundskeeper discovered."

She led Jennings out to the balcony where Elizabeth had been abducted. "Mr. Jennings," she began, and touched his shoulder again. "Christopher. I have known your family since long before you were born. I am aware of your mother's ..." She paused, searching for the appropriate words. "Her gifts," she said finally. "I was one of the few she trusted with the knowledge, in fact, and you needn't fear that I would betray her confidence, or yours."

Jennings felt a stab of nervousness, but he attempted to conceal it as he responded to Lady Morton. "I am uncertain of your meaning, ma'am. To what confidence do you refer?"

Lady Morton gave him a small, sympathetic smile. "I quite understand, dear boy," she said. "How ... how society might view such a gift. And so I kept your mother's confidence all these years, even now that she is gone. But I saw for myself that your poor sister had inherited her mother's talents, and things your mother said cause me to believe that you yourself have inherited them as well." Jennings opened his mouth to plead ignorance once more, but Lady Morton held a hand up. "Your sudden return the other night, and your ability to find Miss Carlisle – hidden as she was beneath the leaves! – are far more proof than you can refute to me."

She looked at him for a long moment, and he at her. He saw nothing in her eyes to alarm him – she held the same kind expression she had always had for almost everyone she met – but he had learned as a small boy to hide the slate and his connection to it, and he was loth to admit to it now. But he did see in her a knowing, and an implacability that silently assailed every argument that came to his mind. His gaze wavered, and he swallowed a slight lump in his throat before saying quietly, "What did you wish to show me, Lady Morton?"

She smiled more broadly, and nodded her head in approval. "Good lad," she said. She gestured to the railing over which Elizabeth had been so violently dragged. "On the other side, sir," she said, walking to the railing and leaning over it. "There is a stain on the stone."

Jennings approached the railing, his nervousness at being discovered quickly replaced with curiosity. As he leaned out to see the spot Lady Morton indicated, he was beset by an uncharacteristic vertigo, and his hand reached out instinctively to grasp the top of the parapet. His vision swam, not so much from dizziness, as from the memory of dizziness – of Elizabeth's abrupt flight through the night air and into the park. As though he were seeing the events through

Elizabeth's eyes, he felt her experiences: being lifted by strong and angry claws, being pulled over the stone rail that ripped at the edge of her gown, being cast down to the ground by something far, far larger than she.

"It's a monster," Jennings breathed, closing his eyes for a moment as his balance steadied. "A great monster that carried her off this balcony in a trice."

"That is what she described," Lady Morton agreed, frowning in concern. "Are you quite all right, Mr. Jennings?"

"I am," he assured her, opening his eyes again and examining the railing. On the outer edge he saw a patch of reddish-brown, flanked along one side by a yellow-green smear. "What is that?" he murmured, leaning closer to it. It had the general appearance of blood, but it seemed too orange at its heart to be so, and the yellowish smear emerged from it as though whatever had bled there had been covered in some viscous substance. "Strange," he said, straightening up and looking over at Lady Morton. "It's almost as though a very large frog scraped up against it!"

"That is rather what I thought," Lady Morton said. "But surely someone would have seen a creature the size of which Lizzie describes? How could it have gone unseen?"

"I'm puzzled by that too," Jennings said. "But I suppose if it was watching her, it might have waited until she was quite alone. It was very late, after all, and most of the guests had moved inside."

Lady Morton's expression had turned decidedly dark. "I considered that, too, Mr. Jennings," she said somberly. "But how could a – well, a giant frog – be the sort of thing that was watching her? It would need to possess some special intelligence, would it not?"

Jennings nodded slowly as he contemplated her words. "It would indeed, Lady Morton," he said. "Something beyond the norm, I would imagine, for the sorts of animals that roam England – even the large ones."

"Good God, Mr. Jennings," Lady Morton breathed, her fingers partially covering her mouth. "What are we saying?" She looked again at the mark on the railing. "If this was a man," she asked. "Then how could he have spirited her away so quickly and silently? If it was a man, how did he leave such a stain on the wall?"

"I think it cannot have been a man, ma'am," Jennings said gravely. "But I think it must have been a man holding the reins." His eyes narrowed. "Who on earth would have wanted so badly to hurt Miss Carlisle?"

"I do not know, sir," Lady Morton said, her eyes filling with tears. "But if it was particular to her, then I fear she is still not safe! And if it was not particular to her, then are any of us safe? Even in our own homes?"

Jennings did not appear to have heard her questions; he stretched his hand out rather tentatively toward the stain, and allowed his fingertips to touch the dark surface of it.

Instantly his hand jerked back as though he had touched fire. He cradled it in his other hand and took a stumbling step backward. "Ring," he gasped. "Kill her! Kill her!" He sank to his knees, still holding one hand in the other, and leaned against the railing. "Take the ring."

"Mr. Jennings!" Lady Morton cried out, quickly bending down beside him. "Christopher! Are you all right? Temple!" she called into the house. "Fetch brandy, at once!"

"I believe I am fine, ma'am," Jennings said, his voice thin. "It took me rather by surprise." When he had touched the stain, he had been overwhelmed by a feeling of being in pursuit of a quarry, that no other thought existed but to capture and kill that quarry. He saw a brief flash of Elizabeth, and then of a necklace she wore – a chain with a ring suspended from it, that he remembered seeing when he danced with her. He could not remember seeing it upon her when he found her. He thought for a moment to go into the park and search for it in the dirt under the trees, but the final image that had assailed him, before his hand pulled away from the stain, was of a huge and hideous claw ripping the chain from around Elizabeth's neck. "It took her ring," he said. "It wanted specifically to kill her and to take her ring." He slumped against the parapet, his breathing ragged as though he had run a long way.

"Good God!" Lady Morton exclaimed again. "Why, for goodness' sake, would anyone want to kill her? Why would a ring be so important?"

"I don't know, ma'am," Jennings said, still winded. "But I plan to find out."

* * *

His intense vision on Lady Morton's balcony had left Jennings a bit rattled, so that he found, to his annoyance, that his hands were still shaking as he climbed the steps to Sir James Carlisle's house. He had met Sir James any number of times at various functions, but they traveled in such different circles that their acquaintance was slight; he was uncertain whether Sir James would recognize him or, if he did, whether such acquaintance would benefit his purpose here or harm it. One never quite knew what to expect from Sir James, especially when he was upset by something.

The porter, a thin, wary-looking man, opened the door and asked in rather abrupt tones, "Can I help you, sir?"

Jennings gave a small nod of his head by way of greeting, and replied affably, "I am Christopher Jennings. I am lately engaged to Miss Elizabeth Carlisle, and I have come to arrange for the delivery of her belongings to my home."

The porter's wariness faded somewhat, and his expression betrayed relief. "Indeed, sir," he said, his voice much warmer now. "Please come in. I will let Sir James know that you are here."

Jennings followed the porter into the front hallway of a very elegantly appointed house. After the porter disappeared through a door at the far end of the hall, Jennings contented himself examining a nearby glass case full of miniature portraits. Tucked into the back of the case, barely visible, was the likeness of what he could only assume was Elizabeth's mother: the colouring was quite different, but the eyes that looked back at him were Elizabeth's eyes, and the dimpled smile was the same. "Please know, ma'am," he murmured, running his finger lightly over the glass above the portrait. "That I will endeavour to bring your daughter all happiness."

Behind him, the porter emerged from the recesses of the house and cleared his throat. "Sir James will see you in the library, sir." He indicated the door through which he had just passed. "Follow me, if you please."

Jennings, in hopes of preventing unnecessary conflict,

suppressed all disapprobation of Sir James' actions or temperament, and put on his face an expression of easy-going amiability. He trotted dutifully after the porter, and walked with as pleasant an air as he could muster into the library.

The room was full of light and windows, but the walls were paneled with heavy dark wood and lined with shelves that groaned under the weight of countless books. The furniture was equally dark and heavy, and the man who sat behind the large, fairly imposing desk complemented the room with his serious and vaguely irritated countenance.

"Christopher Jennings!" he said, speaking much more loudly than was warranted by the size of the room. "Why, I know you!" He came to his feet and made a perfunctory bow, which Jennings returned with exacting politeness. "Hawkins tells me that you are engaged to Miss Carlisle," the man went on, shoving his hands into his pockets and casting an appraising eye over Jennings. "And are you, then, the one who treated her so rough?"

Jennings was surprised that Sir James acknowledged Elizabeth's injuries; his letter to Lady Morton and his absence at his daughter's bedside had caused Jennings to suppose he did not believe anything that had been said of the attack. "Indeed, no, sir," he answered somberly. "I was the one who found her, sir."

"Ah," Sir James said. He looked askance at his visitor for a few seconds, and then continued, still at a near bellow, "I suppose you find me hard-hearted, sir, but I cannot countenance her running off from her chaperone – at near on two in the morning! – and behaving with such total lack of propriety! Crying out now for pity because she received her come-uppance! It can't be borne!"

Jennings' diligently benign expression now revealed a sincere sadness; he tilted his head to one side as he looked back at Sir James. "Quite the reverse, sir," he said frankly. "I can well understand that running off into the park in the middle of the night is a violation of propriety, and that if she was meeting clandestinely with a lover, such behaviour might not be approved of by her father. I can also understand that her account of events – being stolen by force from the balcony – does not sound particularly likely. What I cannot understand, sir," he added, in exceedingly respectful tones. "Is your reluctance to see her or to care for her when she has been hurt so badly."

Sir James, unaccustomed to people giving their true opinions, however respectfully, was somewhat taken aback by Jennings forthright statement. "It was not easy, sir!" he protested, leaning forward and putting his hands on the top of the massive desk. "But the daughter I raised – to be a proper young lady! – died that night in the park, or never existed! She is as much a stranger to me and to all I have attempted to instill in her as you are! I hold myself to the standard I have asked her to follow, and I do not recognize this girl who leaves her poor step-mama for an assignation in the park!" His bellow had become a roar, and his face had become quite red as he defended his position. Suddenly he seemed to remember himself, and he took a step back from the desk and breathed a great sigh. "I do not require your understanding, sir!" he said more calmly, plunging his hands back in his pockets. "But if you are determined to take on a woman who has shown herself to be the veriest trollop, then I wish you luck!" He straightened to his fullest height, and said with some pomposity, "Now if you will excuse me, I am quite busy this day, and do not have time to converse with you on a subject so painful to me!"

"Painful," Jennings repeated softly. He clasped his hands behind his back and said brightly, "I quite understand, sir! Please forgive me; I would not dream of importuning you! As I informed your porter, I have come only to arrange for Miss Carlisle's belongings to be delivered to my house in town." He stood with an air of blithe expectancy.

"I sent a trunk," Sir James said tersely. "With her clothes. I can't imagine she wants for anything else. I have lost my daughter, Jennings," he pointed out indignantly, as though Jennings were cruelly obliging him to think on things better forgotten. "The sweet girl I once knew is clearly gone, and I will not be put to the trouble of collecting her baubles, when the sight of them reminds me so well of what she has become!"

"Then all parties would benefit by the hasty removal of all her possessions," Jennings said congenially. "If seeing her things here disturbs you, then I am most happy to remove them from you entirely."

Sir James' jaw tightened visibly. "Don't think you can fool me!" he exclaimed stridently. "You may not care to trifle with me, my boy!"

Jennings' eyes narrowed, and he took a step forward. His hands, still behind his back, were now clasped rather tightly, but outwardly his entire manner was relaxed, almost languid. His smile had faded, but it lingered wryly at the corners of his mouth. "You are older," he said, his voice barely above a murmur. "But I think not wiser." He glanced briefly at the room around him, and then brought his sardonic gaze back to Sir James, whose outraged response he forestalled by continuing smoothly, "And I am sure – quite sure – that I am much, much richer than you. So perhaps it is you who should not trifle with me." His smile left entirely, and he said crisply, "I expect all of Miss Elizabeth's belongings – all of them – delivered to my doorstep by the morrow." He gave a cursory bow to Sir James, hardly more than a nod of his head. "Sir," he said, and turning abruptly around, he strode purposefully out of the library without looking back.

CHAPTER FOUR

Since her condition and the situation conspired to make time a significant factor, Elizabeth agreed with Jennings' suggestion that they be married within the fortnight, and selected, at his urging, Thursday-next as a perfectly acceptable day for a wedding.

On that day, the minister arrived at Lady Morton's barely an hour after Jennings, and he was shown into a small parlour in the back of the house – a room with huge windows that overlooked Lady Morton's beautiful gardens. Flowers had been placed on every conceivable surface, and platters of cold meat, fruit, and biscuits were arranged on a side table beside the door. As the minister entered, a servant was setting up tea and coffee and lemonade on another small table; she gave a small curtsey to the minister, adjusted a nearby bouquet with a practiced hand, and left the parlour.

A moment later, Jennings came in, bowing a greeting to the minister. "Thank you so much for coming on such short notice, sir," he said sincerely. "Miss Carlisle is not quite able to leave the house, but I thought it best to be married as soon as possible to avoid any further stain on her reputation."

The minister emitted a barking sort of laugh. "It is only her father, I am assured, who perceives any 'stain'," he said crisply. "I have had the pleasure of meeting Sir James, sir, and he struck me as a man much devoted to very antiquated notions. His characterization of the fair sex seemed to me to be most unfair, and not rooted in any actual experience with them that I could perceive."

"Indeed," Jennings said, raising one eyebrow. "The women in Sir James' life seem to be of the most exemplary sort. And," he added, smiling broadly and standing a little taller. "I am most honoured that Miss Carlisle has accepted my hand, and that she will not be obliged to suffer any more from this attack than she already has."

The minister leaned forward and asked quietly, "As to that, sir – you alluded – what I mean, sir, is … has there been any trace of this fellow? Have the constables anything to say?"

"I fear her attacker left few clues," Jennings said, also in a low voice. "But I have reason to think we will bring him to earth one way or another. Hopefully quite soon."

The minister snorted again. "And what will her father have to say then, I wonder?" he said. "When the truth is laid out before him!"

Jennings' smile became rueful. "I do not think," he said. "That it will matter to him a whit. His views seem most deeply ingrained, and I believe they may shield him from the truth, however loudly it speaks to him."

"Sad," the minister said, shaking his head. "He has lost a great deal over this stubbornness."

"He has indeed," Jennings agreed.

Behind the two men, the door to the parlour opened and Lady Morton entered, two of her daughters beside her. All three women were dressed elegantly, and the two girls carried bouquets of flowers in their hands.

"Mr. Jennings!" Lady Morton said, beaming. "Mr. Westlake," she said to the minister, and extended her hand to him. "It is a fine morning, is it not, for a wedding?"

The minister bowed over Lady Morton's hand. "It is very fine, ma'am," he said.

Lady Morton indicated her daughters. "These are Mariah and Jane, my eldest girls. They will be standing up with Miss Elizabeth."

Both Jennings and Mr. Westlake bowed to the girls, who curtsied shyly. They stood close to one another, seeming uncertain about their role as bridesmaids but apparently excited at the prospect.

"And who will stand up with you, Mr. Jennings?" Lady Morton asked.

"My friend, Lord Remington, is here, ma'am," Jennings told her. "In fact, he has agreed to escort Miss Carlisle, and to give her in marriage in the place of her father, since Sir James could not be here."

"Hmm!" Lady Morton sniffed disdainfully. "'Could not'," she repeated. "You are very charitable, Christopher."

"I do my best, ma'am," he said. He turned then as Lord Remington poked his head into the room around the half-closed door.

"Are you ready, then?" he asked jovially. "Your lovely bride awaits!"

Jennings felt his heart beating faster. "I am ready," he said, grinning at his friend.

Lord Remington swung the door wide, revealing Miss Elizabeth standing in the hallway. She stood unaided, but she held herself quite stiffly; her recovery was far from complete. Her face, however, had healed, and when she looked into the parlour at her husband-to-be, her twinkling eyes and dimpled smile were the ones he remembered from their first dance together. Her dress had been made especially by Lady Morton's dressmaker, and, though simple in design and ornament, became Elizabeth very well. Her hair had been curled round garlands of flowers, and she carried flowers in front of her.

"You're as pretty as anything!" Remington exclaimed, offering her his arm.

"Thank you, my lord," she replied, blushing at his compliment. She gratefully took the support of his arm, and allowed him to lead her into the parlour.

He brought her to Jennings' side, and, taking her hand, he put it gently into Jennings' outstretched one. "I wish you very happy, old man!" he said, smiling warmly, and stepped away so that Jennings could stand beside Elizabeth in front of the waiting minister.

"Oh!" Mariah breathed softly, overcome with sentiment. She and her sister both dabbed at tears in their eyes, and behind them, as the minister performed the ceremony, Lady Morton had recourse quite often to her handkerchief.

"What God has joined," Mr. Westlake said at last, grinning almost as broadly himself as the couple he had just wed. "Let no man put asunder!"

* * *

Several days later, the doctor deemed Elizabeth well enough to travel the distance to Mr. Jennings' home. Not knowing for certain her feelings – except a notion that the last few weeks of her life seemed far too surreal to have actually occurred – Elizabeth climbed into her new husband's coach and sat down across from him.

Lady Morton leaned into the coach, her hands anxiously tucking a blanket around Elizabeth's knees. "Take care of yourself, my dear," she said. She placed a loving hand on Elizabeth's cheek and smiled. "You look almost your old self, Lizzie," she said. "I believe the doctor is right, and soon it will be as though nothing ever happened to you."

Elizabeth returned Lady Morton's smile, then impulsively reached out to give her a quick embrace. "Thank you more than I can say, Lady Morton," she said, blinking tears from her eyes. "Without your kindness, I don't know what I would have done."

Lady Morton demurred with a slight shake of her head. "Indeed, my dear," she said. "Your true hero is here." She indicated Mr. Jennings, who flushed at this compliment and attempted to protest. "And he has always been," she went on, before he could speak. "If not for him, I cannot bear to think what might have happened to you!" She squeezed first Elizabeth's hand and then Mr. Jennings. "Take good care of one another!" she told them brightly, stepping away from the coach and allowing the footman to shut the door. "And please do visit me whenever you wish!"

The coach pulled away from Lady Morton's house, and Elizabeth, lost at first in silent reverie, soon found the rocking of the coach to be soothing enough to put her to sleep. She dozed, undisturbed by her watchful companion, until at last the coach turned down a winding lane that was flanked on both sides with rows of trees.

"We are here, Elizabeth," Jennings' soft voice woke her. "At Brightwood."

Elizabeth looked out the window of the coach at the surrounding countryside; Jennings' estate was not as manicured as Lady Morton's carefully sculpted gardens, but it was quite beautiful, and its green hills, meadows full of flowers, and clusters of trees rolled out as far as she could see in all directions.

"My goodness!" she exclaimed, her eyes opening wide. "All this is yours?"

"It is," Jennings said, glad that she seemed happy with it. "I hope it is to your liking, and that you will be happy here."

Elizabeth faced him with an expression of delight. "I cannot imagine anyone who could not be happy here, Mr. Jennings!" she said. She turned back to the view outside the coach window, looking at everything eagerly, as though she might never see it again. "These are the loveliest grounds I have ever seen."

They came presently to the house, a vast stone structure that was made less imposing by the tangles of ivy that crept up its walls and framed its many windows. "My goodness!" Elizabeth repeated, struggling to convince herself that a man so clearly above her family's modest station had agreed to share all of this with her, and to make her mistress of such a grand estate.

Jennings climbed out of the coach and held his hand up to Elizabeth, a warm and inviting smile lighting up his handsome face. "Welcome to your new home, Mrs. Jennings!" he said, as she took his hand and carefully descended from the coach. "It already seems brighter, now you are here."

Her eyes twinkled as she returned his smile. "I'm sure," she said dryly. Growing serious, she surveyed the house and added a bit uncertainly, "I fear I shall get lost in there."

"Devil a bit!" Jennings said jovially, escorting her to the door where several servants stood waiting to greet them. "You'll soon know every part of it, and, of course," he added, pausing a moment and speaking earnestly to her. "You must feel free to make it yours in whatever way you wish. Change anything you desire – it is your home now, as surely as it is mine." He turned then to the row of servants. "This is Mrs. Raleigh, Elizabeth," he said, stopping before a middle-aged woman with a round, pleasant face and faded red hair tucked up into a cap.

"Mrs. Jennings," she said, bobbing a curtsey. "I am the housekeeper, ma'am. If you wish for anything, you've only to ask."

"My butler," Jennings continued, gesturing now to a tall, thin man with black hair and an imposing air. "Combes."

"Ma'am," Combes said, bowing to Elizabeth with his hands behind his back. His voice was deep and gravelly. "A pleasure to welcome you to Brightwood."

Jennings introduced all of the assembled servants, and then, as they passed through the door into the front hall, he waved his hand expansively to indicate the whole house. "It is all yours, Elizabeth," he said, grinning. "I hope that you will be as happy here as I have always been."

Elizabeth, too overcome to absorb her new surroundings fully, gave a small laugh, and put her hand on Mr. Jennings' arm. "I am happier already, sir," she said. "Than I have been in many weeks!" She looked around at the elegantly appointed hall and the sweeping staircase. "I believe it will take me some time to get used to all this, I'm afraid."

"We will start by showing you your rooms," Jennings said, guiding her toward the staircase. "At the moment, they are on the south side of the house, overlooking the lake, but if you find that you would rather be settled in another part of the house, it will be no trouble at all to achieve that for you." They climbed the stairs to a wide hallway, at the far end of which stood a cluster of housemaids falling over themselves in an attempt to flank the entrance to one of the rooms.

"Everyone seems so happy to greet me," Elizabeth noted, wide-eyed. "Do they believe me to be someone particularly important, sir?"

"You *are* particularly important, Lizzie," Jennings said softly. He took her hand and held it to his lips, gazing for a moment into her eyes before turning once more to the cluster of maids. "Is it all ready?" he asked them, nodding his head toward the room behind them.

"It is indeed, sir!" one of them said, curtseying first to him and then to Elizabeth. "We've put all of your things inside, ma'am," she said to Elizabeth. "If you find anything amiss, tell us straight'way, because the man what brought your trunks from your 'ouse was not sure that all 'ad been included."

"I thank you most sincerely," Elizabeth said, tears filling her eyes. "And you, Mr. Jennings," she added, blinking away the tears and managing to smile up at him. "I cannot say how grateful I am."

Jennings dismissed this with a small shake of his head. "It is I who am grateful to you, Mrs. Jennings," he said. "For allowing me to help you." He walked with her then into the suite of rooms that had been given to her, and he smiled broadly in relief as she put both of her hands over her mouth and stared incredulously at what she saw.

"All for me?" she asked, breathlessly. "It's beautiful!" Before her was a large sitting room, decorated in light blues and greens and filled with flowers. Doors opened out onto a wide balcony, and Elizabeth could see, over the stone railing, a park that sloped down to a copse of trees and then curved toward a small lake that glittered in the sunlight. To her left, a set of steps led up to another door, and, behind it, a spacious bedchamber arrayed in sky blue and brown. Flowers had been set in this room as well, and she could see that her belongings had indeed been brought from her father's house, and laid out as congenially as though they had always been here.

Elizabeth no longer tried to hide her tears. "Mr. Jennings!" she exclaimed, impulsively taking his hands in hers. "This is absolutely beautiful! I cannot describe –! Are you sure all this is for me?"

"I am quite sure, Mrs. Jennings," he replied. Behind him, the maids looked to be on the verge of tears themselves, and as happy at Elizabeth's delight as she herself was. Jennings turned to them and said, "Miranda, would you be so good as to arrange some lunch for us? I am sure we are both quite famished."

"At once, sir!" Miranda said, curtseying once more and scuttling off with the other maids behind her. Once they had gone, Jennings brought Elizabeth to the balcony and helped her settle into one of the chairs there.

"I'm so very glad you are pleased!" he said. Nodding his head toward the departing maids, he added wryly, "As you can see, we are *all* most anxious to make you comfortable here."

She laughed and brushed away a tear from her cheek. "When you offered me your hand, sir," she said, gazing out over the park and the lake. "I had no idea what in fact you were offering! I – I hope you find me deserving of it!"

He seemed surprised. "I hope *I* am deserving of *you*, ma'am!" he said with great sincerity. Waving a hand toward her rooms, he went on, "As I said, if you are ever unhappy, simply tell me; all shall be made as you wish." He paused, studying the tops of his boots as

51

though they held important information, then abruptly he sat in the chair across from Elizabeth and, leaning forward, took her hand. "Elizabeth," he said with some intensity, "I know that you have notions of yourself, and of me, and of – of what –" He stopped, cleared his throat, flushed to the roots of his hair, and continued in a rush: "I believe you have notions of what marriage is supposed to be, but I tell you now that I have offered this to you for your own sake, and not for my own, and I expect nothing from you. If – if you wish to – that is – if you wish to – if, after befriending me, you are content to take on all the roles of marriage, and to be intimate with me, then I would count myself most fortunate to have earned your favour. But if your feelings for me do not include such things, I would count it as nothing, and have only ever been gratified to be of use to you."

Elizabeth listened to this whole with the dawning realization that he referred to the marriage bed. Blushing as fiercely as he, she waited until he had done speaking, and then, stammering in embarrassment, she said to him, "As to that, sir, I – well, I – well." She sighed, and smiled gently, and allowed herself to tell him the truth. "I would like, sir, to befriend you ... before – well, before ... beforehand."

They sat in awkward silence for a brief moment, then Jennings laughed, and felt an odd sense of relief. "I would like that, too," he admitted. "So let us proceed from there."

Elizabeth nodded, and also laughed. "That sounds quite nice, Mr. Jennings."

They sat together then for some time, enjoying the afternoon sun and the scenery, and each thinking of the future with a mixture of excitement and curiosity. Then, his face crumpling into a nervous sort of frown, Jennings took a deep breath and broached what, for him, was the more problematic subject. "Lizzie," he began, again looking down at his feet, his fingers drumming distractedly on the arms of his chair. "Lizzie, there is something I would like to show you."

Elizabeth, observing his apparent anxiety, reached out and touched his arm. "What is it?"

He took another breath, and let it out in a gusty sigh. "It is something my family has always had, for many generations," he said, raising his eyes at last to meet hers. "I would like to show you the slate."

CHAPTER FIVE

After luncheon, Jennings led Elizabeth to his rooms, and to the drawer in the desk where he kept the slate.

Although she was smiling encouragingly at him, and he knew even from their brief acquaintance that she was neither judgmental nor skeptical, he felt his heart pounding as he slid the drawer open.

He had never shown any other person what he was now revealing to her.

Nestled snugly in its box in the drawer was a simple piece of slate, misshapen at the edges as though it had been broken unceremoniously off the end of a larger piece. Written on it in an elegant script were the words, "Find my lost child."

Jennings blinked at the slate in surprise. Usually he could sense when the slate was going to deliver a message to him; perhaps his nervousness at sharing the slate with Elizabeth had overshadowed his abilities.

Elizabeth was staring at the words on the slate. "You have a lost child?" she said finally, hesitating in fear that she was mentioning something delicate.

"I don't," Jennings replied, pulling the slate out of the drawer and holding it up in the light from the window. "This slate tells me things that have not yet occurred, or which occurred in secret. I can feel the slate speaking to me –" He put his hand to his chest and pressed his fingers against his heart. "Here, like a strange constriction." He looked at Elizabeth, to find her steadily returning his gaze with kind curiosity and openness. Sitting down on the edge of his bed, he gave her a lop-sided smile. "You must think I'm quite

mad," he predicted. "But my family have always had this ... gift."
He waited then in anxious silence for her response.

She frowned slightly and came to sit beside him. "Indeed, sir,"
she said genuinely. "I cannot imagine why I would find you mad.
Did you not find me hidden under a bush? – no one would ever have
seen me, if they had not known where to look." She smiled gently.
"Either you were my attacker, sir," she added. "And I know that you
were not. Or you had some ability to discover me that others lack."
She looked down then at her hands folded in her lap. "I should not
judge you in any event," she said. "Since I have told you an
unbelievable tale of a clawed monster abducting me from a balcony,
in full view of the house!"

Jennings propped the slate on his knee and put a comforting
hand on Elizabeth's. "Your understanding is a great relief to me,
more than I can say," he told her. "I had not known how to broach
this subject with you in a way that would not frighten you, or cause
you to doubt my sanity." His finger tapped absently on the slate, his
touch smudging part of the words. "And of course," he went on,
squeezing her hands warmly. "We are agreed then? That neither of
us is mad?" He smiled genially, but inside he still feared that she
would not be able to accept his dark talent.

Her eyes twinkled, and he was instantly reassured. "Mr.
Jennings," Elizabeth said, smiling back at him. "We are agreed. And
shall we agree, too," she asked. "That everyone else in the world
must think we are as mad as anything?"

He laughed. "Accepting that fact will certainly make it easier to
bear," he said. He grew serious. "I have inherited this gift from my
mother," he explained. "Who gave it to me and to my sister. My

mother had it from her own mother, and her grandmother, and all the women in her family before her, as far back as she could remember. I am, in fact, one of only four men in my entire family tree who have received visions." He laughed again. "I did not know, actually, if you would be able to see the writing on the slate. I wondered if the letters were simply a part of my gift." He gestured to the smudged letters. "The slate has only been in our family for seven or eight generations; before that, the women of my family had to rely on the accuracy of their feelings, and of the things they saw in visions and dreams."

Elizabeth reached out a tentative hand toward the slate and also touched the letters written there. "So you do not write these words?" she asked. "They appear of their own accord?"

Jennings nodded. "Yes," he said. "And they disappear and rearrange themselves of their own accord as well."

Elizabeth stared at the message and pondered its significance. "How on earth are you to act on such a scant clue? Whoever speaks to you has not even shown who he or she is."

"I see more than the words," Jennings said. He closed his eyes. "When I see the slate," he began. "I also see images in my mind. They are not clear, by any means, and their meaning is often quite … challenging … to suss out. But I see enough, usually, to proceed."

Elizabeth's eyes were open wide. "What do you see now?" she asked, leaning expectantly toward him.

He turned to look at her. Far from criticizing or judging, or being upset by something so unusual, Elizabeth seemed instead to be interested even to the point of excitement. Rather than being one more friend from whom he felt obliged to hide the truth, she could, he thought, become an ally with him in his work of answering the slate.

"I see a house," he said, after gazing on her for a moment. "On Curzon Street. And I see a blue dove and a green box."

Elizabeth looked from him to the slate and back. "Is … is the one who writes these words … is it a spirit?"

"It is," Jennings said. "The slate – that is – I would not wish to distress you. But in fact the words are always written by the spirits of the dead, by those who have some unfinished business in the living world."

"How extraordinary!" Elizabeth breathed. This wondrous talent he showed her was beyond anything she had ever experienced, and she felt both amazed and exhilarated. "So," she began, gesturing to the slate. "You will find this person's 'lost child'?"

Jennings nodded.

"And you will do so by searching for a blue dove and a green box?" she asked.

He nodded again.

She tilted her head quizzically, and her eyes still twinkled. "You do not think that a daunting prospect, sir?"

He laughed. "I suppose I am used to it," he said, giving a slight shrug and leaning forward to place the slate carefully back in its box.

Elizabeth sat quietly for a moment, considering all that he had just told her. "All right," she said at last, squaring her shoulders and smiling up at him. "What do we do first?"

He looked at her in frank surprise, and then a smile spread slowly across his face. "You wish," he said hesitantly. "To help me?"

"I do," she responded matter-of-factly. "I am your wife, am I not? I am to help you in any way I can." She grinned suddenly. "And it all sounds rather exciting, doesn't it?" she said. "I hope you will not prevent me assisting you, since I am now painfully curious to learn what your vision means."

He gazed at her, his face suffused with a mixture of relief and admiration. "I would be very happy to share this with you," he said softly. "But I warn you," he went on. "That it does create some very interesting ... hmmm ... *situations*. This, for instance." He waved a hand in the direction of the slate. "I believe that we should go to Curzon Street, and introduce ourselves where we seem to be led. As you can imagine, that might prove to be an intensely awkward task, pushing ourselves onto a pack of strangers for no good reason."

"Nonsense," Elizabeth said with unexpected conviction. "You said this person was a spirit with unfinished business. This suggests that the person has recently died, and so we are – I am sure they will believe – friends who have come to bid him farewell."

Jennings' admiration grew. "That is an excellent notion," he allowed cheerfully. "But I do not immediately see if this spirit is a man or a woman, or what the name might be."

Elizabeth's shoulders slumped slightly in temporary defeat, but she quickly recovered. "No matter," she said. "It is a skill rather foisted upon a female, I believe, to learn how to find out all manner of gossip without actually being seen to ask anything at all." She grinned again. "You see?" she said. "I shall be ever so useful to you! – and that will make us both feel better!" She came to her feet. "So do we leave for Curzon Street this afternoon, sir?" she asked. "Or do we wait for the morrow?"

He took her hand and raised it to his lips. "We wait until

58

morning," he said. "Perhaps I might have a dream that aids our efforts." He also stood, holding both her hands in his. "And of course you will want to see the whole house, and grounds, and to arrange your rooms as you wish. And Cook is preparing something delightful for supper in honour of your coming."

Elizabeth was overcome, and tears swam in her eyes. "Mr. Jennings," she said, her voice choked with emotion. "Everything is already delightful."

CHAPTER SIX

The next morning found Mr. and Mrs. Jennings on their way to Curzon Street. They had dressed in dark and simple clothing in hopes of being mistaken for grieving visitors; Jennings' experience with the slate suggested that the spirit who had contacted him was in fact only recently gone from the mortal world, and it seemed as likely as not that the household would still be in deep mourning.

"It would help immensely," Jennings murmured to Elizabeth as they walked up the street. "If we knew the name of the family."

"I have in fact turned to Mrs. Raleigh on that score," Elizabeth revealed. She had recovered her strength to a great degree, but their progress was much slower than she would ordinarily have adopted; she leaned rather heavily on Mr. Jennings' arm, and paused every now and then to catch her breath. "She had the *Gazette* from the last few days," she went on. "There are two families in Curzon Street who suffered a loss in this week, one four days ago and one the day before yesterday."

Jennings looked at her in some surprise. "Two?" he repeated. "Were they connected in some way? Some sort of illness?"

Elizabeth shook her head. "I do not believe so," she said. "A young man named Folliott was thrown from his curricle during a race; he did not survive the incident. The other was a man who, while not particularly elderly, had been unwell for some time, and – according to the notice – finally succumbed after a lengthy and bitter struggle."

"This Folliott," Jennings said. "How old was he?"

"I believe it said he was two-and-twenty," Elizabeth answered.

"Old enough, I suppose, to have a child. Neither man was said to have had any heirs, however. Mr. Bertram – the older man – has a daughter, but his estate is entailed on a cousin." She paused, frowning as she attempted to remember the name listed in the notice. "The honourable Clement Parrish," she said finally. "He inherits everything."

"Did the notice list the names of the mother and daughter?" Jennings asked. He had stopped walking and now gazed patiently down at her.

"The daughter is Miss Miranda Bertram," Elizabeth said. "And the mother – Amelia Forster Bertram – passed away four years ago. Mrs. Raleigh seemed to recall that she had been taken in child-bed, and that the infant had also been lost."

Jennings considered this information. "I wonder," he said thoughtfully. "If Mr. Bertram was married before."

Elizabeth shook her head again. "It did not say so in the notice, nor did Mrs. Raleigh know anything along those lines."

Jennings looked at her out of the corner of his eye. "May I ask," he said with a trace of humour. "With what pretense you plied Mrs. Raleigh with these questions?"

Elizabeth's eyes twinkled. "I gave none, sir," she told him frankly. "I was not certain if your servants were aware of your gifts – although I imagine they are – so I simply asked my questions, and she simply answered them." A dimple appeared. "Whatever questions she may have had for me, she did not reveal."

Jennings chuckled. "I am sure she has had many questions that she does not ask, since the first day of her employment." He nodded his head toward the house just before them. "This is the house I saw," he said. "We must be prepared to 'know' whichever family opens the door."

"I will be very circumspect," Elizabeth promised him.

Together they walked up to the house, and Jennings lifted his hand to knock on the door. Before he could do so, however, the door was opened by the butler, and he looked out dispassionately at the couple on the doorstep.

"Good morning, sir," he said soberly. Turning to Elizabeth, he gave a slight bow. "Ma'am," he added. He held the door wide and gestured for the visitors to enter the house. "Miss Bertram is in the small salon," he announced, leading them across the entryway to a closed door. He opened this door and stepped inside, inviting the Jennings to follow him.

They found themselves in a cozy sitting room. The curtains were still drawn across the windows, so that even though the sun was very bright outside, the room remained in a dreary twilight. On a sofa sat a young girl of perhaps sixteen; her eyes were rimmed red from crying, and her expression was one of the utmost sadness. When the butler opened the door, she looked up from her hands that were clasped tightly in her lap, and greeted her guests in a small, solemn voice.

"Good morning," she said, coming to her feet and approaching them with an outstretched hand. "Thank you so very kindly for coming to condole with our family on this dark day."

Jennings bowed over her hand. "It is we who thank you, Miss Bertram," he said sincerely. "To receive visitors when you must certainly wish to be alone."

"Indeed, sir, I do not," Miss Bertram assured him. "I have in fact been looking forward to friends and family being in the house, for it was desperately quiet here last night without..." She paused, struggling to keep her composure. "Without Papa here," she finished, and bestowed on the Jennings a wan smile. "I think I do not know you," she went on, looking at Jennings and then at Elizabeth. "You knew my father?"

"Who did not know him?" Elizabeth said, keeping her promise to be circumspect. "He was, I am sure, the best of men." In real sympathy, she reached out and took Miss Bertram's hand in hers. "I, too, have lost a parent," she confessed. "I feel extremely for you."

A glint of tears shone in Miss Bertram's eyes. "I thank you," she murmured, her voice choked with emotion. "Please forgive me," she said, wiping at the corners of her eyes with a lace handkerchief.

"Not at all," Jennings said quietly. He had never heard of this family in his life, but this girl's grief was so evident that he felt his own heart hurting for her. "Will you not sit?" he asked her, indicating the sofa. "You needn't dance attendance on us. We are here for you, and are entirely at your disposal."

Miss Bertram smiled through her tears. "You are all kindness, sir!" she said, and sat once more on the sofa. "Everyone has been so kind. Even my cousin has not abandoned me, a girl he met only a fortnight ago."

"Your cousin?" Elizabeth asked, sitting next to Miss Bertram. "He is assisting you with all of this?"

"Indeed he is," Miss Bertram replied. "My father has been ill for some time, and..." She looked away for a moment, then turned back to Elizabeth. "We did not have any particular hope of his recovery," she continued. "He was in fact barely able to speak to us. My cousin

Parrish is to inherit my father's estate, and he journeyed here two weeks ago to apprise himself of the estate and to arrange matters." Somehow her woebegone expression became even more melancholy. "He is planning to sell the estate," she said. "And the house here in town. He has no use for them, since his own estate is more … grand … and I believe the money would benefit him greatly. While he was here, he made me the offer to take me in as his ward, and said that I might live in the lake country with him." She gave another wistful smile. "My grandmother too, who lives with my uncle's widow, she and my aunt have also extended an invitation to live with them in the north."

Jennings tilted his head to one side. "You do not wish to accept these offers?"

Miss Bertram gave a slight shrug. "As to that, sir," she said. "What can I be but deeply grateful that so many have considered my situation? It is just that my life is here, and my friends." She wiped away a tear. "You must find me so silly! – to think of such a thing. But I will miss my life here so much, and I will never again be in the place where I lived with my mother and father, where in fact both of them – and my brother too! – took their leave of this world."

Elizabeth leaned toward Miss Bertram and put a comforting hand on her arm. "Brother!" she repeated, her brows drawn together in concern and sympathy. "You have lost a brother as well?"

Miss Bertram nodded. "He died at his birth, and my mother followed him." She dabbed at her eyes with her handkerchief. "And now my father too. All I have left of them is this house and the estate … and I cannot help but wish that I could keep them, just as they are." She looked at her visitors with a sudden look of abashment.

"Forgive me!" she said again. "I did not mean to importune you in such a way!"

"Do not consider it," Elizabeth told her sincerely. "We are all eagerness to help you in any way we can."

Jennings nodded his agreement. "If I can offer any service to you at all, Miss Bertram, you need only say."

Miss Bertram sat for a moment in a state of grateful bewilderment. "It is so gratifying," she said at last. "To know that my father had such excellent friends. It is a great comfort to me." She smiled, and added in a rather conspiratorial voice, "I thought I heard him last night. In his library. I heard the sound of his chair, and the drawers of his desk, and the way he would puff on his pipe. I even thought I smelled the smoke, and because I was not yet used to the notion of his being gone, I skipped into the library as I always did, fully expecting to see him at his desk, or in his reading chair." Her smile faded. "But of course the room was entirely empty." She frowned then, and looked puzzled. "His treasure box had moved, though."

Jennings raised one eyebrow. "Treasure box?"

"His jade treasure box," Miss Bertram explained. "He brought it back from the Orient many years ago. It always sits on a high shelf in the library, but last night it was on his desk, as though he had sat there with it and had forgotten to put it back." She shook her head. "You must think me mad," she said, her voice breaking. "But I *did* believe in that moment, that he had just been there looking in the box. And I know that it is his box of personal things, and that no one else would want it, so I took it off the desk and brought it to my room."

"We do not at all think you are mad, my dear," Elizabeth said.

65

"I believe very sincerely that the spirits of our loved ones make every attempt to say good-bye to us before they travel on. Perhaps your father wanted to remind you of the box, so that you might have it as a memento of him."

Miss Bertram was clearly comforted by this notion. Her shoulders relaxed, and she leaned back on the sofa. "It has my mother's portrait in it," she said. "And portraits of my father's parents. My mother had sewn caps for both me and my brother, and those are in the box. And many, many letters from my mother." She sighed wistfully. "All of his memories in a single box, and now they are all *I* have as well."

Elizabeth took a breath as if to speak, then paused, thinking better of it. Miss Bertram looked at her expectantly, and after a few more seconds, Elizabeth began hesitantly, "Would it be too much to ask, Miss Bertram, to be allowed to see your mother's portrait? I have heard many good things about her, and I was never given the opportunity to know her."

Miss Bertram brightened considerably. "I would be delighted to show you!" she declared, coming instantly to her feet. "I will go and fetch it!"

She left the room and bustled upstairs, leaving her guests alone in the sitting room. Jennings turned instantly to his wife and whispered in her ear, "The jade box must be the 'green box' I saw yesterday."

Elizabeth nodded. "We need only find the 'blue dove'," she said. "And then, of course, we must figure out to what these scant clues direct us."

Jennings smiled. "This work will be made much simpler with

you, my dear," he said. "You are quite resourceful, I think."

She smiled back. "It is a great deal easier than I had anticipated," she said, adding drily, "My life with my father certainly taught me to speak in a way that allows the listener to feel he has all the power – so many things that I have wanted for myself or for the household, I have only been able to achieve by convincing my father that it had all been his notion in the first place."

Jennings gazed at her admiringly. "I believe I shall enjoy getting to know you, Mrs. Jennings," he said softly.

Miss Bertram returned then, carrying an oblong case made of wood and inlaid heavily with green jade. She sat down on the sofa and propped the box up on her knees, unlocking it with a key that hung on a cord around her neck. "Here," she said warmly. "Here are all my family!"

She cheerfully showed the Jennings the small portraits of her mother and her grandparents. "I have a portrait of my father, too!" she said. "And it will be in here, along with a lock of hair from my mother, and a necklace my grandfather gave me." She blinked away more tears. "It is *my* treasure box now."

Elizabeth bent over the box and ran her fingers carefully along the edges of the pile of letters. "All these are from your mother?" she asked.

"Some are from friends, and from my father's mother," Miss Bertram answered. She reached in and pulled out one of the letters. "This one," she began. "Is the letter from the servant girl – Betty – who attended my mother at my brother's birth. My father showed it to me once, and said that he kept it because it was a record of the only moment of my brother's life, and the last moments of my mother's."

She handed the letter carefully to Elizabeth, who opened it with a gentle reverence.

"'Mr. Bertram'," she read aloud. "'I regret I must leave your employ on this day. I am so much stricken by Mistress's death, and the sight of her wee one so still beside her, that I can't bear the sight of it no more. You've always been good to me, and I'm sorry to leave so abrupt, but it distressed me so to watch him laid away, and I can't come back to the house. Betty.'"

"My mother's confinement was sudden," Miss Bertram explained in low tones, flushing slightly at the unusual broaching of such a delicate subject. "The midwife had been summoned but had not yet arrived. Betty attended my mother as best she could, and when all was lost, she took it upon herself to prepare my brother for burial alongside my mother." Tears began to fall unheeded down her cheeks. "Perhaps I am wrong," she said. "Perhaps I *should* leave this house, where so much tragedy has been!"

Elizabeth impulsively wrapped her arms around the girl. "My dear!" she consoled her. "Do not distress yourself! All will be well! – and it seems very clear that your father is looking out for you now just as he did in life."

Miss Bertram collapsed into Elizabeth's embrace and sniffled pitifully into her handkerchief. "I feel that too," she said. "I wish he would tell me what he wants me to do."

"I am sure as long as you are happy, he will be happy," Jennings told her. He reached out and took the letter from Elizabeth; when his fingers touched the paper, his eyes closed, and he shuddered as though a chill had gone through him. "Tell me about this Betty," he said, opening his eyes and looking at Miss Bertram. "Did she have family? Did you ever hear from her again?"

Miss Bertram sat up, attempting to regain her composure. "I believe her family was in Bedford," she said. "I never heard from her or saw her again. I don't believe my father ever did either, although he might have and not mentioned it." She looked up at Mr. Jennings quizzically. "Why do you ask? Is she familiar to you?"

"Not at all," Jennings replied. He shrugged off the chill that had shaken him, and smiled warmly at Miss Bertram. "I just thought – since she was so affected by what occurred – that she might want to be apprised of your father's passing. If you are in agreement, I would be happy to send word to Bedford."

Miss Bertram's eyes widened. "Oh, of course!" she said. "Thank you so much for your suggestion! I do believe she would like to know; I remember her being very affable, and very friendly with my mother. She seemed almost a part of the family, in fact, before she left."

"I will send word to her at once, Miss Bertram," Jennings offered. "You needn't worry at all about it."

She took his hand in real gratitude. "Thank you, sir," she said. "With all my heart. I am as fortunate as my father, I think, to be surrounded by such compassionate people as you two have been, even though I am a stranger to you."

"You are no stranger, Miss Bertram," Jennings said. "I feel strongly that your father wishes us to affect some good here, for you and for him, and I will do what I can in that regard."

"As will I," Elizabeth said. Since Miss Bertram looked dangerously close to breaking down again, Elizabeth hastily added, "Do you happen to remember, Miss Bertram, what Betty's family name may be? It will help us locate her."

Miss Bertram's fingers twisted around her handkerchief as she thought. "I know she had been married," she said finally. "But he was never with her in this house, and I don't know what may have happened to him. So you see," she went on, giving her guests a little smile. "I don't know if her surname was her husband's name, or her family's name. Her name was Betty Cantor, and I imagine she is still Betty Cantor. Her family owned some sort of inn in Bedford." She trailed off, trying to recall things that Betty had said to her more than four years ago. "I can't remember the name of the inn, I'm afraid."

"Do you suppose," Mr. Jennings said. "That it might be the Blue Dove?"

"Oh, yes!" Miss Bertram exclaimed. "Oh, yes, that is it! The Blue Dove!"

CHAPTER SEVEN

The carriage swayed gently to and fro as it made its slow way toward Bedford.

"Shall we have our lunch straightaway, sir?" Elizabeth asked. "I believe it will be rather late when we arrive."

"I had planned to do so," Jennings replied. "Especially since we have no idea what we will find there." He looked in curiosity at Elizabeth's sketchbook, in which she had been drawing intently since they left the house. "What are you drawing, my dear?"

"Oh," she said, looking up at him. It had not occurred to her that he would want to see her drawing; she hoped now that he would not find it too disturbing. "I have been meaning to do it for some time," she explained, turning the book so that he could see the page. "But my courage failed me until lately."

Jennings examined the picture, his only response a sharp intake of breath as he recognized the creature Elizabeth had drawn. "The beast that attacked you," he said finally, his fingers touching the edge of the paper.

Elizabeth had skillfully recreated what she had seen the night of Lady Morton's party. She had never seen the beast's face, and so she had rendered it in dark shadow, but his basic form – easily three times her size and covered with glistening grey skin – was cast in stark relief, the arms particularly seeming to leap from the page with twisting tendons and giant claws. Its feet were also shrouded in darkness, since all she could remember of them was how cruelly they had kicked her, but it stood in the stooped posture of a creature more typically accustomed to walking on four limbs than on two.

"It's what I recall seeing," she said. "And *feeling*." She paused, staring at her drawing with her head tilted to one side. "He was so gigantic!" she went on, shuddering at the memory. "I cannot imagine how I survived at all!"

Jennings quickly reached out to take her hand. "Do not distress yourself, my dear!" he urged her, his brows coming together in a concerned frown as he saw tears swimming in her eyes. Glancing down once more at the drawing, he decided after a moment's consideration to confess what he had himself seen. "I recognize this creature," he told her, his free hand still touching the grotesque image. "I saw it on Lady Morton's balcony." He looked up at her. "In a vision," he finished rather hurriedly. Although she had until now been remarkably accepting of his gifts, he was still secretly sure that at any moment she would become frightened by them.

Elizabeth responded to his statement with her customary curiosity. "You saw it before it attacked me?" she asked. "Is that what prompted you to come back to Lady Morton's for me?"

"No," he said. "The slate only showed me danger, and urgency." He shook his head. "No, I saw it when Lady Morton took me to the balcony where you had been abducted. There was a stain – perhaps the creature's blood, but I think more likely some sort of slime that covered its skin – on the outside of the balcony railing. When I touched it, I was ..." He searched for words. "I was besieged by an image of this beast." He gestured to the drawing. "I saw him carry you into the park, and rip the necklace from your throat – the necklace that held your ring – and all I could feel was the monster's overwhelming desire to kill you, and to steal that ring."

Elizabeth's eyes opened wide. "That was my mother's ring," she

72

explained. "I had thought I had lost it in the park. I – I had not realized – I did not know that this creature had taken it particularly." She frowned, confused and irritated. "Why would it want my mother's ring? It is almost the only thing I have from her."

"I don't know," Jennings said. "I only know that he wanted it, and that his attack had been meant to kill you."

Elizabeth blinked at him in sudden realization. "Do you believe, Mr. Jennings," she asked him, a slight alarm creeping into her voice. "That it will return to finish what it started?"

Jennings squeezed her hand comfortingly. "I had thought of that," he acknowledged. His eyes twinkled. "But I am governing my urge to lock you safely in a cupboard, surrounded by guards."

Elizabeth laughed. "I suppose I am glad of that!" she said. "But of course the thought of it puts things into perspective, doesn't it? Thank you, Mr. Jennings." She smiled and returned the pressure of his fingers. "I will try not to worry." She gazed at her drawing, and grew serious. "But I believe I will be on my guard, sir."

"I have been on my guard since I found you, Mrs. Jennings," Jennings told her with a lop-sided smile. "But I am convinced the best course is to investigate your attack as I do everything the slate shows me; if we can discover this creature's motive, perhaps we can bring its owner to justice."

Elizabeth squinted at him quizzically. "You think that the monster was guided by another?"

"Why would an animal such as the one you have drawn here have a wish to steal your ring?" Jennings said. "Why not simply kill you and eat you?" He shook his head again. "No, I cannot think but that some human has controlled this beast, in hopes of eliminating

73

you and stealing your mother's memento."

"But why?" Elizabeth asked, her frown deepening as she mulled over the incident. "Why would anyone want *me* dead? I've never hurt anyone."

"And, with all respect to your father," Jennings said. "His fortune is neither grand, nor would you ever have been in the way of it. It cannot be the reason." He leaned back and pulled Elizabeth's sketchbook onto his lap. "And why should anyone send such a dire henchman?" he wondered. "Why not just attack you himself?"

Elizabeth considered this. "Perhaps he is someone who could not approach me without great effort," she suggested. "Or someone who would seem suspicious."

Jennings gazed at her in admiration. Although her experiences had deeply affected her, she seemed more interested in solving the mystery than in being brought low by it. "You are remarkable, my dear," he said. "And I think you are likely right about this man."

Elizabeth smiled again, unsure why Mr. Jennings found her remarkable, but pleased by the compliment. Before she could ask him about it, he went on.

"It could be more than one person," he said. "But their purpose is still unfathomable to me."

"And to me!" Elizabeth agreed with a chuckle. "And why my mother's ring?"

They each sat in silent thought for some time, trying to suss out the matter with no success, until the carriage drew to a stop in front of a small inn. The groom quickly opened the door and poked his head inside.

"Bedford, sir," he announced. "The Blue Dove."

The groom helped Elizabeth down from the carriage; she walked around, stretching her legs and neck, as Jennings arranged for luncheon at the inn. She noticed that the Blue Dove was a very pretty sort of establishment, and that the people who came to attend to Mr. Jennings were very affable.

"I believe I rather like Bedford," she said to herself.

Jennings offered her his arm. "Shall we go inside, my dear? I am informed that luncheon awaits us momentarily."

"Wonderful," Elizabeth said, smiling brightly. She took her husband's arm, and he walked with her into the inn. The inside was equally pleasing to her, and she declared herself quite satisfied already with their little journey.

"Now if we can only determine why we have been guided here," Jennings said drily. They followed a serving girl into a tiny salon with a table and four chairs.

"Is this to your liking, sir?" she asked.

"It is indeed," Jennings said. "Excuse me," he added. "Is there a Betty Cantor here?"

The serving girl looked surprised. "There is, sir," she said. "Her father owns this inn."

Jennings nodded. "Excellent," he said. "We've come to the right place." He exchanged glances with Elizabeth, then turned back to the serving girl. "We have sad news for Betty, I'm afraid," he told her, growing serious. "Could we – if it is not an imposition on her time – could we perhaps speak with her?"

"Of course, sir," the girl said, her eyes open wide. "I'll fetch her at once." She withdrew quickly from the room, and a moment later they could faintly hear her calling out for Betty.

They had not waited more than a minute before the serving girl returned to the salon; she held the door open for a second woman who stood behind her. "Mrs. Cantor, sir," she introduced this person, who walked rather tentatively into the room and stood uncertainly looking from Elizabeth to Jennings and back again.

"What can I do for you, sir?" she asked. "Mimsy said you had bad tidings for me."

Jennings stepped toward her, his expression assiduously kind. "I'm afraid we do, Betty," he said gently. "I understand you are very close to the Bertram family?"

Betty's eyes widened, and she looked decidedly wary. "I am, sir," she said. "Or, rather, I was. After Mrs. Bertram was lost, I could not bear to be there anymore." She frowned. "Is something amiss with Mr. Bertram, sir? Or with Miss Miranda?"

Elizabeth, who had taken a seat in one of the chairs, reached forward and put a comforting hand on Betty's arm. "Mr. Bertram has died, Betty," she said, her voice so soft that it was scarcely audible. "I'm so sorry."

Betty's whole body slumped as though all the air had gone out of her. Her eyes closed for a few seconds, and when she opened them once more, they shone with tears. "Well," she said. "Well." She gazed down at her hands, which were clasped in front of her. "I suppose it is no surprise, since he was not a young man, nor healthy, but I've thought often of him, and I'm terrible sad." She gave a sound like a laugh mixed with a sob. "My last memory of him," she continued, her voice choking with emotion. "I had to tell him his wife had gone, and his wee babe as well. Especially now that I have my own child, I can't imagine Mr. Bertram's suffering."

"I'm very, very sorry, Betty," Elizabeth repeated. "Miss Miranda had – well, she showed us your letter to her father upon your leaving, and it was that that prompted us to find you; since clearly you were so attached to the family, a letter filled with such unhappy news seemed frankly cruel. And so we have come here, and we are more than happy to convey you to London if you wish to pay your respects, or to take with us any message you wish to send to Miss Bertram."

Betty perked up a bit at such a thought. "I will gladly write a letter to Miss Miranda!" she exclaimed. She turned toward the door. "I'll just find some paper."

Elizabeth came abruptly to her feet. "If it's no trouble," she said, her hand once again on Betty's arm. "I wonder if – you said you had a child of your own." She smiled apologetically. "It's just that I've had the image of Miss Miranda's poor little brother in my mind, and I have thought of little else these two days. I believe it would do me good to see a *happy* child." Her smile broadened. "Would it be too much to ask if I might meet *your* child?"

If Betty thought such a request to be a strange one, she gave no sign. "Not at all, ma'am," she replied. "I'll bring him in." She left the room then, and Jennings quietly shut the door behind her.

"You believe Mr. Bertram is the father of Betty's baby," he said, more as a statement than a question.

Elizabeth had sat once more at the table. "I thought it was a possibility," she said. She shook her head, frowning slightly. "But it doesn't make a great deal of sense to me."

Jennings looked at her curiously. "Why not?" he asked.

"Well, why would she leave the house if she were carrying his child?" Elizabeth wanted to know. "Even if he never claimed it, better to raise it under his protection than to return home with a child and no husband."

"He does seem – at least through Miranda's eyes – to have been a kind-hearted man," Jennings allowed. "I imagine he would have been content enough to have her child in the house. But her letter indicates that she was quite horribly upset by Mrs. Bertram's death; perhaps she wanted nothing more than to be away from London, and has told her family that her husband left her with child before he ran off."

"But her husband had been gone so long that Miranda had never even laid eyes on him," Elizabeth argued. "Her family would no doubt be aware of that." She shook her head again. "It seems very silly of her to have come home under such circumstances, when she had other choices she could easily have made."

Jennings considered her words. "But if her child is not Mr. Bertram's," he said. "Then why has the slate led us here?"

Elizabeth's eyes twinkled. "That I cannot tell you, sir," she said wryly. "It is your slate, and your vision." Her smile faded as she looked at the closed door. "But if Betty Cantor's child is Mr. Bertram's child, then her actions are quite puzzling to me."

The door opened then, and a small boy came into the room, his tousled chestnut curls complementing enormous blue eyes and a cheerful grin. "Hello!" he greeted them. "Mum said I was to come and meet you!"

Behind him, Betty pushed the door open further, bustling into the room on her son's heels and giving him a gentle push toward Elizabeth. "Give the lady a smile now, William!" she directed him.

"She's been sad."

William looked vaguely alarmed at this notion. "Why are you sad?" he asked Elizabeth, walking up to her.

"For the same reason your mother is sad," Elizabeth said, smiling brightly back at him and taking his little hands in hers. "We have lost someone who was kind and good, and your happy face has been quite the very thing I needed!" She looked up at Jennings. "It is rather a remarkable likeness, isn't it?" she asked him.

"It certainly is," Jennings agreed. He closed the door to the salon and stood casually in front of it with his hands in his pockets.

Upon hearing Elizabeth's words, Betty's wariness returned; in fact, she grew pale, and her eyes darted nervously from one of the Jennings to the other. "What – what do you mean, ma'am?"

Elizabeth gazed at her with maddening placidity. "Why, your child looks so very much like Miss Miranda Bertram," she answered sweetly. "Who, if I am remembering the portraits correctly, takes far more after her mother than her father."

"What are you talking about?" Betty asked, her hands reaching out to rest protectively on the little boy's shoulders.

Jennings decided that it was no longer time for polite circumspection. "Betty," he said, his voice firm even though his posture remained relaxed and, with his hands still in his pockets, almost jovial. "Is William not Mr. Bertram's son?" He was on the verge of asking her why she had not obliged Mr. Bertram to claim William, when Betty suddenly dissolved into tears and sobs.

"Don't take him from me!" she begged, her face buried in her hands. "He's all I got! It's not my fault she died! I did everything I could!" Her sobs turned to wails, and William stood staring at her in absolute consternation.

"Mummy!" he pleaded. "Don't cry, Mummy!"

"There was no midwife!" Betty cried. "I didn't know what to do! It all went so quick, and then she was gone!"

Jennings had been taken aback by Betty's outburst; he put his hands on her shoulders and tried to comfort her. "There's no need to be so upset, Betty," he said. "You're not the first to have her master's child, and to have nowhere to go with it."

Betty lowered her hands and stared up at him in confusion. "What are talking about?" she asked again.

Elizabeth stood and put her own hand on one of Mr. Jennings'. "Miss Miranda takes after her mother," she repeated, gazing at him meaningfully.

Jennings' brow cleared. "You took Mrs. Bertram's infant," he breathed, understanding now what Elizabeth had already deduced. "You took him for yourself."

Betty was rocking back and forth, her arms wrapped now around her stomach as though she were ill. "I never meant no harm," she averred. "I left the other one. I left him there with his mother. I put him in the ground with her, and it broke my heart!"

William, his own cheeks now stained by sympathetic tears, hugged Betty around the waist. "Don't cry, Mummy," he said forlornly, and clutched her to him. "Don't cry."

Elizabeth knelt down and wrapped her arms around the little boy. "Don't worry, dearest," she told him. "We'll sort it all out, and everything will be fine, I promise."

Jennings was not half so sure as his wife seemed to be that anything would be fine at all. "I believe we should summon a constable," he said.

Betty collapsed then, falling against Mr. Jennings. He carefully lowered her to the floor and began chafing her wrists.

"We'll need a doctor as well," he added.

CHAPTER EIGHT

Miranda Bertram hesitated in front of the magistrate's offices, but, after taking a deep breath and, in that brief moment, searching her heart, she raised her gloved hand and rapped gently on the closed door.

It was quickly opened by a young man who seemed to be the magistrate's assistant. "Miss Bertram?" he asked, swinging the door open wide and gesturing for her to enter. "Please do come in, miss."

Miss Bertram entered the room, and saw two stern-looking men sat on one side of a table, and a woman seated between them. This woman was clearly unhappy and a little frightened, and her eyes darted constantly from one to the other of the men flanking her.

Miss Bertram recognized her at once. "Betty," she said, and came immediately to the table. The young man who had opened the door now pulled a chair over for her, and she took it with a murmur of thanks. "Betty," she said again, leaning across the table and reaching her hands toward the other woman. "Will you not look at me?"

Betty was silent and immobile; then, as a strangled sort of sob escaped her throat, she forced her gaze up to meet Miss Bertram's. "Miss Miranda," she croaked, tears in her eyes. "You've grown into such a lovely girl!"

Miss Bertram put a hand on Betty's, which were clasped tightly together on the table in front of her. "Betty," she began, her brows drawn together in a combination of confusion and concern. "Please tell me why you did this."

Betty sobbed again, and tears fell unchecked down her cheeks.

When she did not instantly speak, the man on her right grabbed her upper arm and gave it a shake. "The lady asked you a question!" he barked. "You answer!"

Betty cried out, startled by the man's actions. "I don't know!" she wailed finally. "I don't know why I did it!" She looked beseechingly at Miss Bertram. "I know you'll never believe it, miss, but I swear to you I never meant no harm!"

Miss Bertram still held Betty's hands. She felt tears stinging her own eyes; she had known Betty since childhood, and had never known an unkind word to pass her lips. She had in fact been quite gentle and loving. "Was your regard for us – for me – all a lie, then?" she asked. She found that she was trembling. "Did you never really care for us?"

Betty shook her head vehemently. "The Bertrams was like my own family, miss!" she said. "When Mistress died, I was beside myself!" She hung her head in utter despondence, still moving it back and forth. "When her wee one took no breath, I chafed his arms and legs, and I held him to my own bosom! I –" She faltered, and her voice became choked with emotion. "I did everythin' I could!" Her head sank down until it almost touched the table. "I did everythin' I could!"

Miss Bertram, having wrestled with this dilemma since it had been brought to her two days ago, and having spoken at some length with her cousin Parrish and with Mrs. Jennings, had decided that Elizabeth was quite right: little William had known only love from Betty, and she was, in his heart, his mother; for her part, Betty seemed to be exactly the good-hearted and forthright person she had been when she worked in the Bertram home.

"Betty," Miranda began gently. "Can you not tell me what you were thinking when you took the second baby away?"

For a moment, the room was so silent that it seemed no one even breathed. Betty raised her eyes again to Miss Bertram's face.

"I don't know the right words, miss," she said, her words barely audible even in the stillness. "All I knew was that I'd married a man who left me with nothin', no money nor no children, and here was Mistress dead before me, and p'raps I could've saved her if I had known how, but I didn't." She began weeping again, her shoulders shaking uncontrollably. "And the wee one grew so cold in my arms, and I was heartsick, and I dreaded lookin' on either of 'em. And I just thought –" She gave a helpless shrug. "I saw th'other one stirrin', and I thought – I thought maybe I could save one of 'em." She shook her head again. "By the time I came to my senses, miss, and seen what I had done, I didn't know how to undo it without …" She looked out of the corners of her eyes, first at the man on her left, and then at the man on her right. "I was afraid I would go to prison, miss, or worse." She stopped speaking then, and bowed her head again, awaiting whatever condemnation Miss Bertram saw fit to heap upon her.

"I have met my brother, Betty," Miss Bertram said softly. Suddenly she grinned. "William is the sweetest little boy I have ever seen!" she avowed. "He is still quite confused, I believe, for no one has known just how – or what – to tell him, but he seems very happy at the thought that I am his sister, and that he will come to live in a nice house in town, and go to school."

Betty's shoulders slumped forward. "You'll love him, miss," she said. "I'm glad he'll want for nothing, and that he'll be with you."

Any doubt lingering in Miss Bertram's breast was now

eliminated as thoroughly as though it had never been; she squeezed Betty's hands, and, still smiling, she informed her, "You both will be with me, Betty."

Betty stared, confounded, at Miss Bertram, and the man on Betty's right gave a start and slammed his hand down on the table. "Miss Bertram!" he protested loudly. "You cannot be in earnest!" The man on Betty's left looked similarly aghast, although he checked his emotions more completely than his companion. "Miss Bertram," he said. "Why ever would you take this woman in?"

Miss Bertram, momentarily surprised by the men's outbursts, hastened to reassure them. "I have discussed it at length with my cousin – Mr. Parrish, who I daresay you might remember, Betty – and he has agreed – since there is an heir to my father's estate, after all – that he will be the steward of the estate until William is of age, and he will look after my interests until such time as I am married, and he will take you in as a ward of the estate, Betty, and you will want for nothing, to use your words, and you will have an education if you wish, and you might live in the Bertram house as William's mother for as long as you wish it!" She finished, beaming brightly at the other woman, who still sat in dumbstruck confusion.

"You cannot –" she began, then cleared her throat and started over. "Indeed, miss, you can't mean it! It's not heard of!"

"I completely agree!" the loud man interjected. His face was turning an unpleasant shade of red. "This piece," he went on, indicating Betty, "will only steal everything from you and take William again!"

"No, I won't!" Betty objected, horrified at the notion. "I never took nothin' from them, ever! Nor would I!"

The man glared at her in utter disbelief. "You stole the *child*!" he pointed out, and she shrank down into her chair, abashed.

Miss Bertram put her hand on the man's arm. "Please, sir," she said calmly. "Betty has raised William as her own child, and I can see very well that she has cared for him with all the affection that I remember receiving from her myself." She gave Betty an encouraging smile. "William is so attached to you, Betty, and he has never known any other family; it would be a punishment for him – he who is blameless in this entire affair! – and neither I nor Mr. Parrish could fathom causing William any pain at all. And I believe – however wrong your actions may have been on that day – I believe I see in you here the same good heart I had known in you before you went away."

Before Betty could respond, the man on her left spoke again. "And Mr. Parrish agrees to all this?"

"Yes," Miss Bertram said, nodding. "Of course, now that he is not to inherit the estate, I suppose in large measure the decision is not up to him ... but then again, I would not be skilled at managing the estate, or at having someone be my 'ward'. While I might certainly learn such things over time, for now it seemed best to accept my cousin's offer of stewardship. And, of course, he also had the opportunity to meet William, and to see how well he has been cared for, and how much he loves his mother – you, Betty – and Mr. Parrish was as inclined as I to be merciful in this matter."

"Your cousin," the quieter man said. He leaned forward, his hands spread out on the table before him. "I want to be very clear, Miss Bertram," he continued sternly. "Your cousin *accepts* this woman as a ward?"

Miss Bertram gazed levelly at him. "That part was his own idea," she explained. "If for no other reason than that William's ... well, his *second* mother ... had rightly ought to be from a similar station. And truly," she added, more to Betty than to the others. "Mr. Parrish is quite kind-hearted, and has been very understanding in the loss of my father's estate." She chuckled. "He had been planning to sell it, I believe," she said. "I am sure it must certainly have been quite a blow, but his connection to my father is such that he says he is most honoured and gratified to help both me and little William. Is not that wonderful?"

Betty had given up all notion of comprehending the good fortune that seemed to be shining upon her. She looked in awe at Miss Bertram, and, raising her sleeve to her face to dry the tears from her cheeks, she said humbly, "You are as kind a girl as ever you were, miss, and your heart is so good as I never've seen."

Miss Bertram patted Betty's hand and sat back in her chair. "And so all is decided, yes?" she asked the quieter man. She turned from him to the louder man and then to the assistant that had been standing wordlessly beside the door. "Betty and William come to London with me, and all is well." Her grin widened. "Yes?"

In the next half hour, the quieter man – who revealed himself to be the magistrate for the town – and Miss Bertram discussed the details of the entire matter; as the clock ticked past noon, Mr. Parrish, little William in tow, appeared at the door, and joined his own voice to the account, assuring all concerned that it was proceeding according to his intentions, and that he bore no ill will toward Betty. "For I cannot deny," he said at one point. "That if I had been witness to the death of someone so dear to me, I would no doubt have been so distraught as even to be out of my wits. And then, on the morrow, if I were thus faced with the prospect of prison … well, sir, I do not mind revealing to you that I might well have made the same decision as she." And since he had often heard from both Mr. and Mrs. Bertram a great deal in praise of Betty, and since William was so happy to see his mother – from whom he had been kept for some days – that all efforts to pry him from her side would clearly be in vain, Mr. Parrish was cheerfully committed to implement his plan, and to ensconce William and Betty into their new lives as quickly as possible.

And so, despite the deep misgivings and lingering consternation of the constabulary and the magistrate, the charges against Betty were dismissed, and she was allowed to travel from Bedford to London with the Bertrams and Mr. Parrish.

"Is that not unbelievable?" Elizabeth asked Mr. Jennings, as they sat at supper. "Is it not the happiest ending to the story?" Before he could answer, she went on excitedly, "When I called on them this afternoon, little William was already scampering all over the house as though he had always been there, and Miss Miranda looked so happy!" Her eyes glistened. "It is of all things the most wonderful, to see how all has worked out favourably."

Jennings gazed at her with a soft smile. Silently, he wished that Elizabeth's own father had been nearly so kind as Miss Bertram had been to Betty Cantor, but he would not dampen Elizabeth's joy by saying so aloud. "Indeed, my dear," he said. "It is extraordinary, and I must admit I did not expect such a pleasant outcome when we left Bedford." He reached out and patted her hand before picking up his glass of burgundy. "But you expected nothing less," he added. "I should never doubt you."

She grinned. "Of course you should not!" she seconded. Through the window behind her husband she saw a bright flicker of lightning. "I believe a storm is coming, sir," she noted, as the grumble of thunder reached them.

"Mrs. Raleigh predicted as much," Jennings said, glancing over his shoulder. Outside, a brisk wind had come up, whipping branches to and fro; a few first tentative raindrops spattered against the window. "She has – as she phrases it – a 'knee' which knows more than all the almanacs ever written."

Elizabeth laughed. "My father has a 'shoulder' that is equally good at prediction," she revealed.

Jennings turned back to her. "You don't hate him," he noted. "Even after all that he's done."

Elizabeth's smile remained. "I don't," she said simply. "Indeed, he did nothing *to* me. He has always treated me exactly as he treats everyone, and he evaluates me by the same ruler he has used his whole life to measure everything equally." She shook her head. "No," she went on. "In fact, I could see his heart in the letter he wrote, that Lady Morton read out to me."

Jennings lifted his brows in surprise. "The letter I overheard?" he asked. "You saw his heart in *that*?"

Elizabeth gave a little chuckle. "I did," she averred. "I know that his views on women – and many other things – seem antiquated and cold, but they are his true sentiments. He truly believes his notions, and what he viewed as my 'indiscretion' must have been quite alarming for him. You see, Mr. Jennings," she added, grinning across the dining table at him. "My father is never the sort of person to be outraged by anything. Yet he was outraged at what he believes to be my actions. He would not feel that unless I had particularly disappointed him, unless he had believed before that moment that I would never be guilty of such ... weakness."

Jennings was even more baffled. "And you saw his heart in his outrage?"

"Yes," Elizabeth said. "It means that he had set me apart from others, that I had some significance to him beyond what he might ordinarily feel."

"And the fact that you had this significance," Jennings said. "You perceive that to be his regard for you?"

"Yes," Elizabeth repeated. She shrugged slightly. "We cannot ask people to be more than they are, can we?" She took another bite of her supper. "He felt for me what he could feel for anyone, and he always treated me well, and so I feel no animosity toward him. I feel only the same that I have felt from him since my first memory."

Jennings tilted his head in curiosity.

"He is my father," Elizabeth explained, and shrugged again. "He's my father."

Jennings took a sip of burgundy. "Clearly, you have received *your* heart from your mother."

Elizabeth chuckled again. "Perhaps," she acknowledged. "I have heard endless good of her from all who knew her – even my father – but I never knew her myself."

Jennings finished his burgundy and placed the empty glass on the table. "Can I – do I disturb you by asking? – how your mother died?"

Elizabeth shook her head. "Not at all," she assured him. "I do not remember it." She paused, recalling things her father had told her.

"She died of a sudden fever," she said at last. "When I was only a few months old." A slight frown creased her brow. "She had had a nightmare, apparently. My father said that it took him several minutes to convince her that she was awake and that it had only been a dream. But in the next few days, she became certain that it was a foreshadowing of her own death, and one morning, she did not awaken." She gazed at Jennings, her expression reflecting a sense of epiphany. "She had dreamed that something hunted her, sir, and that it wanted to kill her. My father felt that she sapped her own strength with her irrational belief in her dream, and so allowed the fever to gain hold of her. But if you are correct, and indeed some dark personage has summoned the supernatural to achieve his own ends, then perhaps it behooves us to examine my mother's passing."

"My thoughts exactly!" Jennings said. "This ring that had been your mother's – other than its having been hers, does it have any special significance?"

Elizabeth considered this for a moment. "No," she decided. "It's not even particularly valuable; it's a simple silver ring, set with a green peridot – my mother's birthstone. It had been given her by her grandmother, whose birthstone it also was, and I've always assumed, since my mother was very close to her grandmother, that she then passed the ring to me as a sort of family heirloom." She raised one eyebrow. "But I suppose now that we must assume the ring meant a good deal more."

"Indeed," Jennings agreed. He poured himself another glass of burgundy. "Did your mother leave you anything else? Anything that might point to some story behind the ring?"

"She left me a letter," Elizabeth answered. "She wrote it the day before she died. She was so convinced that her dream had been prophetic, you see, that she felt some urgency in leaving me what legacy – and what sentiment – she could in the time that remained to her." She smiled softly. "I am sure that my father thought she was being silly, but whether she brought the fever on herself, or whether it was visited upon her, she did in fact seem to know that she would die … and so I am very glad that she wrote the letter."

"As am I," Jennings said. He had such fond memories of his mother and sister, and of his father; he could not imagine having only a letter from them, and he wished fervently that he could give Elizabeth her mother back.

"My father gave me some other of her things," Elizabeth continued. "Her family Bible, and journals she had kept; a few pieces of jewelry, and portraits of her and of my grandmother, who –" She broke off abruptly, as chills slid up her spine. "My grandmother died two days before my mother," she revealed. "As my father prepared to send word to her about my mother, a messenger arrived on our doorstep with the tidings of Grandmother's passing."

Jennings leaned forward. "How did your grandmother die?" he asked, his voice taut with dawning excitement.

"She apparently died in the night," Elizabeth said. "She was not ill; everyone considered it quite strange. I don't know if she had had a similar dream or premonition. No one has ever told me that she did, but I suppose it is possible." She too leaned forward, and looked rather anxiously at her husband. "Could what happened to me in fact be connected to my mother's and grandmother's deaths? Could they have been …" She hesitated, almost afraid to say the word aloud. "Could they have been *murdered*?"

Jennings sat back in his chair. Behind him, lightning flashed in the window, and a long rumble of thunder accompanied his words. "I believe, Lizzie," he said quietly. "That your mother was murdered, and that your grandmother was murdered, and that the same entity has tried to murder you."

Elizabeth let this information sink in. "I do not know how to feel about that," she admitted, staring unseeing at her plate. She lifted her eyes to Jennings' face. "Did you see this, sir?" she asked. "Did you see the truth of it?"

"You mean the way I saw the green box and the blue dove?" he asked. She nodded. "No," he told her. He put one hand on his chest. "But I *feel* the truth of it." His eyes glanced this way and that as he pondered what clues had been given him. "You said there were journals?"

"Yes," Elizabeth replied.

"You've read them?"

"Yes," she said again. "But I had not done so with an eye for discovering dark mysteries, sir." She put her hands on the edge of the table as though she would stand, and spoke resolutely. "We must start at the beginning," she said. "And read it all with new eyes."

Jennings nodded, and pushed his chair away from the table. "We must indeed," he said. "But it will have to wait until morning, I'm afraid." He came to his feet, his hand still on his chest. When Elizabeth looked at him inquiringly, he explained with an apologetic shrug, "I believe the slate has something to tell me."

The words on the slate were simple enough: "Save my loved ones."

And the image he saw when he read the words was not a horrible image – a simple cottage nestled in a stretch of woods, next to a stream that might rightly be described as a river under the right conditions. A warm glow of firelight shone through the front windows, and, although he could not see them, he knew that a family was tucked up inside the cottage, gathered together around the fire.

But he knew just as surely that the cottage was in terrible danger, that something threatened it extremely and immediately. The force of this knowing took his breath away for a moment, and he was obliged to sit on the edge of his bed as his vision swam before him.

Elizabeth sat instantly beside him, her brow furrowed with worry. "Are you quite well, sir?" she asked him. She put a hand on his arm. "What did you see?"

Jennings shook his head. "I saw an ordinary peasants' cottage," he said. "But I *felt* overwhelming dread – something bad is about to happen." He came to his feet. "I'm prompted to head northeast," he went on. "I believe the house is along that road, not too far from here."

Elizabeth's eyes widened. "You cannot mean to go *now*!" she exclaimed. "Into this storm? It's madness!"

Jennings shrugged, closing the drawer where the slate still lay. "I must do what the slate bids me do," he explained. "I've been given this gift for a reason."

Elizabeth blinked, contemplating his words. She knew that if he had not been willing to act immediately on the night that she met him, she would now certainly be dead; she had no reason to think that this vision was any less accurate, or that his actions should be any less urgent.

"All right," she said at last. "But I won't watch you go out alone."

Jennings, who had been on the point of departure, stopped abruptly. "You are not coming with me," he informed her firmly. "I have no idea what sort of danger imperils this cottage, and the storm is quite fierce." Indeed, the thunder booming outside seemed to be shaking the house as well as the windows. "It's not safe."

She stood, and raised one eyebrow. She had thought at first to remonstrate with him, but realized in the same instant that it would be entirely fruitless, and would only waste time which Mr. Jennings clearly deemed to be in short supply. "I will not watch you go alone," she repeated. "If you will not take me with you, I will follow you."

He stared at her, bereft of speech. He opened his mouth to ask her if she was in earnest, but he could already see the answer in her eyes, which looked coolly back at him with utmost conviction. "If I leave," he said. "You will follow me."

"Yes," she replied simply.

He squinted at her. "Why?" he asked.

Her direct gaze faltered slightly. "I don't want you to be hurt somehow without anyone's knowing where you might be," she said truthfully. "When you say you're walking deliberately into danger, who can tell what might befall you!" Her shoulders twitched in a slight shrug. "Besides," she added. "I want to know what's going to happen to the cottage."

She continued to watch him, and his eyes never wavered from her face. "Short of tying you to something," he said finally. "Or locking you in a cupboard, is there any way to dissuade you?"

She gave him an apologetic half-smile. "Not really, no."

At a loss to explain how he had let himself be talked into such a ridiculous course of action – and unwilling to acknowledge that in fact very little talking had marked the conversation – Jennings put a hand on Elizabeth's shoulder and walked with her toward the door. "As you wish, then," he said, trying to make his voice crisp but succeeding only in sounding wearily resigned. "We must move quickly."

* * *

By the time Jennings steered the curricle onto the road, the storm had whipped itself into a veritable frenzy; rain flung down from the heavens in heavy sheets that quickly drenched them both, even though Jennings had put up the curricle's hood before leaving the house.

Still feeling strongly that the cottage lay to the northeast, he guided his horses in that general direction, eventually ending up on a narrow lane that wound its way into a section of thick forest. His route was illuminated only by the flickers of lightning that lit the black sky, and he had set such a wicked pace that finally Elizabeth, her hands gripping tight to the side of the curricle, voiced her concern.

"Mr. Jennings!" she shouted over the noise of the storm. "We'll be overturned! You cannot even see your path!"

Jennings looked askance at her. "I told you to stay home!" he reminded her.

"And you wish to kill us both to prove a point to me?" she asked him, pushing rain away from her face before clamping her hand once more on the edge of the seat.

Jennings did not answer; his attention was riveted on what little of the path he could see ahead of him. The sense of urgency that had been thrust upon him was now growing by the minute, and his heart pounded in his chest. He had no wish to die – and certainly no wish to harm Elizabeth in any way – but the urgency drove him forward as though no other thought could enter his brain.

After what seemed an interminable ride, the curricle passed underneath a canopy of trees, and the rain beating against the Jennings slackened. Elizabeth was able to peer ahead into the darkness. "Is that a light?" she asked hopefully, nodding her head toward what she thought – prayed – was a circle of yellow glowing faintly in the distance.

Jennings spied the tiny light and felt a glimmer of relief. "I believe so," he said. Soon they had drawn close enough to make out the shapes of windows through which the yellow glow emanated, and then, a moment later, the cottage itself became visible – a blot of greyness contrasted against the black woods around it. "That's the cottage I saw," Jennings revealed.

Elizabeth was examining the cottage as best she could through the rain. "It does not seem to be in any danger," she noted. "Are you sure it's the one you saw?"

"I'm sure," he said. He drove up to the front of the cottage and pulled the horses to an abrupt stop not ten feet from the door. "Ho there!" he shouted, but his voice was drowned out by the thunder and wind. "You there, inside!"

He climbed down and strode up to the house. "Ho there!" he yelled again, thumping the side of his fist on the door. Behind him, Elizabeth gathered her cloak around her shoulders and carefully slid down from the seat of the curricle.

"It is quite late," she said to him, coming to stand beside him on the stone stoop.

"Lizzie!" Jennings exclaimed, surprised to see her. "I'm sorry!" he said contritely. "I should have helped you down!"

A dimple appeared, and her eyes twinkled as she looked up at him. "I believe I am quite capable," she said drily. She tucked her hand under his arm. "But I am sure these poor people have long since gone to bed."

As though to contradict her, the front door was flung suddenly open, and a middle-aged man glared angrily out at them. "What the devil is this about, then!" he demanded. "It's near the middle o' the night!"

"I apologize, sir," Jennings said. "But I must ask that you leave this cottage at once!"

The man became angrier, and, squinting at Jennings in deep suspicion, he barked at him, "Are you out of your senses? What are you on about?"

From inside the cottage, a woman called out. "Who is it? Is it someone for Mama?"

The man looked briefly over his shoulder. "It's someone I've never seen in my whole life," he informed her. "He wants us to leave our house!"

A cluster of children of various ages appeared then, circling the man who seemed to be their father. They stared out in open curiosity at the strangers on their doorstep, until the woman who had spoken came up behind them and began shooing them away.

"Get back from the door now!" she admonished them. "Your father will take care of it." She eyed the Jennings with the same suspicion that still lingered on her husband's face. "Whoever in the world are you?" she asked. "You're not here for Mama?"

Elizabeth, seeing an opportunity to turn the tone of the conversation, stepped forward and asked, as kindly as she could muster, "You're expecting someone to fetch your mother?"

To her dismay, the woman's expression became even more mistrustful. "My mother is dead, ma'am," she said curtly. "She left us not two days ago."

"And," her husband interjected, his brows drawn together starkly over his nose. "If you were any acquaintance of her, I daresay you would know that she is gone." He placed both hands, balled into fists, on his hips, and positioned himself protectively across the doorway. "So whatever your business is here, you'd best be off!"

"Please, sir," Jennings said, wiping a hand across his face to clear the rain away. "I know it must sound exceedingly strange to you, but I assure you, you are in danger here!" He gazed pleadingly from the man to his wife, and then all around him at the raging storm. "Please! You must leave at once!"

The man in the doorway puffed his chest out, and his irritation suffused his entire person. "We will do no such thing!" he avowed.

A deafening explosion of thunder answered him, as a bolt of lightning split the center of the large tree to the left of the cottage.

Elizabeth, at first startled nearly out of her wits, watched wide-eyed as the tree, its trunk now decorated with a few tongues of flame and a cloud of bitter-smelling smoke, slowly listed to the side.

"Come out now!" she ordered, stepping away from the house and beckoning frantically with both arms.

Jennings grabbed the man by the front of his shirt and dragged him outside. "Now!" he shouted.

The woman, rattled by the blast of lightning, hastened to follow Elizabeth's instructions, grabbing her children and pushing them before her into the storm. She had not even cleared the doorway herself when the tree, groaning monstrously in protest, fell crashing down onto the roof of the cottage. The roof caved in, and the cottage walls bowed outward; the branches of the tree brushed against the woman, eliciting a terrified scream from her, and causing her to jump forward several feet in alarm.

"Good God!" the man exclaimed, standing in awe at what had just happened. Before him lay the crushed remains of his small cottage, pinned beneath a smoldering tree that had, until this moment, been as welcome a sight of homecoming as the house itself. The worst part of the destruction was over the sitting room, and the man realized that, had the Jennings not come by and brought the whole household to the door, the roof would have fallen on all of them.

"You've saved us," he murmured. "We would have been killed if not for you." He shook his head in shock and wonder. "We would surely have been killed."

The woman, clutching her children as close to her bosom as possible, gazed with unabashed gratitude at Mr. Jennings. "How did you know?" she asked him breathlessly. "How could you know?"

Jennings, breathless himself, released his grip on the man's lapels. Putting his hand on the man's shoulder, he shook his head, and replied, "I did not know, ma'am. I believe – but perhaps you will think me mad – I believe your Mama – her spirit, I mean – led me here."

"Mama," the woman repeated, and her eyes filled with tears. "Thank God for it, sir! Thank God!"

* * *

Jennings found Elizabeth at the breakfast table the next morning.

"I did not think you would be up, my dear," he said, sitting across from her. "After returning home so late, I thought you would sleep the day away."

She smiled at him. "Much like you, I suppose," she said. "I woke when I usually do, and could not go back to sleep." Her smile broadened. "I slept very well for all that," she added. "It was most gratifying to have saved someone, and to have had such an adventure!"

Jennings laughed. "An adventure indeed!" he said, pouring himself a cup of coffee. "And I daresay they'll have their cottage rebuilt in a trice, and none the worse for wear."

Elizabeth tilted her head. "As to that, sir," she said. "Do you routinely pay for people to rebuild their cottages? And for their accommodation in town?"

Jennings looked down at his coffee cup, and waved his hand dismissively. "They had to stay somewhere," he explained diffidently. "And rebuild somehow."

"Of course," Elizabeth said, still smiling softly. "You are a very good man, sir," she told him.

He looked up at her. "I try very much to be so, my dear," he told her. "And I thank you for your good opinion, for I believe no one's counts for more."

Elizabeth felt tears stinging her eyelids. "And yours to me," she managed to say around a sudden lump in her throat. "But I believe," she went on brightly. "That we were tasked with reading my mother's journals, and her letter to me." She patted a stack of leather-bound books that lay on the table beside her. "I have brought them, as well as the family Bible, that we might go through them together."

Jennings leaned forward. "Excellent!" he said, his interest piqued.

After their breakfast, they made their way outside, to a shaded spot of grass not far from the house. After Jennings put down a blanket, he and Elizabeth sat, alternately enjoying the warm day, reading through her mother's journal entries, and wading through the copious family tree that had been traced onto cream-coloured paper and tucked carefully into the cover of the Bible.

As she read, Elizabeth became gradually aware that her mother's peridot ring had been one of a pair, that a second ring of amethyst had also been passed down to various women in the family.

"Mr. Jennings," she said. "I can trace both the peridot and an amethyst ring back at least five generations on my mother's side." She gestured to the entry she was currently reading. "The amethyst was given to my grandmother on *her* birthday, the same year that my mother received the peridot ring."

Jennings raised one eyebrow, his eyes quickly scanning the entry. "Who gave your grandmother the amethyst?"

"My great-grandmother," Elizabeth said. "Each ring was the birthstone of the recipient, and my mother writes that they had been 'passed through the family for over a hundred years'." She gazed at Mr. Jennings. "But what indeed could be the significance of them? They're not precious stones, or expensive rings. They're both silver, quite ordinary." She frowned, pondering. "If they had some sort of *magical* significance, would that not act more as a protection?"

"One would assume," Jennings murmured. He also frowned, puzzled by this matriarchal mystery, but then abruptly his brow cleared, and he looked at Elizabeth with dawning revelation. "The rings marked them," he guessed. "They marked them, and yours marked *you*."

Elizabeth's eyes opened wide as she digested this. "It makes sense," she decided finally. "But why would my mother wish to mark me in such a way?"

Jennings shook his head. "I cannot imagine she would do so," he said. "Even if I entertained the notion that she would harm you — which I cannot do — it seems apparent that she had no idea what the ring represented. It targeted her as well, after all, if I am correct; I believe to her it must simply have been an heirloom."

Elizabeth had grown very serious. "What on earth could my mother have done?" she asked. "That someone would want her dead? What on earth could *I* have done? I've barely been allowed out of my home since I was a little girl!"

Jennings put a comforting hand on hers. "It can't possibly be anything either of you *did*," he said. "You are clearly the kindest and best of women, my dear, and I can see through these pages that your mother was very much the same. No." He shook his head again. "No, I believe the deaths of your mother and grandmother, and the attack upon you, were orchestrated for some magical purpose."

Elizabeth was both intrigued and horrified; a "magical purpose" would perhaps explain how such a dire creature had been summoned to murder her, as well as the dark and secret manner of visiting a fever upon her mother and stealing her grandmother away in her sleep. But at the same time, the notion that such magic existed boggled the mind and crushed the spirit – how could anyone hope to combat or elude such a supernatural force?

"Surely we're letting our imaginations run away with us, sir," she said. "Although I have seen your gift, and know that it is real, surely it is not possible to *arrange* a fever, or for a woman to be taken in the night, dead from no apparent cause!" She took a deep breath, struggling to contain her emotions. "Surely not," she repeated, rather nervously.

"I'm not saying it's something commonly seen," Jennings replied, gently squeezing her hand. "But when the notion occurred to me, I felt strongly –" He held his other hand against his chest. "That I was heading in the right direction." He looked at her out of the corners of his eyes. "And what I have read here," he began, speaking with a sudden air of delicacy. "Prompts me to believe it."

"What do you mean?" Elizabeth asked. With a mixture of curiosity and dread, she went on, "What have you read?"

Jennings ran his fingers over the front cover of the Bible. "According to your mother's family tree, at least two women – sometimes still children – died in each generation. There were other deaths, of course, and by the dates given it seems that more than one woman died in childbed, but every nineteen years, two or more women died within a fortnight of each other. Most recently are your mother and grandmother, and now, nineteen years later, your own life has been threatened."

Elizabeth blinked, nonplussed. "Nineteen years?" she repeated. "What significance could 'nineteen' have?"

"It is the cycle of the moon," Jennings offered. "It will be in the same location in the sky at a particular time, every nineteen years."

Elizabeth did not know what to think. To be sure, something diabolical had been dispatched not only to murder her but also specifically to take her mother's ring. In her mother's Bible was a record of deaths in which Jennings had seen so sinister a pattern. And it had in fact been nineteen years since her mother died. But the moon had never held any special relevance to her family, as far as she was aware, nor had magic ever been the subject of any discussion. It all sounded so unbelievable.

She leaned forward and picked up a carefully folded paper. "Allow me, sir," she said. "To read you the letter my mother left me." She unfolded the paper, holding it delicately as though it might break apart, and began reading:

"Dearest Elizabeth, I am looking on you now as I write this for you, and I have never seen such a sweet and beautiful creature in all my life. I am desolate to consider the possibility that I might not be here to share your life with you. But we all are here according to God's design, and none of us knows which moment will be our last. My dreams told me that my time here is finished, but they have also

told me that you will grow to be happy and strong and good, and that all is happening as it should.

"Please know that you are the only thing in my life that makes me so proud, and that I have never known happiness as I know it since you have been with me. Whatever occurs, I will watch over you and love you, and I give you my peridot ring, given to me by my own dear grandmother, both as a keepsake and as a connection to me. If ever you find yourself in harm's way, call upon me, my dear sweet girl, and I will render you what aid I can.

With all my heart, forever,

Mama."

Both Jennings and Elizabeth sat quietly for a long moment, each affected by the heartfelt simplicity of her mother's words. Finally, Elizabeth raised her head and said softly, "I have always felt that she meant the ring to be a protection." Momentarily overcome, she blinked away tears and cleared her throat. "I think she sought to protect me, sir, perhaps from the very forces that had haunted her dreams."

"I believe you are right," Jennings said gently. "She seemed even to feel that the ring possessed a magical quality – one that would allow her to come to your aid, even from beyond the grave. Whether she meant that literally or symbolically, I cannot know. But it would be silly, if she were part of some dark family secret, even to hint at a magical aspect to the ring. Even if all we had heard of her were false, which I cannot believe, to bring such attention to the ring would be illogical, and perhaps even detrimental to the purpose."

"But what purpose could it be?" Elizabeth asked. "What usefulness could a family find in eliminating its own members?" She shook her head. "It makes no sense."

"No," Jennings said. "But perhaps your mother did in fact work some magic on the peridot ring." When Elizabeth looked inquiringly at him, he continued, "If the rings are a mark of some type, then they have been part of a series of deaths in your family going back to the beginning of the record written here. For you to escape that fate is, as far as I can see, unprecedented." He reached out and once more took Elizabeth's hand in his. "Perhaps it was your mother who guided me and who wrote on the slate. Perhaps she somehow altered the nature of the ring – possibly without even realizing it herself – and in so doing caused *your* attacker to fail in his attempt."

Elizabeth considered this. "I find a good deal of comfort in that notion," she said. "The thought that she would wish ill upon me had been rather distressing. But," she went on, frowning. "Who then *has* placed these rings into my family? And why?" Her frown deepened. "And since, whatever the reason, it must be of extreme importance, will my attacker not be made desperate by my escape? Will he not find me?"

Jennings's expression was grave. "I have thought of that since the moment I found you in the park, my dear," he said soberly. "Your mother and grandmother were taken in a – shall we call it a 'clandestine' manner? – that implies there is no place where this power cannot reach. If in fact they were murdered, then I cannot understand what has prevented your being taken away in the night as well."

Elizabeth gave a small smile. "If my mother was the one who spoke through the slate, sir," she told him earnestly. "Then it was no doubt because your gifts would offer me protection. You are the reason the creature does not return."

Jennings looked vaguely embarrassed. "I've done nothing," he said, worry still creasing his forehead.

"You saved my life," Elizabeth pointed out, squeezing his fingers.

"But I've done nothing to protect it since," Jennings protested, his cheeks flushed. "My 'gifts' have told me very little about your attack."

"Perhaps it is something about *you*, sir," Elizabeth said, still smiling. "Perhaps your very presence is keeping something at bay."

Jennings raised one eyebrow. "I shall be afraid to let you out of my sight, my dear," he said. "If you put such thoughts into my head." He raised her hand to his lips. "I have a task for you," he added, gesturing toward the journals. "You must correspond with all your relation, and discover who had each of these rings."

Elizabeth blinked, somewhat daunted by the prospect of contacting a score of people she had never laid eyes on. "For the last hundred years?" she asked.

A sudden grin dispelled Jennings' solemnity. "Yes," he said. He leaned toward her. "If we can learn who had the rings originally, then we will have found your attacker."

Elizabeth cast a sardonic eye at him. "That person would be well over a hundred years old," she said drily.

"That would explain why he sends monsters to do his work for him," Jennings said, his eyes twinkling.

CHAPTER TEN

Elizabeth sat at the breakfast table, drinking coffee and reading over several letters that had come to her in the past two weeks. She often put the letters down to jot something onto a piece of paper that lay beside the remnants of her breakfast. When Jennings entered the room, she greeted him without looking up, but instead continued reading first one letter and then the next, her thoughts spinning as she cobbled together what clues these folded pages revealed.

"I have traced the amethyst," she announced rather proudly. "Not one but three different cousins have been quite happy to correspond with me, even though I do not remember our ever having set eyes on one another. My cousin Elinor Dreling in Devonshire has written me some rather interesting details."

"What does she say, my dear?" Jennings asked, sitting down across the table from her. His voice seemed subdued, and Elizabeth tore her attention away from her task and looked at her husband.

"Are you quite well, sir?" she asked. "You seem a bit out of sorts."

"I had a particularly restless night," he explained, giving her a reassuring smile. "Strange dreams that I don't quite remember." He indicated the letters. "Does Elinor in fact have the amethyst?"

"Indeed no," Elizabeth said. "If she did, I would have told her at once to cast it as far from herself as possible! – but she did recall my great-grandmother taking the ring back after my grandmother's death. She made rather a scene over it, sobbing that it was a reminder and a connection to her daughter. But then, not a month later, she gave the amethyst to a nephew – Elinor's younger brother, who had been living in London but has since moved his family into the north. Elinor has not seen him these two years."

Jennings frowned slightly. "It is strange indeed that your great-grandmother would crave the ring so desperately only to give it to a nephew. But why not give it to Elinor? What I saw in your family tree suggests that women are the targets."

"As to that," Elizabeth replied, taking another sip of coffee. "Elinor is the daughter of her father's first marriage; her younger brother is in fact only a half-brother, and she is not actually related to me by blood."

"That *is* very interesting," Jennings noted, his fatigue countered somewhat by his growing curiosity. "It supports our thought that the rings mark women in your family." He sat back in his chair and put his hands in his pockets. "But should we not contact this half-brother? It will mark him too, I believe, or the unfortunate relative to whom he gives it."

"I wrote him three days ago," Elizabeth said. "I have not yet received a response." She leaned forward, her eyes gleaming. "But I have not told you the whole of it, sir," she went on. She pointed to one of the letters. "My cousin Elliott – a more distant relative – said that my great-grandmother had given the amethyst to his mother, and that, after her untimely death, Great-grandmother came and retrieved the ring, explaining that it was a family heirloom that should 'stay with the living', and saying that it had only been 'loaned'. That was thirty-eight years ago, sir," she added meaningfully, and took another sip of coffee, waiting for Mr. Jennings' reaction to her words.

All traces of fatigue had vanished from his face, as a dawning excitement suffused his features. "And how," he said, "did Elliott's mother die?"

"Well, as I explained to my great-aunt's granddaughter Mariah Davies," Elizabeth said. "As much as my curiosity was piqued by Cousin Elliott's letter, I could hardly be so unfeeling as to ask him such a forward question. And so Cousin Mariah has very kindly sent a missive which arrived only this morning, in which she explained in some detail about the disturbing and much talked-about misfortune." She folded her hands together and rested them on the table. "Apparently Mrs. Elliott had gone walking – as was her daily habit – and had been attacked by some animal – whose identity no one has ever been able to deduce – and left on the creek bank. Cousin Elliott's father found his poor wife, her clothes bloody and torn, her life quite extinct. She was covered with deep gashes, as though from gigantic claws, but Mr. Elliott could neither imagine a creature of such size wandering about the countryside, nor track the animal. Despite its apparent size, whatever had attacked Mrs. Elliott had done so without leaving so much as a mark in the dirt."

Jennings sat quietly, digesting all that Elizabeth had said. "It would seem," he said at last. "That my interpretation of your family tree is correct. But how far back does your exploration trace the ring? Can we follow the amethyst to any others?"

Elizabeth shook her head. "I fear not, sir," she said. "But my mother mentioned in her journal that the amethyst – as well as the peridot – had come to my great-grandmother from *her* grandmother." She closed her eyes to better recall the journal passage. "Great-grandmother had said that receiving the rings had been part of a family tradition, one that designated her as a member of a most illustrious clan." She opened her eyes and went on wryly, "My mother felt that her receiving the ring had been part of that same tradition, but clearly this 'illustrious clan' is far more selective than one might ordinarily believe."

Jennings squinted at her curiously. "What do you mean, my dear?" he asked.

Elizabeth raised one eyebrow and gazed pointedly at him. "Why, sir, only this: if giving the ring to my mother had been part of the same tradition that brought the rings to my great-grandmother, then I would imagine my great-grandmother would have been targeted as well. But she lived a long and happy, prosperous life until only three years ago, and at that time died peacefully in her bed surrounded by family." She frowned. "No," she continued, a slight edge to her voice. "It seems clear that my great-grandmother received the rings as an initiation into some segment of our 'clan' to which my mother, her mother, and myself are apparently not worthy to belong, and that part of her membership included finding new targets."

Jennings watched her silently, as outraged as she at the apparent iniquity of her relative, but as uncertain what to do with a theory based on so little information. "Elizabeth," he said at last. "It may be that your great-grandmother was as taken in as you have been – that someone controlled her actions as he controls the dark forces that kill the bearers of these rings. We are speaking of magic, are we not? – a creature from the netherworld summoned to murder you and poor Mrs. Elliott, an unseen entity that visits fever and death upon women in their sleep … these are not ordinary attacks. Whoever orchestrated them must possess extraordinary power; we cannot underestimate his ability to control others to do his bidding."

Elizabeth gave him a small smile. "You're only saying that," she said sardonically. "Because you cannot imagine a woman being able to sacrifice her own daughter and granddaughter. This does you credit, sir, but I believe it is unlikely that my great-grandmother's actions are unwitting. After all, sir, the transfer of these rings caused us to be suspicious in the first place! – they are central to this matter, I think." She smiled more broadly. "And you yourself *felt* that we were correct, no matter how strange our deductions might seem to others!"

Jennings returned her grin. "That is true," he said. "But it still does not follow that every participant is a willing one." His smile faded. "I admit, however, that it does pain me to think of a woman behaving so heartlessly toward her own children."

"And it remains a mystery *why* these women would be targeted," Elizabeth complained, her brow furrowed. "Money would be the most obvious reason, I suppose, but none of those you felt were part of the nineteen-year pattern were actually in line for the family fortune of which my great-grandmother was most recently the matriarch; even my grandmother would have been excluded because of her marriage to my grandfather, since he could not claim even distant cousinship with our 'illustrious clan'. My entire branch of the family tree, therefore, was really in no position to affect my great-grandmother in any conceivable manner, any more than could any of the others who had been given the rings. Only Elinor's brother is an exception."

"And men have never been the targets," Jennings mused. "In truth, however much your great-grandmother was the family matriarch, those in our sphere are required, I believe, to transfer fortunes from father to son, from man to man. These women would have presented no particular impediment to anyone's scheming, and since three of them were under the age of ten, I can't imagine any harm they could possibly have posed – especially to someone who – as we've said – has a great deal of power."

"Hmm," Elizabeth murmured. "I believe I might correspond with my cousin Isabelle."

"Isabelle?" Jennings repeated. "You believe she knows something about all this?"

"Well," Elizabeth said. "Her grandfather is my great-grandmother's eldest son, and his younger brother's son Fitzhugh is engaged to Isabelle. Her marriage to Fitzhugh is seen as an excellent match, and will in effect consolidate a family fortune that had split off in various directions over the generations; it will indeed be a 'family fortune' again – as it was over a hundred years ago – but of course much, much larger now. I suppose, given that, that Isabelle will now replace my great-grandmother as the matriarch of our family."

"Is it wise to contact her?" Jennings asked. "If she has indeed inherited your great-grandmother's place in the family – rings and all – it might be rather dangerous to reveal to her what we suspect. Especially when our list of known facts is woefully tiny."

"I would not ask her anything about it," Elizabeth told him. "I have had the misfortune to meet my cousin Isabelle on more than one occasion. She is a very shrill and peremptory sort of person, always looking down her nose at others; it is quite difficult to spend more than a few moments with her. But I believe that she would be very capable of inadvertently revealing things to me, since it seems to please her to have secrets from those she feels are of lesser consequence."

"Your father's fortune is by no means inconsequential," Jennings noted. "Did that not allow her to see you as an equal?"

"Well, in a way," Elizabeth said. "It allowed her to give me some small measure of respect, rather than dismissing me out of hand, as she has done with so many of the rest of our family."

"It sounds like she will make a delightful matriarch," Jennings said drily.

"Agreed," Elizabeth said, her eyes twinkling. "I will contact her – with the pretext of trying to connect with her now that my father has put me out – and see if I can glean from her any reason why certain members of our family might wish harm on other members." She chuckled. "My supplication to her superiority will no doubt be a welcome beginning from her point of view, and my obvious inferiority as an outcast will likely prompt her to list – in a very haughty manner – every conceivable thing that would render my life expendable."

"Wonderful," Jennings said, grinning.

* * *

Later in the day, he found her walking in the gardens beside the house. "I've had a message from the slate, my dear," he told her. "I must go to town."

"Might I go with you?" Elizabeth asked, her eyes lighting up. "I am very much enjoying our little adventures!"

"I would have it no other way, ma'am," Jennings replied, offering her his arm.

Within twenty minutes they were on the road toward town, and

Jennings was explaining to her what the slate had shown him. "The words were remarkably unhelpful," he noted. "It said, 'I am Joshua.' What significance his name could have, I don't know."

"Well, I imagine *he* was quite attached to it," Elizabeth said. "Did you see any images connected with it?"

"Only the house," Jennings said. "And a letter tucked into a book."

"What sort of book?"

Jennings shrugged. "A tiny one," he said. "Perhaps a book of poems or some such?"

"Hmm," Elizabeth mused. "That is indeed very little to start with."

"Yes," Jennings agreed. "Yet the message was delivered with a sense of some urgency. Not quite so much as the other night, but a good deal more than would be warranted by a spirit declaring his name."

They came presently to a row of houses that Jennings recognized from his vision. Stopping the carriage, Jennings hopped down and reached up a hand for Elizabeth. "I believe we are in the right place," he said, looking around him. "If anything, the matter seems *more* urgent, but I can't imagine why. I saw absolutely nothing alarming."

"Perhaps," Elizabeth offered, stepping down onto the street, "our experience with the house in the woods has inflated our notion of urgency. I suppose a thing might be urgent without involving falling masonry."

Jennings chuckled. "I suppose you are right," he allowed.

He walked with her a little way down the street, coming at last to a door before which stood a pair of young women. One of them was clearly comforting the other, who was overcome with quiet sobbing.

"It will all be well, Caroline," the first woman was saying. "Surely our cousin cannot be so cruel as he seems."

"He is!" the sobbing girl wailed, her voice muffled by a handkerchief pressed desperately to her lips. "He is taking all, and we are thrown out into the hedgerows!"

The first woman noticed the Jennings, and quickly pulled the other girl more closely into her embrace. "Yes?" she asked, one eyebrow raised rather defiantly, as though daring the Jennings to importune her.

"Forgive us, ma'am," Jennings began, bowing and taking a small step forward. "This young lady is clearly upset; can we not assist you in some way?"

The woman shook her head. "I thank you, no," she said. "We have received distressing news, but we are quite well."

Behind her, through an open window on the floor above them, came the distinct sound of a woman crying, and the more subdued sounds of her maid attempting to console her. This prompted Caroline to renew her wails of despair, and to bury her head in the other woman's shoulder.

"Please, ma'am," Elizabeth said, her heart moved by the women's obvious unhappiness. "Perhaps there is some design in our coming here; perhaps we are *meant* to help you. Will you not take us a little way into your confidence?"

The woman at first seemed disinclined to change her mind, but, after seeing the open sincerity and compassion so evident on the

118

Jennings' faces, her expression softened. "You may be right," she said quietly. "I did pray for deliverance from this fate." She guided Caroline carefully to a bench that stood along one side of the stoop. "Sit here, dearest," she instructed, and gently deposited the woman onto the bench. Straightening up, and squaring her shoulders, she turned once more to the Jennings and folded her hands placidly in front of her. "We are all put out of our home," she announced, in a calm voice that belied the disastrous nature of the news she imparted. "Our dear Papa has died not a week ago. His estate is entailed on his cousin, and his cousin has arrived this morning to inform us that he wishes to sell Papa's house and lands at once, and that we must remove ourselves immediately." Her demeanour remained entirely passive, and would perhaps have been mistaken for coldness, except that her eyes now swam with tears, and the corners of her mouth trembled. "He has given us until the day after tomorrow."

Caroline pulled the handkerchief from her lips long enough to deliver one quivering sentence: "And we had been so thoughtful as to send him an invitation – to welcome him!" She dabbed at her eyes with the handkerchief and struggled to regain her composure.

Jennings spoke, and his voice was so cold that Elizabeth was startled by it, and cast a sidelong glance up at him. "Ma'am," he said crisply. "May I ask if you have anywhere to go?"

The first woman shook her head. "Indeed we do not, sir," she informed him. "We do have some money left to us by our Papa, and I suppose we could cast ourselves on the mercy of our relatives, but since Papa had assured us that his cousin was a very kind and generous man, we had not thought to seek out such alternatives."

"I greatly sympathize," Elizabeth said earnestly. "I found myself in a similar situation not so long ago." She indicated Mr. Jennings. "But you see? Everything can work out perfectly well, even out of the most desperate of straits."

The woman's stoic façade faltered slightly in the face of Elizabeth's genuine concern; she cleared her throat, and looked for a moment down at her feet. "I thank you," she repeated, raising her eyes once more to gaze gratefully at the Jennings. "Forgive me; I cannot at the moment see how it could work out at all." She glanced at Caroline, who had stopped crying but now sat with slumped shoulders and an expression of absolute dejection. "But I am sure we will manage somehow," she added. "If our cousin is indeed amenable to our staying through tomorrow, I will have time to arrange for the storage of our belongings. I believe my friend Anne will allow us to impose upon her, and keep our things in her father's unused stables." Doubt and hopelessness flickered across her face. "I have already sent word to her," she said. "And so I am sure you are correct, ma'am, and that we will manage somehow."

Elizabeth was at a loss; no words that came to mind seemed helpful in the slightest.

"Ma'am," Jennings said. "May I ask you – please excuse me for being forward – is your father's name Joshua?"

The woman blinked in surprise. "It is not, sir," she said slowly. "Joshua is our newly-arrived cousin."

CHAPTER ELEVEN

The Jennings had been shown into a sunny sitting room at the back of the house. Elizabeth had deposited herself into a chair by the window, while Jennings stood beside her, one of his hands on the back of her chair and the other in his pocket. He stared pensively out of the window, but when a knock sounded at the front door, he turned and gazed curiously out of the sitting room and across the entryway.

A maid, first setting down on a nearby table the tea tray she carried, bustled to the door and opened it. Jennings could not see who stood at the door, but assumed it must be someone delivering a letter, since the maid reached out for something that she then tucked into the pocket of her apron. Whatever it was, he noticed, did not immediately fit into the pocket, and the maid was obliged to slide it carefully in beside a thin book that had already been there. She reached into a second pocket and retrieved a small bag, out of which she pulled a coin to give to whomever stood at the door.

"Who is there, Bettina?" a woman called from the stairs that descended into the entryway. "Have our guests been shown into the sitting room?"

"Yes, ma'am," the maid responded, quickly closing the door and picking up the tea tray again. She entered the sitting room, gently pushing the door further open with her shoulder. "Beg your pardon, ma'am," she said to Elizabeth, and then bobbed her head toward Jennings. "Sir." She placed the tea tray on the table beside Elizabeth's chair. "Tea and biscuits, ma'am," she said, pouring the tea for Elizabeth. "Would you care for tea, sir?" she asked, glancing at Jennings.

He smiled warmly at her. "Thank you, Bettina," he replied urbanely. "That would be wonderful." He looked again toward the door into the entryway. "Did I hear the lady of the house? Is she able to join us?"

"Mrs. Gilbraith'll be down directly, sir," Bettina said. "She needed to – that is – I – she's been preoccupied, sir, with Mr. Heron. Miss Louisa and Miss Caroline have gone to her and informed her you are here."

"Of course," Jennings said. "Thank you." He tilted his head to the side. "You will be going with the Gilbraiths when they leave here?" he asked.

Bettina was startled. "As for that, sir," she said after a brief pause. "I have a new position waiting. I –" She paused again, and her cheeks turned bright red. "I had thought it might go this way, sir," she went on. "When Mr. Gilbraith fell ill, I thought it might be best to try to make arrangements that didn't depend on the situation here." She stopped, her brow furrowed as though she worried that speaking at all had been improper. "Beggin' your pardon, sir." She bobbed a curtsey and left the room; Jennings' eyes followed her, and his scrutiny was obvious enough that Elizabeth commented on it.

"You are taken with her, sir?" she asked teasingly.

Jennings flushed. "Not at all," he hastened to assure her. "I –" He looked from her to the now-empty entryway and back, his consternation evident.

She laughed aloud. "I am only joking, sir," she said, her eyes twinkling. "But something has captured your attention. Something Bettina has done? Someone she reminds you of?"

Jennings, still slightly flustered, cleared his throat and, keeping his voice low, said, "I am curious only about the letter that was delivered."

Elizabeth carefully lifted her teacup to her lips and sipped from it. "She put it beside a book she carries," she said. "And – although of course we do not know the family's ordinary ways – it seemed strange that she did not answer her mistress' query about who was at the door." She took a bite from one of the biscuits and another sip of tea.

Jennings gazed down at her, a soft smile curving his lips. "I noticed that as well," he said. He put his hand to his chest, a gesture that, as Elizabeth was learning, indicated a feeling of supernatural intuition. "I am certain," he said. "That the book in her pocket is the one the slate showed me. And the letter seems somehow important as well."

"I believe you are right, sir," Elizabeth said. "But how best to get at it?"

Miss Gilbraith appeared at the door to the sitting room, on the arm of a gentleman. This gentleman seemed quite affable, not at all what Elizabeth had expected from someone she and Mr. Jennings suspected of nefarious pretense, and so she was quite surprised when Miss Gilbraith introduced the gentleman as her cousin Joshua Heron.

"He has inherited my father's estate," she explained in a carefully modulated voice. "He has been gracious enough to give us this opportunity to make arrangements for ourselves." If she intended any sarcasm in this remark, it was entirely hidden by her placid demeanour. "Cousin, these are the Jennings. They have come to condole with us about our dear father."

Mr. Heron stepped forward and bowed first to Elizabeth and

then to Jennings. "Your most faithful servant, ma'am," he said brightly. "Sir." He smiled at his cousin and continued, "My lovely young cousins have been so kind as to accept me into the house even while they are still residing in it – I am most appreciative, Miss Gilbraith – and I am most happy – most happy – to help them find a new situation where I am assured – most decidedly assured – they will be quite contented." He finished this with an even brighter smile, and looked rather expectantly from Elizabeth to Jennings to Miss Gilbraith.

"You are indeed all kindness, sir," Jennings said, returning Mr. Heron's joviality. "I understand you are selling the properties?"

"I am, sir!" Mr. Heron said cheerfully. "I already have more than one person willing to take the whole thing off my hands right away!" He chuckled and sank his hands into his pockets. "It's all been extraordinarily easy!" he announced. "I had thought it would be much more difficult!"

"Ah, no," Jennings said, nodding his head. "When people wish to sell, others always want to buy; one need only know whom to talk to." He paused, frowning in puzzlement. "I would rather have wanted to put my offer into it; is it all arranged, sir, or may you and I contract?"

Elizabeth stole a quick glance at her husband out of the corner of her eye. Was he planning to save everyone by purchasing their houses? She smiled softly. *We will soon ourselves be in the hedgerows at this rate*, she thought.

Mr. Heron raised his eyebrows, and he blinked his eyes several times. "Why, as to that, sir," he said. "I believe it is all arranged, with a Mr. Cornwallis who contracted with me about the house even before I made the journey here, and with a Mr. Davis who will be taking the country estate and who spoke with me just yesterday. I have spoken with both of their stewards, and expect them here any time this day."

"Unfortunate," Jennings murmured, then grinned. "For me, at least!" he amended. He chuckled. "Mr. Cornwallis must have seen Miss Gilbraith's letter delivered to your door, to have made his offer so quickly!"

Mr. Heron frowned in confusion. "Letter?" he asked.

"The letter inviting you here," Jennings clarified. He turned to Miss Gilbraith. "Did you not say you had sent him a letter?"

Mr. Heron's brow cleared. "Oh, of course!" he said. "The letter. The letter they sent me."

"You seem upset, sir," Elizabeth said, still quietly sipping her tea. "Is all well?"

"Of course!" Mr. Heron said again, adjusting his cravat. "I am only annoyed with myself that I had forgotten the letter; Mrs. Gilbraith had been so obliging as to send it, and indeed how else would I have known to come?" He laughed, a trifle nervously.

"Miss Gilbraith," Elizabeth said. "I am sure you must have put a notice in the *Gazette*?"

"There was a notice, ma'am," Miss Gilbraith replied. She did not know the purpose of the Jennings' conversation with her cousin, but his responses to them so far told her that the day was on the verge of being very interesting. "We put it in three days ago."

"Why, then," Elizabeth said, turning to look at Mr. Heron. "I am sure anyone might know of it now. Word spreads so quickly, really." She smiled at Mr. Heron.

Mr. Heron's affability had entirely faded. He looked over his shoulder and into the entryway, where Bettina stood at the foot of the stairs. She stared back at him, her eyes wide. Turning back to the Jennings, Mr. Heron said hesitantly, "Well, I am sure ... of course, by now ... I'm sure everyone might know by now."

Jennings leaned toward him. "Are you quite well, sir?" he asked solicitously. "You have grown pale."

Mr. Heron forced another chuckle. "I am very well!" he assured him with a wave of his hand. "Very well! I am sure I am just affected by the passing of my dear cousin. I had not seen him in some time, you know, and I believe I regret that now."

"That is always sad," Elizabeth agreed. She took another bite of her biscuit. "As I'm sure Miss Gilbraith can readily understand. I believe, Miss Gilbraith," she said, gesturing toward the entryway. "That a letter arrived. Perhaps it will offer you good news."

At this, Bettina's eyes opened even wider, and she took an involuntary step backward.

"Bettina?" Miss Gilbraith asked. "Did a letter come for us?"

"W-Why," Bettina stammered. "Why, yes, miss." Her face was flushed to the roots of her hair, but she walked forward into the sitting room and handed Miss Gilbraith the letter she had earlier tucked into her apron pocket. "Just after your guests arrived, Miss," she said. "I was bringin' in the tea. I must've forgot it."

"Thank you, Bettina," Miss Gilbraith said, taking the letter. "I will take it up to Mama directly."

"I beg your pardon, Miss Gilbraith," Jennings said. "But –" He put his hand once more to his chest. "I cannot explain why," he went on. "But I believe that letter may contain very important news that should not be delayed even a moment."

Miss Gilbraith looked shrewdly at Jennings for a minute, then, deciding that the appearance of such odd visitors must indeed be a sign of an answered prayer, she broke the seal on the letter and unfolded the pages. She had not read more than a few lines of its contents before her face suffused with bewilderment, and she gazed up at Mr. Heron in absolute incomprehension. "Why, this letter is from you, sir!" she informed him. "You have written that you will journey here on the morrow."

The room became so silent that Elizabeth imagined she could hear others' hearts beating. Bettina's red cheeks had turned stark white, and she appeared on the verge of panic. Jennings was as still as a statue, and only his eyes moved as he looked between Miss Gilbraith and Mr. Heron.

"How extraordinary," he said softly. "You've arrived before you left, Mr. Heron. How did you manage it?"

Miss Gilbraith had returned her attention to the letter. "Good God!" she breathed, then began reading aloud. "'My dear Papa – the elder Joshua Heron – has also left us, not even a month ago. But having learned of your own excellent father's passing, and being made aware that the entailment has fallen upon me, I am most anxious to call on you at once and to make whatever arrangements will help you.'" She looked up, tears falling unheeded down her cheeks. "He is worried about us!" she said, her voice choked with emotion. "He's –" She glared darkly up at Mr. Heron, and her whole form shook with suppressed anger. "He is not you, sir!" she exclaimed. "And you are not he."

"Cousin Joshua" did not respond, but instead stood in rigid

silence, looking first at Jennings, then at Bettina, and finally at Miss Gilbraith. He opened his mouth to speak, but, discovering that nothing he could say would be likely to help explain his situation, he pivoted on one foot and bolted out of the sitting room.

In an instant, Jennings had leapt after him, catching him by the arm and dragging him backward. The erstwhile Joshua spun around and punched Jennings in the face; Jennings fell back as blood spurted from the wide cut on his cheek, but he managed to keep his grip on the other man's sleeve. Using his own weight as leverage, he twisted the other man's arm at the shoulder and forced him to his knees.

Desperately, the man struggled against Jennings but to no avail. Every movement seemed to twist his arm even further behind him, and finally he collapsed onto the floor, grimacing in pain.

"Please do stay, Mr. Heron," Jennings said, a bit breathlessly. "We've hardly had any chance to get to know you!" He released the man's arm and turned to face the ladies who still stood, gaping, in the sitting room. "Bettina," he continued, touching the side of his face. "If you wouldn't mind fetching some water for me."

With some difficulty, Bettina regained her composure. "O-of course, sir," she said. She inched her way out of the sitting room, casting her eyes briefly on the man who now sat on the entryway floor, massaging his wounded arm and looking decidedly alarmed.

"Bettina?" Jennings said. "Might you also – if you don't mind – show us the book you have in your pocket?"

Bettina frowned, startled. "Sir?"

"Your pocket," Jennings repeated amiably. He reached into his own pocket and pulled out a handkerchief, folded it into a small, padded square, and pressed it against the cut on his cheek. "Your book. In your pocket."

By now Miss Gilbraith had accepted wholeheartedly that the Jennings had been sent to deliver her family from peril. Although she could not fathom why the contents of her maid's pockets would be of any significance, she held in her hand proof that without the intervention of her unusual guests, her family would have fallen victim to a chilling deception. "Bettina," she said sharply. "What is Mr. Jennings talking about?"

"Miss Louisa, I don't know!" Bettina splayed her hands to the sides in apparent confusion. "It's only the housekeeping book, where I jot down what's needed at the market!"

Miss Gilbraith lifted one eyebrow. "Then there can't be any harm in showing it to us," she pointed out.

Bettina stared helplessly at her mistress, her breathing becoming fast and shallow. After an awkward silence during which Miss Gilbraith's unsympathetic gaze remained fixed on Bettina's face, the unhappy maid burst into tears. "No!" she cried, and attempted to run from the house just as "Mr. Heron" had done.

But Elizabeth had predicted that if one tried to flee then so might the other; while Jennings was asking about the housekeeping book, she had edged her way out of the sitting room and along the wall toward the front door, and now, as Bettina ran toward that door, Elizabeth slid her foot out and tripped the other woman.

Bettina fell headlong, landing in an undignified heap in front of Elizabeth. Wasting no time, Elizabeth bent down and snatched the housekeeping book from Bettina's pocket.

"What could be such a secret?" she mused aloud. She opened the small book, and, upon examining the two letters she found tucked inside, said in a voice tinged with genuine shock, "Bettina, how could you lend yourself to such a scheme?"

Bettina had pushed herself to a seated position, and was now sobbing, her hands covering her face. "I'm tired of workin'!" she wailed. "Why should *they* have everything?"

Miss Gilbraith stepped toward Elizabeth. "What does it say?" she asked, not sure she really wanted to know.

Elizabeth handed her one of the letters. "I believe you recognize this," she said. "It seems to be the letter you and your mother and sister wrote to your cousin Joshua, telling him of your father's passing. Bettina was entrusted with it, no doubt, and chose not to send it."

Miss Gilbraith ran her fingers over the letter. "We invited him here," she murmured. "He does not even know it." She smiled suddenly. "But his son is coming to help us, even though we have never set eyes on him at all!"

Elizabeth put a comforting hand on Miss Gilbraith's arm. "I am certain," she said warmly. "That we were indeed destined to walk down your street today, Miss Louisa! I am so glad to have been of help to you."

Jennings nodded his head toward the second letter. "What does that one say, my dear?"

Elizabeth looked at him and then at Bettina. "Why, this would be Bettina's letter from her *beau* here," she said crisply. "Saying that he will have the properties sold before anyone knows any different, and that the two of them will be away and settled within a fortnight. Apparently his name is Richard."

Miss Gilbraith's eyes narrowed to angry slits. "I cannot believe that *anyone* could be so heartless!" she cried.

Caroline Gilbraith appeared at the top of the stairs. "Whatever is all the commotion!" she asked, irritated. "Poor Mama's nerves are shattered!" She saw Bettina and Richard sitting on the floor. "What on earth?" She frowned at her sister. "What is going on, Louisa?"

Richard took this opportunity to stagger to his feet; swinging wildly, he slammed his fist into Jennings' stomach, but Jennings had seen it coming and had steeled himself to the blow. Ignoring the pain as best he could, he quickly lunged forward and punched Richard squarely in the jaw. Bettina screamed as Richard fell to the floor beside her.

"You've killed him!" she shrieked.

"No," Jennings said gruffly. "But I imagine he is not happy."

CHAPTER TWELVE

Elizabeth had prepared herself for bed but found that she was not tired at all. She sat next to her bedroom window, a shawl wrapped around her shoulders, and looked out over the wide lawn that shone silver in the moonlight.

She and Mr. Jennings had spent the day helping the Gilbraiths; the imposter Richard and his equally deceptive lover Bettina had been ejected from the Gilbraith home and into the waiting hands of the constabulary. Word had been sent immediately to the real Joshua Heron, whose letter painted him as a most amiable and caring man, in hopes of apprising him of all that had happened before his arrival. Word was also sent to the two men with whom Richard had contracted to sell the Gilbraith estate, and Jennings had spent some hours of the afternoon conferring with Mr. Davis, the gentleman who resided in London. When everything had been explained to him, the man was deeply appalled, not only at Richard's deplorable scheme but at the part he himself had been about to play.

"If you have any trouble with this other fellow," he said to Jennings, referring to Mr. Cornwallis, the second potential buyer. "You just let me know. I'll set the fellow straight about what's done and what's not done!" His cheeks were flushed and puffed out, and a dreadful scowl sat determinedly on his face; he was clearly offended by Richard's actions, and anxious to be of assistance to the Gilbraith ladies, with whom he had been already, though only slightly, acquainted. "I only hope Mrs. Gilbraith will forgive me!" he murmured gruffly.

"I am quite sure she will, sir," Jennings assured him sincerely.

"She – and the Misses Gilbraith – are simply relieved and glad to have the whole thing exposed and corrected." He frowned. "They were as taken in as anyone," he said darkly. "I am more shocked than I can say, frankly."

"As indeed so am I," Mr. Davis agreed, still scowling and shaking his head. "Most shocked."

For her part, Elizabeth had stayed with the Misses Gilbraith and their mother, a woman who, though overcome and quite disposed to weeping, showed herself to be very capable of handling unusual circumstances.

"What a dog!" she exclaimed more than once, quivering in anger. "To mislead us so!" At one point she owned to feeling some foolishness, but immediately dismissed this notion, since she had never laid eyes on the man in her whole life, no, nor his father either, but had only ever heard her husband speak of the Herons. "And always he was very kind toward them," she said. "And spoke highly of them. But one never knows the truth about another, does one? And now that Mr. Gilbraith is gone, I confess I thought it was simply Mr. Heron's revealing his true nature, as does often happen after someone has died." She sipped gratefully at a cup of tea that her daughter Louisa had brought her. "But that Bettina!" she added, almost hissing the name out. "I cannot stomach the realization that she has been here, under my roof, for I don't know how many years, and now to treat us so shabbily! When we have been so good to her, and pay her a very good wage!"

Mrs. Gilbraith's rather one-sided conversation continued for nearly an hour, interrupted from time to time by some supportive comment from one of her daughters or from Elizabeth. Caroling

Gilbraith had traded her earlier tears for uncontained grins of joy, and she attended her mother's monologue with only a partial ear, her relief and gratitude drowning out, for the moment at any rate, whatever anger she might have felt. Louisa, too, was all smiles, and the tension with which she had carried herself since "Cousin Joshua" had arrived had completely left her, so that she could do little more than sit in the chair across from her mother and feel utterly exhausted. She only roused herself upon the Jennings' departure, impulsively catching Elizabeth in a brief, tight embrace.

"I cannot thank you enough," she said, tears shining in her eyes. "It seemed so odd for you to take such an interest in a stranger, but I see now that my prayers were answered."

Elizabeth flushed at the praise. "We were guided here, Miss Gilbraith," she said. "We were most happy to help in any way possible."

Mr. Jennings would likewise take no particular credit for the day's events, but he took Miss Gilbraith's hand in his and bowed low over it. "I am your most humble servant, Miss Louisa," he told her. "It has been truly an honour to assist you and your excellent family."

He and Elizabeth had left the Gilbraith house with an air of tranquility, as though they had just stopped by for tea and were now on their way home. As heinous as Richard's and Bettina's actions had been, Elizabeth was so gratified to have had a hand in discovering them that she could feel only an abiding cheerfulness that lingered with her throughout supper and into the evening. Now, as she gazed out over the lawn, she still felt a buoyancy of spirit that made it almost impossible to contemplate sleep.

A soft knock sounded at her door. "Come in," she called out.

The door opened, and Jennings poked his head into the room. "Do I disturb you, my dear?" he asked.

She turned to him. "Not at all," she said, her eyes twinkling. "I am rather restless, in fact, no doubt from the excitement of the day."

He returned her smile. Coming into the room, he shut the door behind him and sat in a chair opposite her. "It was not quite as exciting as the woods," he said drily, leaning back in the chair. "But it was certainly very *interesting*."

She glanced at the cut on his cheek. It was small, but surrounded by an unpleasant-looking bruise. "Are you sure," she said, frowning a little in concern. "That you're quite all right?"

He reached up and gingerly touched his cheek. "I'm sure," he said, grinning ruefully. "I used to get into much worse scrapes," he confessed. "In my school days."

She laughed. "I admit, I cannot picture it," she said. "You are so gentle, sir."

He laughed too. "A couple of the lads might disagree with you," he said. "I was forever getting in a row with some upper-classman."

They sat quietly for a moment, looking out the window at the moonlight; then Elizabeth, giving in to her curiosity, spoke.

"Mr. Jennings," she began. "Earlier, when you told that horrible Richard person that you would like to make an offer for the Gilbraith estate, did you in fact mean to purchase it from him?"

Jennings smiled softly. "I had entertained the notion," he admitted. "But I could hardly afford to buy the whole Gilbraith estate, and if I bought only the house, why, the ladies would be in the same position – struggling to maintain a household without any money. No, I was only trying to call Richard's bluff; I was drawn most insistently toward that letter, even before Bettina opened the door. I knew it must possess some sort of good news within it."

Elizabeth regarded him with admiration. "Your kindness is extraordinary, sir," she told him. "You are truly the best of men."

Jennings stared at her, startled and embarrassed by her compliment. "I – I do what any man would do," he said. "I do not believe my actions are particularly out of the common way."

She lifted her eyebrows in surprise. "Then you have not spied yourself in a mirror, sir," she said. She gestured toward her dressing table. "Please," she went on. "Take the opportunity to do so now." She leaned forward, and gazed steadily into his eyes. "You cared so much for *me*, sir, a woman you had barely met, that you offered me *marriage*. You have been more kind that any words can say." Tears stung her eyelids, and she looked away from him, her fingers fumbling clumsily for the shawl that had fallen from her shoulders. "To do such a thing for a stranger," she said, her voice now choked with emotion. "Is extraordinary. To me, at any rate."

The room became completely silent. After a long moment, Jennings reached out his hand and touched Elizabeth's knee with the tips of his fingers.

"Elizabeth," he said, so softly that she barely heard him. She raised her eyes once more to his, and found something in his expression that she had never seen before, something that was not quite sadness, and not quite joy.

"Elizabeth," he said again. "I like to think that I am the sort of man who would have married you to help you out of your predicament." He gave her a lopsided smile. "But I will never know. The night that I met you, when I danced with you ..." His fingers

136

tapped lightly on her knee, but otherwise he was as still as a statue, and his eyes never wavered from her face. "When I heard your laughter, and saw your smile; when I held your hand, even for those few short seconds; when I stood beside you ... I never wanted to leave. I was – I am – deeply honoured to have saved you from a situation that –" He paused, struggling to maintain his composure. "That you might have avoided altogether if I had been able to run faster." He paused again, then went on in a voice hardly more than a whisper: "But I married you because I wanted to, Elizabeth. I can't imagine life without you now, and I will spend the rest of my days trying to capture your heart, because you have had mine long since."

Elizabeth thought to tell him that she, too, had been drawn to him from the moment he approached her at Lady Morton's party. She thought to tell him that her heart had been entangled with his since his first visit to her sick-bed at Lady Morton's, that, even though she had not been properly awake, she had known he was there, worrying over her. She wanted to say that, when all she could think to do that night in the park was to drag breath into her tortured lungs, she had been aware somehow that he was searching for her, that he had found her, that she would be safe. She wanted to tell him all these things, but the words stuck in her throat. She wanted to show him her most beautiful face, but, against her will, tears began streaming down her cheeks. Not knowing what else to do, she leaned forward and kissed him.

She watched as a thousand expressions flitted in an instant across his face. Then, taking her by surprise, he cupped his hands on the sides of her face and pulled her toward him, and kissed her deeply. Her fingers clutched at the cloth of his shirtfront and brought him closer to her; she hoped that this moment would never end.

* * *

Later that night, he dreamt – as he had every night for two weeks – of a tangle of trees, beneath which he could see a dark gash in the ground that marked the entrance to a cave. As he had a dozen times before, he walked toward the cave, and with every step his heart beat faster. Something horrible waited for him in the cave, and although he could neither see nor hear it, he approached it with a mounting dread.

The entire scene was clearer this particular night than it had ever been; for the first time he could see out past the small woods where he stood, but he did not recognize the surrounding lands. He became aware, too, of a smell – the smell not only of the rotting vegetation that swam in the mud at his feet, but also of blood, and decaying flesh. More than ever, he did not want to keep walking, but something compelled him, and he soon found himself ducking into the cave entrance, into a darkness that was absolute, yet somehow he could see even blacker shadows dancing around him.

The dread was almost overwhelming and he wanted to run away, but still he stood, encircled by darkness and the clamminess of wet earth.

As always, he sensed a presence behind him, blocking his escape. As always, he tried to turn to confront it, but his body would not listen to his urgent commands. Before, this was the moment when he would awaken, but tonight was different. Tonight, he felt the presence sliding closer to him, felt its scrabbling fingers on his arms and its icy breath on the back of his neck. Tonight, he was assailed by a single thought – one even stronger than the crippling dread.

Betrayal.

Turn! He ordered his resistant limbs. *Turn and face this thing!*

But he remained frozen in place with the dark presence behind him, until suddenly a great bellowing shook the air, and a sharp blow to the back of his neck launched him forward onto the ground. He tasted blood in his mouth as it poured out of him into the mud.

He woke then, shouting in shock and anger.

Beside him, Elizabeth woke too, alarmed by his outburst. "What is it!" she cried.

He shouted again, startled; he was unused to someone being in the bed with him. Quickly he reached out for her hand and gripped it. "I'm all right," he assured her. She looked at him skeptically, taking in his ragged breathing and the sheen of sweat that covered him. "I'm all right," he said again. He turned toward her and laid his head in the hollow of her neck. "I had a nightmare."

Elizabeth wrapped her arms around him. "Good God!" she said, amazed at the effect this nightmare had had on him. "What on earth was it about?"

His breathing was more controlled now; he held Elizabeth to him gratefully, and allowed her presence to comfort the lingering sensation of peril. "I've been dreaming about a cave for many days now," he told her. "But tonight I saw violence – murder – and a knowing, in my bones, that the murderer was a close friend."

"A friend?" Elizabeth repeated, frowning in concern. She gasped, and asked, "Was it a vision? Is it something that's going to happen?" She hoped with all her heart that it was *not* a glimpse into the future. "Is it – is it something that's going to happen to you?"

He sat up so that he could look at her. "I believe it is a vision," he said. "But it is not of a future event. I am only able to see things that have already occurred, and, occasionally, the imminent events that the spirits choose to show me. Sometimes I have insight into something – like Mr. Heron's letter – but I cannot see what will happen."

She sat up as well, relief washing over her. "So you are not the one who is murdered?"

"No," he said, shaking his head and smiling softly. "But someone was killed, someone in a cave the location of which I cannot suss out." He shook his head again. "Usually, when the spirits have contacted me through the slate, they guide me to where I need to be; I feel ..." He searched for the words. "I feel a *pull* in some direction or other. That is how I find these houses scattered all over London, and how I found the cottage in the woods. But even though I saw more of my surroundings tonight than I ever have before, I still have no idea where this cave is." He sighed. "I have had dream-visions before," he added. "But they were always a bit clearer than this, and I have never had a recurring dream such as this one has been."

Elizabeth considered for a moment. "This spirit does not speak through the slate," she noted. "But the slate usually offers a very simple message; perhaps this spirit's needs are more ... complex. Perhaps the slate is not enough for this message, and so he has entered your dreams."

"He says very little," Jennings complained. "Yet he is most persistent!"

"Is there a sense of urgency, as you felt with the cottage?" she asked.

"Not at all," he said. "For such a persistent person, he has not impressed upon me any urgency at all!"

"If he was in fact murdered – and by a friend, as you said – it may be that he simply wants you to find him."

"When I get the chance?" Jennings said drily.

She shrugged, her eyes twinkling. "It's better than nobody finding him at all. Unless," she added. "You are somehow already where you need to be."

Jennings frowned. "I do not know how that could be," he said. "The cave was nowhere that I have ever been. It certainly is not nearby."

"But the spirit says very little," Elizabeth reminded him. "Perhaps you must brave the dream again before his true intentions become clear to you."

"An unpleasant prospect," Jennings murmured, but he knew that she was right. Realizing suddenly that it was the middle of the night, and that he had given her as much of a fright as he himself had experienced, he reached out a hand and lovingly stroked her cheek. "I apologize, my love," he said. "I have disturbed your sleep."

She leaned against his hand. She opened her mouth to speak, paused, then said, "I am where I need to be."

* * *

The next morning, Elizabeth preceded her husband to the breakfast table; Mrs. Raleigh greeted her cheerfully, and handed her a stack of letters that had been delivered to the house for her. "Three for you, ma'am," she announced.

"Thank you, Mrs. Raleigh," Elizabeth said, examining the letters. One was from her stepmother Charlotte and the next from her dear friend Mariah Lansing; the third, however, was the one she opened first, since it came from her cousin Marcus Tate, Elinor Dreling's younger brother, to whom she had sent a letter some time ago and whose response she had been rather impatiently awaiting.

"My dear Cousin Elizabeth," it began. *"I hope this letter finds you well. Forgive me for being so late in my response to you. Our family here has been obliged to suffer the most horrible calamity – my little daughter Eliza, who had just turned four this past spring, has been taken from us by a sudden fever. We are all desolate here, and Eliza's poor mother has taken it most desperately, and is confined to her bed in her grief. I too barely know what I am about; I walk the house hoping to see my sweet girl, but all the rooms are quite empty and cold, and I fear my heart will break from this sadness.*

"I am desolated to send you such wretched tidings as these, but I did not wish you to wonder why I had not answered your kind letter. To hear from you indeed lifted my spirits, and I hope perhaps someday soon to journey to London to visit you; perhaps it might soothe Mrs. Tate's heart as well.

"I had heard of your own troubles, and have been worried for you. I am greatly heartened to know that you have recovered so well, and that you have found such happiness.

"With my most sincere regard for you and for Mr. Jennings,

"Your obedient servant,
Marcus Tate"

"Good God," Elizabeth breathed, putting her fingers over her mouth. "Little Eliza was the target." Cousin Marcus must have given the amethyst ring to his young daughter – indeed, why would he not? – and the poor girl had been targeted as she herself had been, though thankfully not by a dread creature. "I cannot believe it was just a 'fever'," she murmured to herself. She had no doubt that the little girl had been eliminated by the same person who had wanted Elizabeth dead – a diabolical person who evidently possessed no scruples or soul, and who would steal the life of an innocent child to suit his hidden purpose.

"Christopher!" she called out, standing up abruptly and hurrying out of the room. With the letters crumpled in her hand, she flew up the stairs to her husband's room. "Christopher!" she called again, stopping in his open doorway.

He stood, bent over the drawer where the slate lay; apparently he had found a message there, one that he was taking seriously. He turned to her, a frown creasing his brow. "Is anything amiss, my love?" he asked.

"I have found the victim of the amethyst, sir," she told him solemnly. "And you? What has the slate revealed?"

He glanced down at the slate and then back to her. "It is Joshua again," he said. "I cannot say how I know it is he; I simply do. But his message does not seem to be anything for me to *do*, and it feels ..."

He placed his hand on his chest. "It feels connected in some way to the dream of the man in the cave."

"Do you feel that Joshua *is* the man in the cave?" Elizabeth asked.

Jennings shook his head. "I did not inquire how the elder Joshua Heron died," he responded. "But I do not believe that he is the man in the cave. No, the connection seems to be more remote, yet, according to the slate, there may be more people involved than just Mr. Heron and the man in my dream." He opened the drawer wider, inviting Elizabeth to come look at it herself.

She approached the drawer a bit hesitantly, but, as was often the case, the actual writing on the slate did not convey for her the emotional impact that Jennings, with his gifts, typically experienced. Given the intensity of his dream, however, and the unusual nature of the Heron-Gilbraith matter, she was not surprised that he found it at best extremely puzzling, and at worst rather sinister. Were there other imposters out there? – ones willing to kill for the privilege? And what part did she and Jennings have to play in it? Where, indeed, could they even begin?

They both stood silently then, staring somberly at the slate's simple, seemingly innocuous sentence: "There are many more like me."

CHAPTER THIRTEEN

Jennings was not happy to hear about little Eliza. Through clenched teeth, he muttered darkly, "I know in my bones that her 'fever' was not a natural event!"

"I feel that very strongly myself," Elizabeth said. "Though I have never met her, the poor little thing, and I have only the slightest memories of meeting my cousin Marcus when I was very small, I remember him being a kind man. Indeed, he is the most selfless man imaginable, if he thinks he importunes *me* when he is suffering so!"

"We cannot tell him about the ring," Jennings asserted. "It would no doubt crush him to think he had done anything to hurt her." He frowned deeply. "But how then do we get the ring away from him? We must intercept it, surely, before Isabelle – or whoever has taken your great-grandmother's place – takes it and passes it on to some new unsuspecting victim."

"I had not thought of that," Elizabeth said, horrified by the notion. "It seems a strange thing to request, since I had never laid eyes on the girl, to ask for such a personal memento. But outside of that, I cannot immediately think of a plausible reason." She gasped, stricken. "It has been some days, sir," she noted. "I am sure Eliza has already been laid away. Whoever controls the rings now, this person must already have taken the amethyst!"

"Of course," Jennings said. After a moment, his brow cleared, and he looked meaningfully at Elizabeth. "Could you – you have been so resourceful these past weeks – could you contrive to ascertain the identity of the person who took the amethyst?"

Elizabeth smiled. "I believe I can, sir," she said brightly. "I will write my cousin at once."

* * *

While Jennings lingered over his coffee, Elizabeth opened the other letters that had come for her. As she read through the pages her stepmother had written, she abruptly leaned forward and reached a hand across the table toward her husband.

"I fear we have received this letter too late to do aught about it, sir," she said. "My stepmother is informing me of her planned visit here. She will arrive later this morning, if the roads favour."

"That is excellent news, my dear," Jennings said placidly. "Why would we wish to do 'aught about it'? I had thought you liked your stepmother."

"I do," Elizabeth asserted. She considered his question for a moment, then answered, "I suppose, sir, that I do not wish to disrupt your household without warning, when you are so preoccupied with this mystery."

Jennings smiled softly and took her hand. "It is your household too, my love, and I could use a distraction from the mystery." He sighed and rubbed his forehead. "It gives me headache."

It was uncertain if a visit from Charlotte Carlisle would rid him of his headache; Elizabeth's stepmother was bubbling over with excitement at seeing Elizabeth, and hastened to share all news in a blur of words that was, functionally, a single sentence, delivered with unabashed grins and a dozen embraces.

"It has been so very long, dearest Lizzie!" she cried happily. "I have missed you so terribly!" She and Elizabeth had settled in the small sitting room at the front of the house, and Mrs. Carlisle more than once looked over her shoulder and out into the hall. "I am not alone," she explained presently, after all the gossip she had stored in her brain had been revealed to her stepdaughter. "That is, he said that he would be following close on my heels."

"Father?" Elizabeth asked dubiously.

"Indeed no," Mrs. Carlisle said with a slight scoff that she quickly smothered. "He is much as he has always been," she went on. "But he at least made no objection to my visiting you. No, I have come here with Mr. Cedric Delacourt, your father's cousin, upon whom your father's estate is entailed." Her smile faltered slightly. "Of course, one hopes that there will be heirs soon enough," she said, as brightly as she could muster. Her five-year marriage to Sir James Carlisle had been childless so far, but, as she had confided in Elizabeth long ago, her doctor had told her that all was well, and that she would no doubt be able to provide her husband with any number of male offspring who would inherit his rather large estate. It had been a source of some upset for her, but on this even Sir James seemed optimistic and unaffected, telling her that she was a young and healthy girl, and that there was plenty of time. If Elizabeth secretly believed that her father simply didn't care who inherited his estate, or what might happen to the females attached to it, she kept this opinion to herself, and contented herself to pray with her stepmother that that lady might soon be with child.

"But it is always best," Mrs. Carlisle continued, looking once more into the hall. "To prepare for whatever may befall one. And so I thought it prudent to invite Mr. Delacourt to visit, and to make friends with him, so that – well, if your father were to – well, so that I would

147

not be unknown to him."

"You are quite wise to do so," Elizabeth said placidly. "It is always better to foster friendship in such situations, I believe."

"Just so!" Mrs. Carlisle agreed. "And when his visit unexpectedly coincided with my plans to come here, I naturally thought he might like to make your acquaintance as well, with which notion he readily agreed, but he did insist on driving himself because he did not wish to importune me or to do anything that might have even the semblance of impropriety." She smiled. "Is he not the most gentlemanly man? I think you will like him very well!"

Mr. Delacourt did not arrive for another fifteen minutes; he explained, amidst a number of earnest apologies, that his curricle had slipped into a muddy rut, and there was some difficulty in extricating it.

He was a tall young man, and rather lanky, and Elizabeth thought, as she looked on him, that he seemed very familiar to her. Perhaps it was the faint resemblance to her father, she mused, for he and this cousin shared a similar quality around the eyes. In all other respects, he was nothing like the austere and peremptory Sir James. His clothes and hair were simple but elegant, and arranged extremely meticulously; his manner was one of easy-going self-assurance, bordering on arrogance, but his smiles were genuine, and he greeted Elizabeth with a warm and friendly handshake.

"Dear Cousin Elizabeth!" he said, beaming at her. "I have long heard so much about you from Sir James! It is most gratifying indeed finally to make your acquaintance!"

Elizabeth could not help but like this man, whose gaze and demeanour were so frank and direct that she felt it impossible to doubt his sincerity. "Cousin Delacourt," she responded. "I am also pleased to meet *you*. My father has spoken highly of you."

"And for that I am doubly grateful!" Mr. Delacourt announced, still grinning. "For he and I had never met before yesterday! Except that I believe he visited my father when I was a very tiny boy, but I can't think that signifies, can you, Cousin? – for I have no recollection of it, and to be sure I am not the same as that little boy your father would, I am sure, have entirely ignored." His eyes twinkled merrily, and Elizabeth laughed.

"You are quite right, sir," she agreed. She gestured into the front sitting room where she and Mrs. Carlisle had just been ensconced. "Shall we not sit?" she invited. "I will have Mrs. Raleigh bring us refreshments."

"That would be absolutely delightful!" Mr. Delacourt said, offering one arm to his cousin and the other to Mrs. Carlisle, and escorting both ladies into the sitting room. They conversed quite comfortably for some time, and Mr. Delacourt was very complimentary of his cousin, of her household, and of her refreshments. He told her that she seemed a first-rate sort of person, and that he counted himself fortunate to have two such excellent ladies among his friends. "For we are friends, are we not, Cousin?" he asked, with an air that suggested he would be quite unhappy to hear otherwise. "I know – that is, I would not wish to say anything to upset you, dear Cousin, but I am aware – and most distressed by it, I assure you! – that my Cousin Carlisle has distanced himself from you, but I would not want you to think, even though I am his heir, that I would consider any such circumstances to be part of my inheritance!" After this lengthy but heartfelt speech, he patted her hand reassuringly.

"We shall be great friends!" he decided. "And you and your stepmother need never have any concern for your futures!" He stopped then, and laughed rather loudly. "Of course," he said. "I had crafted these words well *before* I heard that Mr. Jennings had asked for your hand. I daresay my humble offers must seem a trifle silly when your future is so completely assured!"

Elizabeth leaned forward and touched Mr. Delacourt's arm. "Not at all, sir," she said earnestly. "Kindness is never ill-timed. That you would hear of the rift between me and my father, and think first of how best to *help*, speaks greatly to your character." She smiled. "I will gladly call you friend, sir." She tilted her head, looking at him quizzically. "Are you quite sure that we have not met?" she asked. "I had thought that I only spied a resemblance between you and my father, but now I am convinced that I have met you somewhere before."

"Well, as to that," Mr. Delacourt said. "I am often in London. I adore balls and assemblies." He squinted at her. "But I am certain that I have never seen you in attendance at any of them."

"No," Elizabeth said, smiling wryly. "My father is not fond of those sorts of amusements. In fact, the party at Lady Morton's where I – where I met Mr. Jennings, is one of the only parties I have attended in my life." She frowned slightly, considering her cousin's words. "You come often to London?" she asked. "Why, then, have we not met you?"

Mr. Delacourt made a face, and looked sheepish. "Well, Cousin," he explained. "I thought it might be a bit *rude* to descend uninvited on your father, for although I am his heir, that state of affairs was not *his* idea. I did not wish to appear to be ingratiating myself, or to be *assessing* the property, or any such distasteful thing."

Elizabeth raised an eyebrow. "And my father never invited *you*?"

Mr. Delacourt opened his mouth to speak, paused, and, twisting his mouth ruefully, said, "No." He laughed. "But as I said, I hardly expected him to be anxious to meet me, and he has quite often corresponded with me on matters of the estate, and has been perfectly courteous in those letters. I had no reason to complain or to feel slighted, and I will say that he has been all that is cordial since my arrival yesterday!"

Mrs. Carlisle scoffed. "I cannot see how!" she averred drily. "I have not seen him above ten minutes these past two days!"

Mr. Delacourt laughed. "He sat with me for some time," he assured her. "While you were visiting your friend – Mrs. Stoke, was it?"

"He left you there alone!" Mrs. Carlisle pointed out, apparently feeling this slight to be quite scandalous.

Mr. Delacourt laughed again, and shook his head. "I was not alone more than half an hour before your return, dear Cousin! And he very graciously invited me to dine with him at his club, and to introduce me to his cronies." He leaned forward and once more patted Elizabeth's hand. "And I am so very delighted to have been able to follow Cousin Charlotte here!" he announced cheerfully. "And to meet you!" A thought occurred to him, and he added, "Where, indeed, is your Mr. Jennings, Cousin Elizabeth? One hears nothing but good of him, and I had hoped to make his acquaintance."

Elizabeth smiled broadly. "He is truly the best of men," she said. "He is gone out with his steward, Mr. Davies, to inspect some part of the grounds – an issue of engineering governing one of the boundary walls, I believe. He did not think it should take long, and I expect him any moment. You will be staying to lunch with us, will you not, Cousin?"

Mr. Delacourt seemed sincerely flattered by the invitation, and hastened to tell his cousin that he would be more than glad and honoured to stay. "I had intended to return to Everdale – my estate – this afternoon, but I have been persuaded by both Cousin Charlotte and Sir James to join them for a week at the lake lodge."

"You will love it there!" Elizabeth informed him enthusiastically. "It is the most beautiful part of the country!"

"Will you and Mr. Jennings not join us, Cousin?" Mr. Delacourt asked. "It has been nearly three months since the *rift*, as you called it; do you not think he might have softened his heart by now?"

Elizabeth exchanged a glance with her stepmother. "I believe my father's heart has not changed overmuch in all the time that I have known him," she said, her words delivered gently and without rancour. "He is who he has always been, and I would expect nothing else."

Mr. Delacourt looked as though he wished very much to disagree with her, but even his brief acquaintance with the gruff Sir James led him to see that Elizabeth was likely quite correct, and he contented himself instead to suggesting gently, "Perhaps in the coming years – when there are grandchildren to think of, you know – he will change his mind."

"Perhaps," Elizabeth acknowledged. "I think that would be nice." She smiled warmly. "But do not let it concern you, Cousin," she told him. "I believe you will enjoy yourself prodigiously at the lodge. You will not want to leave at the end of the week!"

"So I told him as well!" Mrs. Carlisle said, adding teasingly, "But he *will* go to some ridiculous wedding!"

"Of my oldest friend, dear Charlotte!" Mr. Delacourt defended himself. Turning to Elizabeth, he explained, "My boyhood friend Ned Fitzhugh is to be married in less than five weeks' time, and I must – of course – abduct him in the meanwhile for one last round of adventures!"

"That sounds very exciting!" Elizabeth said, her eyes twinkling. "But does the young lady approve of your abduction of her bridegroom so soon before the event?"

Mr. Delacourt let out a bark of laughter. "She has been most understanding!" he said. "More so than one might have thought, given her circumstance." He lowered his voice and spoke rather conspiratorially. "She is a prominent member of a wealthy clan, and this union with Ned has been something of a to-do since they first set eyes on one another. Both families have sizable fortunes to bring to it, and this marriage is being viewed as a *most* eligible political alliance."

Something tugged at Elizabeth's memory. "What is the lady's name?" she asked.

"She is the honourable Miss Isabelle Fetherston, daughter of Sir Richard Fetherston." He looked quizzically at her. "Are you acquainted with that family?"

"Oh, my, how famous!" Mrs. Carlisle exclaimed, clapping her hands together.

Elizabeth blinked, incredulous at the coincidence. "Why, she is my cousin, sir!" she said. "On my mother's side. Not close enough a

153

cousin for her family fortune to be in any way *my* family fortune, but still, what an extraordinary thing! We had just learned of her engagement some days before Lady Morton's party!" She thought briefly of the haughty, rather acerbic girl who had, during their brief and infrequent encounters, looked down her nose at Elizabeth, and considered herself to be much superior to those who made the grave mistake of *not* being a Fetherston; it seemed strange and almost unbelievable that such a woman might now be described as 'most understanding.' Of course, Ned Fitzhugh's family was only one step away from the Fetherstons, and his fortune by all accounts was quite large; Isabelle might have reserved her good conduct for such a worthy object – and for his particular friends.

Mrs. Carlisle did not attempt to be circumspect. "I'm quite surprised to hear that she is understanding, Cousin Cedric, I don't mind saying! She was always very cool to us here, and not just to me – who is not properly her family at all – but to Lizzie as well, who never did a thing to her except to be kind! But she was very young when she last visited; I suppose time might have changed her."

Mr. Delacourt raised his eyebrows at Mrs. Carlisle's words. "I am sure so, Cousin," he said. "For she is now very much the gracious hostess, most pleasing indeed!" He chuckled. "Perhaps it is Ned's doing! He is a very open and friendly man, and doesn't stand on ceremony. One can't know him for more than an hour and not be affected by his good nature!"

From the hallway came the sounds of the door opening, and of dogs milling about, and of Mr. Davies commanding them to clear away and to be quiet.

"Here is Mr. Jennings now!" Elizabeth said brightly, standing

154

and walking to the door of the sitting room. When Jennings saw her, he broke into a happy grin, and, pushing the energetic dogs away from him, he moved quickly to join her.

"Your stepmother has arrived, I take it?" he asked her, taking her hand and bringing it to his lips.

"She has," Elizabeth informed him, inviting him into the sitting room. "As well as my cousin, Cedric Delacourt, who is my father's heir."

Mr. Delacourt had come to his feet, and now greeted Jennings as though they had been old friends. "It is indeed a pleasure to meet you, sir!" he said jovially, shaking Jennings' hand in both of his. "I – that is, Mrs. Carlisle and I – can well see how happy you have made Elizabeth, and that is worth the world to me, I assure you!"

Jennings, much as his wife had done, could not help but like this amiable visitor. "I am much obliged to you!" he said. Feeling an odd sensation of recognition, and fruitlessly searching his memory for Mr. Delacourt, he asked him, "Have we already met, sir? I have the distinct impression that I have seen you somewhere before."

Mr. Delacourt cocked his head to the side and scrutinized Jennings' face. "I agree, sir," he said after a moment. "I believe I have met you before. I suppose it must have been at some assembly or other." He grinned suddenly, and clapped Jennings on the shoulder. "But I am quite sure that we were never introduced, and so today is a most pleasant day indeed!"

Mrs. Carlisle, her heart overflowing with joy at the realization that her plan had worked – her husband's heir seemed *very* ready to befriend Elizabeth and herself, and would no doubt be kind to her if anything should happen to Sir James – smiled and once more clapped her hands together. "Most pleasant!" she echoed. "And it is only just noon!"

They spent the afternoon touring Brightwood; Mrs. Raleigh, having predicted that these guests would wish to take advantage of the beautiful weather, had prepared a picnic lunch while they chatted in the sitting room, and they set out thus fully stocked to explore the estate. Cedric Delacourt proved to be an extremely easy man to know, and to be very contented to spend time with his cousins. It was with apparent reluctance that he and Mrs. Carlisle decided to end their visit – the sun already hanging rather low in the sky – and, as he climbed into his curricle, he said earnestly, "We must do this again very soon! Very soon!"

"We look forward to it!" Elizabeth assured him.

After the curricle and Charlotte Carlisle's coach had driven up the lane and out of sight, Elizabeth turned to her husband. "And how do you like my Cousin Cedric?" she asked him, her eyes twinkling.

"He is most affable!" Jennings said. "He may come here as often as he likes!" He smiled wryly at Elizabeth. "It is a comfort to see such affection from your father's side of the family."

Elizabeth chuckled. "It is!" she said. "And I believe Charlotte is much relieved to make friends with him, for she has been concerned, I think, that upon my father's death she would be cast out into the streets!"

Jennings raised an eyebrow. "Did it not occur to her that we would never allow her to be cast out into the streets?"

"I don't know," Elizabeth admitted. "But I imagine she would not wish to importune us by asking." She turned then to go into the house, only to stop in her tracks. "The portraits!" she cried, clapping her hand to her forehead. "I *knew* I had seen him before!"

"Portraits?"

"The portraits in my father's house. Most are hanging on the walls in the small sitting room, but several of them are kept in a glass case in the front hall." She looked perplexed, and stood apparently mulling something over.

"Is it unusual for his portrait to be among them?" Jennings asked. "Is he not part of your father's family?"

"Yes," Elizabeth answered. "But he is a young man, and the portrait is of a young man, and has been displayed in the case for as long as I can remember. And it sits with others from my *mother's* family." She frowned and bit her lip. "That makes no sense."

"I'm sure it is just a resemblance, and is a portrait of some other cousin," Jennings suggested. "Perhaps on our next visit into town, we could stop and look at them."

"Oh, yes!" Elizabeth agreed eagerly. "Charlotte and my father will be gone to the lodge, and I am sure I shall be allowed in, just to look!" She shook her head, still frowning. "For I am sure it is Delacourt's portrait, and that makes no sense. No sense at all."

CHAPTER FOURTEEN

Their next visit to town came much sooner than the Jennings had planned, and for a reason that left neither of them anxious to make the journey.

The morning after Cousin Delacourt's visit, the *Gazette* arrived, announcing, amongst the engagements and weddings, the untimely death of a young woman. She resided, apparently, in Whitechapel, and had been walking home from her work in one of the dressmaking shops not a stone's throw from her front door. She had been found, in fact, by her own mother, who had been expecting her daughter for over an hour before venturing out to look for her. A constable and a doctor were immediately summoned, but the poor girl had been lifeless for some time, and had, according to the doctor, been "ravaged as though by a wild animal."

If Elizabeth was hesitant at all to assume that this "wild animal" was the monster that had attacked her, her doubts were dispelled by her husband's expression; he sat staring at the notice in the *Gazette* as though a puzzle had suddenly been solved.

"You feel this is the same creature?" Elizabeth asked him.

He nodded. "I do indeed," he said. "More to the point, I believe this young woman left a message on the slate this morning: 'Eldest,' it said. And I saw a vision of a girl who looked very much like she might work in a dressmaker's shop, and a dark street, and a sensation of something coming up very quickly behind her."

"Eldest?" Elizabeth repeated, frowning. "How could that signify in such a tragedy?"

"I have no idea," Jennings admitted. He looked at his wife, and then at the letter she held in her hands. "You were displeased with its contents?" he asked. "I thought I heard you scoffing over it?"

Elizabeth chuckled. "Several times!" she said. She laid the letter on the table and, smoothing out the paper that she had crumpled in irritation, began to read it aloud:

"'*My dearest Cousin Elizabeth*' – a promising beginning, to be sure, but don't be fooled, sir! – '*It was such a pleasure to hear from you. After hearing – as one does – of all that had befallen you, I was most concerned for your well-being! The polite world knows all too well your father's rigid opinions, and my friends – with whom I spoke about the matter at some length, it being of such a serious nature, and enough to prompt more than one of my acquaintance to vow never to go to London again if such ruffians wander the public parks! – my friends all agreed that it was most unfair of Sir James to cast you out, only because you were walking alone.*'" Elizabeth sighed at this thinly-veiled aspersion on her conduct, but continued without comment: "'*I well understand how unhappy your father's actions must have left you – wondering upon whom you could rely in such a troubled time – and that naturally you wish to satisfy yourself that your family has not all deserted you. And so you may rest your mind on that score, dear Elizabeth, for I assure you, from the very depths of my heart, that I feel all the same friendship and tenderness for you that I always have!*' – I'm sure I know how to take that! She has never felt even the slightest regard for anyone on our branch of the family, except her rather obvious fawning in deference to my father's money! – '*And I would most certainly have invited you to visit if I had not thought of your sensibilities – for I know how kind you are, dear Lizzie, and that it would hurt you to think that you had importuned anyone! – and everything here is in such a hubbub planning for the wedding! It is only five weeks away, you know! And of course to have visitors now would be very distracting, and I would not be able to spend any amount of time with you, and I fear you would be quite unhappy and neglected!'* – well, I'm certainly happy she thought of my sensibilities – *'But as soon as my dear Ned and I have settled in, we will be quite delighted to bring you for a visit! – and your dear father, too, of course, if you think that he would be willing to make the journey with you. I trust this letter finds you well! Your Mr. Jennings seems to be a decent sort of fellow; I'm so glad you found someone willing to look past all of this dreadful unpleasantness! Yours most sincerely, Isabelle Fetherston Fitzhugh.'"*

Elizabeth sat back after reading this, her disgust evident on her face. "She is the most dreadful girl!" she said of her cousin, and pushed the letter away from her.

"Well, now," Jennings said in soothing tones. "At least she told you what you wanted to find out." As soon as these words left his lips, he frowned, contemplating them in puzzlement.

"How so?" Elizabeth asked, her own baffled expression mirroring his. "She has said nothing of any consequence whatsoever." She lifted one eyebrow. "Much like always," she added drily.

"I don't know," Jennings said. "It simply seemed to me that she had done so, but now that I consider her words, I have no earthly idea what I was thinking."

Elizabeth tilted her head to the side. "Perhaps it was part of your gift," she suggested. She reached out and picked up the ill-used sheets of the letter. "Perhaps some part of you sees something here that we cannot otherwise recognize as any sort of clue." She folded the letter. "I will keep this, I think," she decided. "In case I am correct. In time, the clue might be better revealed."

Jennings nodded. "Wise, my love," he said rather abstractedly, his mind still searching for the reason for his odd pronouncement. It had come unbidden from him; Elizabeth was no doubt correct about its origins. But it was unlike him to receive information without an accompanying vision, and he remained preoccupied with the mystery all morning, not able to abandon it until he and Elizabeth climbed into the carriage to go to town.

"Although I cannot fathom how they would be willing to discuss it with us," Elizabeth noted as she settled into the carriage seat. "We are no acquaintance of this girl – what was her name?"

"Ann Baker," Jennings said, sitting next to his wife. "She and her mother, according to the *Gazette*, have lived in Whitechapel for many years." As the carriage pulled onto the high road, Jennings took Elizabeth's hand in his. "I am in hopes," he went on. "That where our words and arguments might fail us, a few coins might suffice."

Elizabeth stared at him. "You mean to bribe the coroner?" she asked.

"Or the undertaker," Jennings said. "Whoever is in charge of the poor girl at the moment. But of course I am not 'bribing' them; I am simply paying them for their services."

"Their 'service' of telling us information that is none of our business?"

Jennings eyes twinkled. "Yes," he said, and raised her fingers to his lips.

When they arrived in town, they went first to Sir James' house, and, as the carriage pulled up to the door, Elizabeth realized that her heart was beating rapidly, and that she was almost trembling with nervousness.

"I have not been here in so long," she said, gripping Jennings' hand tightly. "Well, I suppose it has only been several weeks," she amended. "But it seems a lifetime."

Jennings gazed at her in some concern. "Are you sure you wish to do this?" he asked. "I believe your stepmother said that they would leave for the Lake house today, but if you think they might still be here – if you do not wish to encounter your father just now ..."

She shook her head. "I am sure they are gone," she said. "If they are not, we will simply leave again." She squared her shoulders. "It's silly to be nervous to enter my own house!" she said, as much to herself as to him. "I have as much right to visit it as anyone."

They climbed down from the carriage and approached the door of the house, and Elizabeth, to her irritation, felt even more trepidation than she had a moment before. *Why is it so difficult to be here?* she wondered. *I grew up here.*

When the door was opened by the porter – a man whose face she had seen every day of her life for nineteen years – her anxiety vanished. "Simmons!" she said, smiling warmly at him.

Simmons, abandoning his habitual stern expression, broke into a wide grin. "Miss Elizabeth!" he cried. "Or – forgive me – Mrs. Jennings!" He ushered them in, his face beaming. "If I may say so, ma'am," he said. "You look most well, and it's the most excellent thing to see you!"

Elizabeth reached out impulsively and shook his hand. "I *am* quite well," she said. "And it is indeed the most excellent thing to see *you*!"

"Miss Elizabeth?" a voice called, and a woman bustled in from the far end of the hall. "Miss Elizabeth!" she said again, overjoyed to see the visitors. She looked from Elizabeth to Jennings, and then, with a cluck of disgust, at Simmons. "Take Mr. Jennings' hat and coat!" she said. "Have you forgotten yourself?" She herself helped Elizabeth out of her travelling cloak, and draped it over her arm as Simmons hastened to do as he had been bid.

"Beggin' your pardon, sir," he said contritely. "I was just that glad to see her – to see you both!"

"I quite understand," Jennings told him. "Am I correct in assuming that Sir James is not currently at home?"

"He is not, sir," the housekeeper said. "He and Mrs. Carlisle and Mr. Delacourt have all gone to the lake house, just this morning." She turned again to Simmons. "Simmons, tell Cook to prepare a luncheon for the Jennings!" She smiled cheerfully at the guests. "It won't be twenty minutes, Miss Elizabeth!" she said. "Shall I show you to the back sitting room?"

Elizabeth, relieved to hear that her father was already away, and as pleased to see the servants as they were to see her, laughed and nodded. "But in a moment," she said. She pointed to the cabinet where rows of miniature portraits were displayed. "I wanted to see one of the portraits," she explained. "Someone who, I think, was an ancestor of my mother's."

By this time, other servants had made their way to the front hall, all of them delighted to see Elizabeth, and several of them breaching the ordinary conventions of propriety to shake Jennings' hand and thank him earnestly for saving "Miss Elizabeth". Without going so far as to criticize their master, or even to acknowledge how painfully aware they were of his ways, they made it clear to Jennings that they felt every tenderness toward his wife, and that they had all been quite worried for her since the attack, and that his being there for her was a relief to them greater than they could say.

"For I don't mind saying, sir," the housekeeper said solemnly. "That when we saw how Sir – how things were going to be, that you were very much the answer to my prayers!" Her eyes had actually misted over with tears, and she turned away. "And I'm ever so grateful!" She left the hall, hurrying to ready the back sitting room for company, and surreptitiously wiping her eyes with a handkerchief.

Elizabeth, amidst animated responses to the servants, who had begun peppering her with questions as though she had been gone for years instead of weeks, had made her way to the cabinet. "Here it is!" she said to Jennings, gesturing for him to come see the portrait. "I was right! – it looks exactly like Cousin Delacourt!"

Jennings leaned over the cabinet and looked at the portrait. It seemed, at first, to be a portrait of Cedric Delacourt, so much so that Jennings asked his wife, "Is this a new portrait? The one you remember has perhaps been removed?"

"Oh, no, sir," one of the servants said, bobbing a slight curtsey to excuse her intrusion. "That's a portrait of Jonathan Fitzhugh, and I had noticed myself, sir, that it was all over Mr. Delacourt. But that's been there for all the time I've been here."

Elizabeth nodded her agreement. "It's been there as long as I can remember," she said. "In exactly that spot, with exactly that face.

Cousin Cedric's face."

"I did find it uncanny, ma'am," the servant said. "I had even thought to mention it to Mr. Delacourt, but Frimmy told me not to be rude."

The housekeeper had returned to the hall. "And don't you be oppressin' Mr. and Mrs. Jennings!" she said tartly. "Bring them into the sitting room, and I'll check on Cook."

The servant, casting a sheepish glance at the housekeeper, quickly showed the Jennings into the back sitting room, still asking Elizabeth questions about her new life. For the duration of the Jennings' visit, and even while they ate the lunch that Cook had prepared, she and the other servants milled in an out of the sitting room and the small dining room, and made constant conversation with Elizabeth. They were clearly very attached to her, and Jennings was glad to see that the cold and haughty Sir James had not by any means been the only person in Elizabeth's household. She had apparently been quite surrounded by loving people, and she in turn was vastly contented to spend these hours with them.

After luncheon, as the Jennings prepared to leave, Elizabeth asked the housekeeper to tell her about the man in the portrait. "Is he not one of Mama's relatives, Frimmy?" she wanted to know, as she carefully reached into the cabinet and pulled the miniature out. Where it had been, a circle remained, a darker patch against the faded surface of the cabinet shelf; the portrait had been there for some time, and had not been moved until now. "Is this not a very old portrait?"

"Aye, Miss," Frimmy replied. "Much too old to be Mr. Delacourt, which I told Tina, but she said it was most uncanny, and I suppose she's right, but it can't be Mr. Delacourt, nor even his father or grandfather." She pointed a finger at the miniature. "That man is the head of the Fitzhugh clan, which was your dear mother's clan, and that portrait is over a hundred years old."

* * *

As they made their way to the coroner's, Elizabeth was unnaturally quiet and serious. Although she had much enjoyed her visit to her father's house, she was puzzled, not only by the strange similarity between her cousin Cedric and the long-dead Jonathan Fitzhugh in the portrait, but by her fascination with it. People often resembled one another, after all, especially in miniature paintings the accuracy of which depended completely upon the skill of the painter. It was true, too, that family trees often intertwined at more than one place; perhaps Mr. Delacourt was her relation on both sides of her lineage, and perhaps those connections had simply been forgotten over the intervening decades. It made no sense, really, that this should bother her so.

Jennings noticed her altered mood, and asked her solicitously, "Are you disturbed to be going with me to the coroner? It would be most understandable if you did not wish to go."

She looked up at him. "Oh, not at all, sir," she said. "Although her death saddens me, it has already occurred; what would a fit of sensibility on my part benefit her – or myself – in the least? She has reached out to us through the slate, and I take rather seriously our responsibility to help her as best we can – I will not shirk it simply to avoid the coroner." She gave a small laugh. "When one is being contacted by the spirits of the dead, one might reasonably expect to be required to *see* the dead, and to deal with the consequences of death. I cannot suppose it would do very well to be squeamish!" She shook her head. "No, especially since you feel her death to be connected to the attack on me, I am in fact rather curious to discover more about her. I am only thoughtful at the moment, about the portrait and about why the matter is so pressing to me. I cannot decide how it should seem so important." She laughed again. "You must think me rather silly!" she said. "To fret so much over such a small thing!"

Jennings shook his head. "Not at all, my dear," he told her. "I have spent my life acting upon feelings the nature of which others could not understand. If you feel this portrait is more than a remarkable coincidence, then by all means you should consider it. Perhaps, indeed, we should examine your cousin Delacourt."

This thought struck Elizabeth as being distasteful as well as unwarranted. "But that would be so ... *rude*!" she protested. "He is the most affable man! And completely forthcoming! I cannot imagine that he would be involved in any sort of plot to hurt others!"

"I quite agree," Jennings said. "I felt nothing upon meeting him other than warmth and friendliness." He pondered the matter silently for a moment. "We might instead look the other direction," he suggested. "It may be your mother's ancestor who is the key here; his direct descendent is marrying your Cousin Isabelle, after all, and is Mr. Delacourt's closest friend."

"But that also feels rather wrong," Elizabeth argued. "I have never met Ned Fitzhugh – although I knew *of* him, as part of a list of distant cousins I had no expectation of ever laying eyes on in my life – but I have not heard anything other than good about him."

Something in her turn of phrase triggered a sensation in Jennings' chest, a familiar sort of tingling breath that typically prefaced a vision, but no insights came immediately to him. "We've heard nothing but good of him," he echoed. "From your cousins Isabelle and Delacourt."

"His fiancée," Elizabeth said. "And his best friend." She regarded her husband curiously. "Are you seeing something?" she asked. "Something about the portrait?"

"No," he said slowly. He had stopped walking, and he now turned to Elizabeth with a somber expression. "My dream," he went on. "Betrayal. The man who was killed was betrayed by someone he trusted implicitly."

Elizabeth's eyes widened. "But Cousin Cedric is very much alive," she pointed out. "The man in your dream was killed." A thought occurred to her. "Unless," she continued. "You believe your dream might in fact be a vision of the future after all?"

"No," he said again, shaking his head emphatically. "I could sense the man," he explained. "He is dead, killed by a friend. And whoever killed him seems in some way to be connected to your cousins – all three of them, perhaps." He seemed suddenly worried. "It may be that they are in danger."

"In danger?" Elizabeth repeated in consternation. "From whom? From my mother's ancestor? – who has been dead nearly a hundred years!"

Jennings looked askance at her. "Do you believe Eliza Tate was killed by a fever?" he asked. "Or that the creature that left you for dead was of this world?"

Elizabeth blinked, staring at him mutely. "No," she said at last.

"I do not." The things they had been discussing these past weeks – the deaths, the notions of dark magic and family secrets – had never seemed more real to her, and, as she thought again of the portrait, she could feel that her mind had been guiding her to this conclusion. "My ancestor," she began soberly. "Is in some way still manipulating his family."

She turned then, and continued walking. Jennings walked beside her, neither of them saying a word as they each contemplated the mysterious situation.

Upon arrival at the coroner's establishment, they were informed that Ann Baker had already been delivered to the undertaker, who, even as they spoke, was no doubt preparing the girl for burial. The coroner was a stout middle-aged man named Oxley, who, once Jennings had indicated that Miss Baker was a relative, seemed perfectly inclined to discuss the matter.

"The poor girl was ripped apart!" Oxley said, clearly troubled by the incident. "Clawed all about as though by some animal, but the *size* of the animal passes all believability! – it should have been a bear, I would imagine, of considerable size, and I can't imagine how such a thing would make its way into the heart of the city! Twice, too! – for another young lady was attacked in such a way not two months ago, from what I understand not a stone's throw from her home!"

Oxley did not seem aware that Elizabeth was in fact this other young lady, and Jennings did not offer the information. "Strange," he murmured. "For a bear to roam undetected for two months."

"Indeed!" Oxley agreed vehemently. "It's almost as though it's being *released* to hunt, and then disappears whence it came."

Jennings thrust his hands into his pockets. "Can't be," he objected. "Surely not. What sort of wretch would train a bear to go out hunting young ladies?"

"Just what I was wondering!" Oxley said. "And *how* would one do it? How would one control a creature of such size and strength? It makes no sense, sir, I tell you. But it makes even less sense that such a beast would simply be wandering loose, and no one the wiser." He shook his head, and frowned. "The poor thing was most viciously savaged by it," he went on. "There was hardly anything left of her."

Elizabeth stepped forward. "Dr. Oxley," she said softly. "Was Miss Baker wearing a ring, by any chance?"

Dr. Oxley, who had forgotten to some extent that Mrs. Jennings was in the room, was for a moment worried that his frank discussion about such delicate matters had upset Elizabeth. When he saw that she was unaffected, he was too relieved to concern himself with the reason for her question. "In a way," he answered. "I found a ring upon examination, one that had fallen into …" He looked at Jennings, and then back to Elizabeth. "But I do not wish to offend you, ma'am, with any depiction of Miss Baker's injuries."

Elizabeth gave him a small smile. "The girl is connected with my family," she reminded him, convinced as she spoke that this was no fib. "I am quite willing to hear whatever I must to learn what befell her."

Dr. Oxley, still hesitant, nodded his head. "Of course," he said. "Of course. Well." He coughed, and continued, "There was a ring hidden deep inside one of the girl's wounds. All of her fingers were broken – nearly wrenched from her hands! – so I surmised that the ring had fallen." He was unused to speaking so graphically before a

170

lady, and he coughed again, and flushed awkwardly.

"Do you have the ring, sir?" Elizabeth asked him. "I would very much like to have it back, so that we may deliver it to Mrs. Baker."

"I do not, ma'am," Dr. Oxley informed her. "I gave it – and some other things found with Miss Baker – to her mother yesterday."

"Mrs. Baker and I have not spoken in some time," Elizabeth said. "I don't suppose – would it be too much to ask you for her direction? I daresay she may not wish to see us, but news of Ann's death has brought my heart to her, and I would like to try, if I can, to offer some comfort to her."

Oxley's brow cleared. "Of course," he said again. "Mending fences. Of course." He cheerfully gave them direction to the Bakers' house in Whitechapel, and within a very few moments, the Jennings found themselves on their way to visit a stranger – a situation that was daily becoming less unusual to Elizabeth. As they made their way to Whitechapel, she composed several avenues of conversation with which they might speak to Mrs. Baker without arousing her suspicions or putting her on her guard.

In the end, however, no subterfuge was required, for Mrs. Baker seemed eager to bring them into her home and to speak with them. "For I'm not sure how to feel, ma'am," she explained to Elizabeth as they seated themselves in her small front room. "I still can't believe it. I keep calling to her as though she was just in her room, and then remembering that she's not." She looked up at her guests, her face pale and stricken. "Forgive me, ma'am," she said. "I should have offered you tea." She moved as though to get up, but Elizabeth put out a hand to stop her.

"We are quite fine, Mrs. Baker," she said with sincere

compassion. "We are here to offer *you* condolence."

Mrs. Baker pressed a handkerchief to her mouth. "Thank you," she said, her voice muffled. "I suppose you are friends of Annie?"

Elizabeth exchanged glances with Jennings. "This will perhaps sound strange to you, Mrs. Baker," Elizabeth began delicately. "But I believe that whatever attacked your daughter also attacked *me*, some weeks ago."

Mrs. Baker looked startled, and stared for a long moment at Elizabeth. In a small voice, she asked, "Do you – do you know what it was?"

Elizabeth felt tears welling up, and blinked them back as best she could. "I do," she said. "But I believe the monster was dispatched by some wretched master, who targets his quarry by means of a ring."

Mrs. Baker's eyes opened wide. "A ring," she repeated. "What kind of ring?"

"I know of two," Elizabeth answered. "One is a peridot, and the other is an amethyst. But I suppose there is the possibility of more."

Mrs. Baker got up from her chair. "Please excuse me," she said. "I'll be back directly." She left the room, returning not thirty seconds later with something clutched in her hand. "Is this one of them?" she asked, opening her hand to reveal a green peridot ring resting in her palm.

Elizabeth did not bother to hide the tears that now fell onto her cheeks. "That is my ring," she said. "My mother's ring, that the monster stole from me."

Mrs. Baker held it out for Elizabeth to take. "Please, ma'am," she said. "Please take this. It is of no particular significance to me; I only took it because Dr. Oxley said that I should have Annie's things.

172

But it was not hers for more than a fortnight, and I had thought to return it to the one who gave it to her, but I never cared for him much, and have no knowledge of where he might be, and since it is yours, ma'am, you should have it."

Elizabeth thought of Mrs. Baker's pain at losing her daughter. "I do not wish to take something that will remind you of your daughter, Mrs. Baker," she said somberly. "I am content to part with it if it will give you some comfort."

Mrs. Baker shook her head. "No, ma'am," she said. "I have many other things to remind me, things that mean a great deal more. This was given her not two weeks ago," she reiterated. "By a 'gentleman' suitor who never even told her his name, other than 'Edmond'."

Elizabeth reached out tentatively and touched the ring, but did not take it. "I have no proof for you that it is mine, Mrs. Baker."

Mrs. Baker smiled faintly. "It's clearly yours, ma'am," she said. "I saw your face when you looked on it. It means a great deal more to you than it does to me or, I daresay, to my daughter." She placed the ring into Elizabeth's hand, and closed Elizabeth's fingers around it. "It is yours, ma'am, and I am happy to give it to you." She sat once more, and, revealing a touch of anger behind her grief, continued, "This 'master' … do you know who he is? Can he be held accountable for what he's done to my Annie?"

Before Elizabeth could answer, Jennings leaned forward and, speaking as gently as he could, said, "His identity is unknown to us, ma'am. But we believe he has taken issue with members of Mrs. Jennings' family. Are you connected, ma'am, with the Fitzhugh clan?"

Mrs. Baker did not answer at first, but then, looking down at her hands folded in her lap, she responded in a voice heavy with resignation. "I am not," she murmured. "But Annie is. Was." She sighed, and raised her eyes to Elizabeth's face. "Mr. Baker," she went on with a pained expression. "God rest his soul, he was not Annie's father. He was her stepfather, and as kind to her as any man could be to his child." She began to weep, and pressed her handkerchief once more to her mouth. "Annie's father never knew that he left me with her; I knew I would never be accepted by his family, and that coming forward would ruin him. I suppose that sounds stupid – I suppose I *was* stupid – but I chose to raise Annie on my own, and not tell her father about her, and when Mr. Baker proved to be such a good-hearted man, and very accepting of my situation, and loving toward my girl, I thought that I had made the right decision."

Elizabeth clasped Mrs. Baker's hands in hers. "I am sure you did, Mrs. Baker," she told her. "No one is stupid who considers the welfare of others."

"Mrs. Baker," Jennings said. "Do you mean to say that Miss Baker's father was a Fitzhugh?"

Mrs. Baker nodded. "His name was Tate, but his mother's family was Fitzhugh, and he was very proud of it. He was so young, sir," she said. "I knew it then as I know it now. We thought – well, we thought our actions would have no consequence, as the young typically do, and I know he never meant me harm. I know he would have done right by me if I'd told him, but I think it would have ruined his life, and I cared for him, and I didn't want that for him. He moved away from London; he's married now, and is happy. And I had Annie and Mr. Baker, and I was happy." She sobbed. "Now what do I have?" she asked Elizabeth. "Now my Annie is gone!" She abandoned any pretense of composure, and lowered her head into her hands.

Elizabeth's heart broke for the woman's loss. She was stricken too by the misfortune that had befallen her cousin Marcus – for it must be he! – that he should lose two daughters in a week. Indeed, he had never been given the chance to know Annie, and would now never know her. His little Eliza had been so cruelly snatched from him. The only consolation was that he could not feel grief for a daughter he was unaware had ever existed, but anger swelled up in Elizabeth, and flushed her cheeks, as she thought of the soulless deeds committed by her family's unseen foe.

"We have to stop him, Christopher!" she said tersely. "We have to find him and stop him, before more girls are lost!"

"Yes," Jennings said simply, his jaw tight and his expression cold. "And I have a notion where he might be found."

Mrs. Baker stifled her weeping abruptly, and both women turned to stare in astonishment at Jennings.

"You cannot think it is Cousin Marcus!" Elizabeth said.

Jennings raised one eyebrow. "Indeed no," he said. "Although I suppose we should not dismiss anyone out of hand. No, I refer to this 'suitor' who gave Miss Baker the ring. You said, I think, that his name was 'Edmond'?" When Mrs. Baker nodded, he went on, "And you said you did not care for him?"

"No, sir," she said. "Even though Annie thought he was the moon and the stars, something in the way she talked about him made me suspicious of him. She said he was engaged, but that he planned to break off the engagement, and that he had given her the ring to show his intention to marry her as soon as he had spoken to the other lady."

Elizabeth scoffed. "I can well understand your suspicions!" she said drily. "At best, this is a man of inconstant affections."

"Just so, ma'am," Mrs. Baker agreed. "But Annie found him to be very charming and sincere, and I could say nothing to dissuade her." She indicated the ring. "Annie wore that as though it were a wedding band. She was so in love with him!"

"Did he mention the name of this other lady?" Jennings asked.

"He did, sir," Mrs. Baker replied. "Annie said the girl's name was Isabelle."

CHAPTER FIFTEEN

They sat for some time with Mrs. Baker, speaking frankly about Ann and her father. Elizabeth supported Mrs. Baker's decision not to tell Marcus Tate about Annie now, feeling that it would be unnecessarily cruel, and injurious to his family who were already suffering so dreadfully the loss of their little Eliza. But after reminding Mrs. Baker that they were, in fact, family, Jennings insisted that she call on him if ever she were in need. "After all," he explained. "However prepared and conscientious Mr. Baker might have been, he no doubt had planned to grow old with you, Mrs. Baker, and to see Ann safely married, and for her children to be there for you in the future. He could not have predicted such a bizarre circumstance, or that you would be left on your own."

Mr. Baker had indeed left money for his widow, but Mrs. Baker admitted that she depended a great deal on Ann's wage from the shop, and she accepted Jennings' generosity gratefully. "I should refuse, I suppose," she said, her expression one of overwhelming heartbreak. "But without Annie, I don't know how else I would manage." She pressed her handkerchief to her mouth, and tears glistened in her eyes. "I don't know what I will do without her," she went on. "All the riches in the world cannot fill this hole in my heart!" She sat for a moment, quietly weeping into her handkerchief, while Elizabeth held her hand. "But I thank you most extremely, sir," she said finally, struggling to collect herself. "Your help is most welcome and appreciated, and I believe without it that I would lose these rooms as well, and be put out on the street."

"We will not let that happen," Elizabeth assured her. "And we *will* discover this 'Edmond' who gave Annie the ring; whether or not it is my cousin remains to be seen, but we will bring him to earth and hold him accountable for his crimes!" She scowled, and a dark anger welled up in her. "He has taken so many lives!" she said, her voice gruff. "He cannot be allowed to take any more!"

Although Mrs. Baker could not fathom how the Jennings might combat a foe who commanded forces so far outside the ordinary, she was too grateful to them to say anything of her doubts. Indeed, when she had suggested to the constables that Ann's suitor was a possible suspect in her murder, they had rather condescendingly declared to her that only a large animal could have caused such wounds, and, while she had no reason to question this conclusion, the Jennings' assertion that it could be both Edmond *and* a wild animal supported her misgivings about Edmond without denying any of the evidence. As unlikely as such a notion would have seemed to her three days ago, Mrs. Baker could see the truth behind the Jennings' words: Annie may have been brought down by claws and fangs, but they were those of some otherworldly creature commanded by human sorcery.

"Human sorcery," she said aloud softly. She lifted her eyes to Elizabeth's. "That's very strange to say, isn't it?"

"Yes, it is," Elizabeth agreed. "And I see what you're feeling – how can anyone hunt down such a man, or even find him? How can his guilt in these deaths be made plain? Where would we even begin? I assure you, I have asked myself these questions a thousand times in the past weeks." She sat up taller and squared her shoulders, and managed a smile. "But if it can be done," she added. "We are as suited to do it as anyone, and maybe more so!"

Eventually they took their leave of Mrs. Baker, Jennings insisting once more that she not hesitate to call on him for anything; Mrs. Baker, so obviously shattered by her loss, did at least, upon their departure, seem a little less overwhelmed, and as she saw them to the door, a slight bit of colour had returned to her cheeks.

Elizabeth turned to wave one last time at Mrs. Baker, who watched them from a window. Mrs. Baker returned the wave before retreating into the house, and Elizabeth said anxiously, "I hope our visit has done her some good."

Jennings offered his arm to his wife, and walked with her down the street. "I believe it has," he said. "As strange as our news must certainly have been, I think she is heartened by the thought that Miss Baker's killer will be found. And she seemed glad to hear that you would call again soon; however sad the origin, your kind heart has brought you a new friend."

She looked up at him. "Your generosity," she pointed out. "Has put her mind greatly at ease." She looked down at the ground, frowning. "I wish we could bring her Annie back to her."

"So do I," Jennings said, and patted Elizabeth's hand. They walked a moment in silence, then he added resolutely, "But since we cannot do what we would rather, we will do instead what we can: we will find Miss Baker's body, and I will try to glean some sign from it."

Elizabeth stopped walking. "You cannot do that," she told him. "The body has already been given to the undertaker. She's to be buried tomorrow."

Jennings looked quizzically at her. "All the more reason to find her now," he said. "If I can touch her, it may trigger a vision – of her attacker, of his face, of his motives. It could be a crucial clue, and Miss Baker herself directed us to her."

"That is true," Elizabeth said. "And I know that on our journey here, I myself spoke of doing what must be done, however difficult or unseemly it might prove to be. But even I cannot think on what pretext we would accost the undertaker to allow us to see her body for no good reason. If she had still been with Dr. Oxley, I think it would not have seemed particularly odd at all, but to pursue her now would be highly unusual."

"My entire experience with the slate has been highly unusual," Jennings argued. "I have fabricated dozens of pretenses, faced countless strange looks, and endured hours of awkwardness. Why should today be any different?"

Elizabeth reached into her reticule. "Because I do not think we need to fabricate, face, or endure anything," she answered, pulling her mother's ring out and holding it up. "Do you not see?" she went on, pointing at a smudge that ran along the inside of the band. "It is a smudge of blood, I think, and also of some green liquid that might belong to the creature that attacked her – that attacked *us*."

Jennings looked at the ring, and at the smudge. A smear of yellow-green residue lay over a dark brown stain – no doubt Miss Baker's blood, covered by a substance that he recognized from Lady Morton's balcony. "It is," he breathed, reaching out to take the ring. "It's what I saw at Lady Morton's." Remembering the intensity of that vision, he hesitated suddenly, and pulled his fingers away, but a second later, he willed his hand to close around it, and his finger pressed against the stain.

Instantly his head rocked back as though he had been struck in the face. He grimaced in pain, and cried out; Elizabeth, alarmed, took his hands in hers and called his name, but, other than to squeeze her hands almost convulsively, he could do no more than stand before her, his features pale, his eyes clenched shut. He could hear Elizabeth's voice faintly, but, as the vision washed over him, he was unable to speak.

The street he saw was much the same as the street where they walked now, but it was shrouded in darkness, filled with horrible smells and strange noises. He could see through someone else's eyes, and he could feel that this person was used to this street, to this nightly walk home and to the vague unease of wending through unsavoury alleyways, past innumerable faceless strangers whose glances seemed to Jennings to be lecherous at best.

The walker came to the end of a better street – a cleaner place, with fewer people and a sense of fresher air. Jennings could feel the walker's relief at reaching this point.

Out of the deep shadows of an alleyway came the beast that had carried Elizabeth off the balcony. It ran out on massive, sinewy legs, leering at the walker with glittering eyes and a slavering mouth. Its claws were enormous; its muscular arms swung through the air toward the walker, and Jennings was besieged by the walker's fear and panic. It threatened to overcome him, and he doubled over, his arms wrapped around his stomach.

"No!" he cried. "No! Leave me alone!"

Elizabeth realized that these were not her husband's words. "Who is it?" she asked, bending over him and putting her arm across his shoulders. "Do you see Ann?"

"He's clawing her apart!" Jennings gasped, watching helplessly as the monster in his vision slashed again and again at the defenseless walker. Blood sprayed up onto the creature's head and torso, driving it into an even greater frenzy, and its growls became more like shrieks as it ravaged its victim. Just as it had with Elizabeth, the creature tried to wrench the ring from the walker's hand, but in the distance came the sounds of revelers, stumbling their way home down the same alley, and the creature abandoned its efforts. Pivoting on one foot, it spread massive wings that stretched across the street and touched the buildings on either side; with a rush of wind, the monster disappeared into the night sky. The revelers, emerging into the street, stopped dead in their tracks, and Jennings watched as their drunken smiles turned into abject horror.

"We need a doctor!" one of them shouted, and Jennings echoed his words with a raspy hiss. He sank to his knees, and Elizabeth put both her arms around him.

"Christopher!" she cried. Two men who had been walking on the other side of the street hurried quickly to her aid, one of them gripping Jennings' shoulders and pulling him to his feet.

"Are you well, man!" he barked, frowning at Jennings in concern. "Shall we fetch a doctor?"

Jennings was still lost in his vision. He saw the creature flying away over the rooftops; he saw the revelers circling the body that the creature had left behind. Then a face appeared, floating incongruously in front of him for a brief second before evaporating. Abruptly the vision ended, and Jennings leaned gratefully against the stranger who had helped him up.

"Thank you!" he said weakly, trying to catch his breath. "It – It must be something I ate."

It took some effort – and a fair bit of both Elizabeth's charm and her storytelling abilities – to convince the men that Jennings was all right, and that they needn't summon a doctor. But the men insisted on escorting them both to their carriage, and admonished Jennings more than once about eating at the sorts of shops one found in this area, for, as one of them noted, "One can never be sure what's in the meat, you know. Could be anything."

As the carriage moved down the street, Jennings sank back against the seat and closed his eyes. "I believe you're right, my love," he said, his voice still a little breathless. "I don't think we need find poor Miss Baker's body. She has said quite enough."

Elizabeth put a hand gently on his cheek. "Are you recovered, Christopher?" she asked. She had never seen him react in such a way, and it had affected her deeply.

"I am," he assured her. "Blood is … very powerful."

Elizabeth looked down at her mother's ring, which Jennings had placed on the seat beside him. "You saw Ann?" she asked, picking up the ring and putting it back in her reticule. "What did she say to you?"

"Well, nothing, really," Jennings said. "I saw through her eyes," he explained. "I saw her walking home from the shop, down a rather unpleasant looking side street, and then the beast that abducted you descended upon her." He paused, frowning at the memory. "It tore her apart; I could feel its claws and teeth sinking into my – into *her* skin. I could feel the blood pouring from the wounds. And then the monster tried to take her ring, but a group of men came down the

183

street, and the monster was obliged to fly away."

Elizabeth was puzzled. "Why would it feel the need to flee?" she wondered. "If it is truly a wild animal of some sort, let loose into the city, would it not attack any who approached it?" She shook her head. "It must indeed be controlled by someone who does not want it to be discovered."

Jennings had opened his eyes and was watching Elizabeth. "You're correct, I believe," he told her. "But even then, why would this person be concerned over the discovery of his beast? I do not think the beast had the capability to speak, after all. It must be over concern for the beast itself."

Elizabeth's brow cleared. "The beast is not invulnerable," she said with relief. "It hunts solitary prey because larger numbers scare it. It is mortal."

Jennings nodded. "It can be killed," he said.

Elizabeth's joy at this news was short-lived. "But its master is still hidden," she said. "And we cannot know if this beast was the only beast under his control. You said it flew away; it is, then, not a creature of our ordinary world. What sort of power does this master possess, that he can summon such things and send them to do his bidding?"

"More to the point," Jennings said. "If it is Miss Baker's suitor, why did he not kill her himself? She trusted him, apparently, and was in his company unattended. He could have taken her life at any time."

"Perhaps he feared to leave clues behind," Elizabeth suggested. "To have another do it would hide his identity and his guilt."

Jennings sat quietly for a moment, lost in thought. "I saw his face," he said eventually. "He was not *actually* there, in the street

184

with Miss Baker. He appeared before me for just an instant."

"Did you recognize him?"

"No," Jennings said. "But he looked like the portraits in your father's house."

"Cousin Cedric?" Elizabeth asked apprehensively. She did not want to believe that he could be involved in this matter; she had become so instantly fond of him.

Jennings had recovered somewhat, and was able to sit forward and turn toward his wife. "No," he replied. "It is clear, to be sure, that at some point in the past, Mr. Delacourt's lineage and yours were one and the same. But the man I saw did not so much resemble Delacourt – or Jonathan Fitzhugh – but rather simply seemed to be a member of your mother's family." He took Elizabeth's hand. "We must assume," he went on. "That Miss Baker's Edmond is possibly your cousin Ned Fitzhugh, and that he is the man responsible for this creature, and its attacks."

Elizabeth digested this, and her expression became both sad and angry. "My 'cousin'," she repeated scornfully. "Who murders his own relations, and has clearly made a pact with diabolical forces!" She gasped, and stared wide-eyed at Jennings. "Isabelle!" she exclaimed. "She is no doubt in danger from this man! As dreadful as she is, she does not deserve to be murdered; we must warn her away from him!"

"I had considered that," Jennings said. "I believe on the morrow, we should venture north, and take rooms in Isabelle's neighbourhood." He raised an eyebrow, and his eyes twinkled. "We shall call on her in a most uninvited fashion!" he announced. "And, since I doubt she would listen to – or believe – any warning we might deliver to her, we will attempt to suss out Ned's guilt, and prevent him doing whatever he plans to do next."

Elizabeth smiled at this. "I would very much like that!" she said. "It would be most irritating for her, I daresay!"

* * *

They left quite early the next morning, heading north in a carriage laden with weeks' worth of luggage. The day at first was quite fine, the sun burning off a slight mist and shining down warmly on the travelers; by mid-day, however, clouds had rolled in, and a chilly breeze came up, so that Elizabeth was obliged to close the carriage window.

"Do you think we'll arrive before it rains, sir?" she asked, glancing at the darkening sky. The driver and the groom apparently wondered as much themselves, gazing often up at the clouds and conferring with one another.

"We may be forced to wait in the next town," Jennings said. He signaled for the driver to stop, and, letting himself down from the carriage, communicated to the driver his plan of taking lunch at the village just in sight on the horizon. "We'll wait there until the rain has passed," he said. "We may need to stay the night, but I imagine not. We are only two hours or so from our destination."

"Aye, sir," the driver concurred. "It doesn't look to be a big storm. We should be able to travel on by mid-afternoon, and reach Northampton before tea-time!"

"Good man!" Jennings said. He turned to climb back into the carriage, but stopped abruptly as his glance took in the surrounding countryside. "Perry," he said to the driver. "I know you will think me quite mad, but we must wait here for a bit; I need to go for a walk."

"Go for a walk, sir?" Perry asked skeptically. He looked in the direction that Jennings was looking, but he could see nothing but rolling hills and a distant copse of trees. "It's turnin' a bit blustery for that, sir."

"Yes," Jennings said. "Nevertheless, I am compelled." He opened the carriage door and spoke to Elizabeth. "I recognize this place," he said. "It's what I see in my dream."

"The one with the cave?" she asked, instantly intrigued. She leaned out the door and surveyed the landscape. "We are but five miles from Cousin Cedric's lands, sir," she noted, and looked at him enquiringly. "Could your dream be prophetic after all?" she asked. "Cedric is Ned's particular friend; could Ned be planning to harm him? Could that be the sense of betrayal you felt?"

Jennings pondered this. "I have never had a prophetic vision," he said. "But I suppose it could be." He looked at her askance. "I don't suppose you are willing to wait here while I look for the cave?"

Elizabeth frowned at him. "Why on earth would I do that?" she asked, and, gathering her cloak tightly around her shoulders, stepped down from the carriage.

It was not the first time that Jennings had done something that his servants found strange, but as he and Elizabeth walked out into the field that separated them from the copse of trees, Perry watched them with a disapproving and worried eye. It was one thing to be odd for your own part, he thought. But to bring the young lady into it seemed unwise. He knew better than to criticize, however, and contented himself with telling the groom to keep watch on the couple.

"He gets some crazy notions," the groom observed.

"Aye," Perry agreed. He sighed. "But he's the best master there ever could be."

Elizabeth, stepping carefully over the uneven ground, felt as content as she ever had; her sense of adventure was certainly satisfied by her husband's visions, and this current journey seemed very much to bring many pieces of a puzzle finally together. What shape they would take remained to be seen, but she cheerfully accompanied Jennings into the trees, certain that they would find here the answer to both his recurring nightmare and her family's dark mystery.

"Perhaps," she said teasingly. "Cousin Ned will have left a note for us: 'I am the killer, and listed here is the way to stop me.'"

Jennings laughed. "That would be very welcome!" he said.

They walked far enough into the trees that the field and the road were almost completely hidden from view, and Jennings, pausing to look around him, felt a strong urge to step some yards to the west, where several trees had grown up on a small hill, their roots and branches intertwining.

"Here is our cave," he said. Its entrance was little more than a gash in the earth, wrapped on either side by tree roots and tangled bushes. He recognized it at once, but, against his expectations, he felt no urgency or trepidation. He had thought that finding this site, which had plagued his sleep for so many nights, would trigger more intense sensations of discovery or foreboding, or even an overwhelming relief at fulfilling the wishes of a most persistent spirit; instead, he experienced only an anticlimactic sort of curiosity, and, as he walked toward the cave, he wondered if perhaps the dream, however unpleasant, had been only a dream after all.

Behind him, Elizabeth stood still as a statue, and, when he turned to offer his hand to her, Jennings saw that she had grown pale, and was staring unblinking at the cave entrance.

"What is it, my dear?" he asked, concerned. He came quickly to her side. "Are you unwell?" He glanced at the cave entrance, and then back at her. "If you are uncomfortable in such a dark place, please do not think you must accompany me. You can wait here, and I will return in a moment."

She looked at him as though his suggestion were the most ridiculous thing she had ever heard. "I will not let you go in there alone," she told him emphatically. "But I wonder if either of us should go in there at all." Her gaze returned to the cave entrance. "It fills me with the strangest dread," she explained. "As though something horrible will happen if we go in there."

Jennings thought of the nature of their foe: whoever he was, he clearly possessed otherworldly abilities, and had covered his own tracks through mystical means. Perhaps he had worked some magic on this place, so that ordinary people would be afraid to approach it; Jennings' own abilities may have caused the magic to affect him very differently, so that he could not see it as he normally would.

"Perhaps that is why I feel nothing special," he murmured aloud. He took Elizabeth's hand. "I think I must go in there," he said. "But I do not think there is any present danger; I believe you may safely wait for me here."

"No," she said, squeezing his hand. "I'll go with you."

They stepped together into the uninviting crevice, ducking their heads to avoid tendrils of roots and spindly branches. The cave was not more than five feet across, and hardly that high, so that Jennings had to stoop. Everything was exactly as it had been in his dream.

"We should have brought a lantern, I suppose," Elizabeth said. She was struggling with little success to control the sensation of panic that had welled up inside her. She could not account for it, and she trusted her husband's judgment, but it was all she could do to stand in this place and not sprint madly back to the carriage. "If the events in your dream have in fact already happened, then there should be blood stains here, and possibly other clues."

The faint light that made its way through the narrow opening was not enough to illuminate the cave, especially since they stood blocking the entrance, but Jennings scanned the ground as best he could, and ultimately was rewarded with a slight glint in the furthest recess. "There," he said, stepping forward and crouching down. "A piece of metal."

"Be careful," Elizabeth advised, watching him anxiously. Her panic threatened to overwhelm her, and she trembled violently; only her promise to stay by his side prevented her from fleeing.

"I believe it is a ring," Jennings said, reaching out for the golden band that lay half-buried in the dirt. "A signet ri–"

As his fingers closed around the ring, a blast of cold assailed him, and searing pain gripped his stomach. He fell back and out of the cave as though flung by an unseen hand, and lay gasping for breath. He felt again the dread he had encountered in his dreams, and the now-familiar sense of betrayal. Yes, there it was: the relief he had expected, now that he had come where the spirit had led. He was transported once more into the dream-vision, but the details were no longer obscured by shadows. He could see the victim this time, and the creeping shape with a weapon raised to strike; he could see the

190

face of the assailant as the weapon descended upon its target. It was a face devoid of any emotion – neither anger nor hatred nor joy, but only a cold intensity, as though this brutal act were as necessary and as easy as shutting a door. It was a face he knew.

"Christopher!" Elizabeth cried, kneeling on the ground beside him. When he had picked up the ring, her panic vanished, as instantly as though she had awakened from a nightmare. Her only thought now was for Jennings, who lay in obvious pain, his arms clutching his stomach. "Christopher!" She grabbed his hand and pried the fingers apart, and wrenched the ring from his grasp. "Christopher!"

The pain subsided, and after a few seconds, Jennings opened his eyes. "Lizzie," he said, trying to sit up. The blast had taken a great deal out of him; he was able only to lift his head, and then to set it back down on the ground. "Lizzie, we need to go home."

"Why?" she asked, perplexed. "We need to protect Isabelle!" She put her arm under Jennings' shoulders and helped him sit. "We need to find Ned."

Jennings shook his head. "It's too late," he said. "I saw the murderer. I saw his face." He looked up at Elizabeth; she could see that he did not want at all to tell her what he now knew, and she felt her heart sink.

"Ned?" she asked, her voice a whisper.

Jennings leaned forward and put his hand on the side of her face. His fingers curled around her hair, and he brought her close to him, so that his forehead touched hers. Finally, he spoke.

"The spirit is Ned," he said. "And Cedric killed him."

191

CHAPTER SIXTEEN

Having found a suitable inn at the nearby village, Jennings and Elizabeth took shelter from the rain and arranged to have luncheon in one of the inn's small sitting rooms.

Jennings had recovered from the shock he had sustained at the cave, but he felt now a strong urgency to bring Cedric Delacourt to earth, and his mind raced to fit together the pieces of the puzzle he had been given. "Clearly," he said, almost as much to himself as to Elizabeth. "The spell on the cave was prodigious. If we can be so deceived in our own feelings, how can we ever know for certain that we have finally stumbled onto the truth?"

Elizabeth shook her head, and bit wearily into a sweet biscuit. "I do not know," she said. "But one way or another – no matter which way we consider it – I believe we must act in haste now to avert calamity."

Jennings looked at her curiously. "What do you mean, 'which way we consider it'?" he asked. He drank deeply from a mug of ale. "Cousin Delacourt is our man, is he not? As much as it pains me to say, both of this generation's victims have already been taken; if he is true to form, then there will be no more sacrifices from your family for another nineteen years." He leaned back in his chair and added wryly, "But your father is a direct impediment to Cedric's fortune. We must, then, go as quickly as possible to the lake house, and prevent him doing your father a harm."

"Yes, if indeed your dream has been of past events," Elizabeth replied. "But I question its being so." She saw that Jennings would argue this point, and hastened to continue. "The enchantment on the cave was prodigious, as you said, but would it affect those already dead? Perhaps Ned could not communicate through the slate because he is not yet a spirit. Perhaps your dreams are echoes from a future that we can, in fact, forestall. Why else would we be drawn on this journey, and to the cave and the signet ring, except to hear the warning of what may be?"

Jennings shook his head. "The signet ring belongs to the Fitzhugh clan," he reminded her. "It is very likely Ned's. And I have never had any sort of prophetic vision in my entire life; why would I now?"

"Picking up the ring dispelled the enchantment," Elizabeth said. "Why would the murderer use his victim's ring to create such magic?"

"I know very little of magic," Jennings said drily. "I suppose there might be any number of reasons he would do so."

"And Ned's body?" Elizabeth asked. "Why would Cedric take it from a place that is entirely removed from anyone, hidden from view, and protected by an enchantment? There was no body, sir, which suggests to me that Ned is still alive. Someone may very well have been posing as Ned to trick Annie Baker, and Ned himself is in danger from that person who, at some future time, will lure him to that cave."

Jennings considered this in some surprise. "I had not thought about the body," he acknowledged.

"You said you felt urgency," Elizabeth went on. "But is it directed toward the lake house, or toward Cedric himself? If it is toward Cedric, then I believe we must consider the words of Joshua Heron – that 'there are many more like' him. He told us this for a reason, did he not? Just as that horrible *Richard* fellow posed as Mr. Heron, so there is a possibility of someone *posing* as Cedric; if that is the case, then he could even now be on his way to Northampton, while the real Cedric is at the lake house with my father and Charlotte."

Jennings lifted one eyebrow. "You may very well be correct," he said. He could not easily dispute the importance of evidence from the slate, but he felt strangely troubled by the notion of being able to see into the future. Perhaps it was the burden of it; he did not want to be obliged to know what *should* be, as though his guesses were better than another's. He took a long drink of ale. "It may be that the man who betrayed Ned was not the real Cedric," he said after a moment. Sighing in resignation, he added, "Perhaps I *can* see future events. Perhaps that is the meaning of my dreams." He leaned forward and folded his arms in front of him on the table. "But where does this take us?" he asked. "Either Ned is alive and in danger from Cedric, or from someone pretending to be Cedric; or Ned is dead because Cedric – or a false Cedric – killed him and assumed his identity; and Cedric is either in danger himself from a false Ned, or he is himself the danger that faces Sir James and Mrs. Carlisle." He gave a sudden bark of laughter. "Have I forgotten anything?"

Elizabeth laughed in spite of herself. "I believe those are all the possibilities that we have as yet encountered." She grew serious once more. "I cannot justify my sense of haste," she admitted. "I only know that the situation feels both urgent and dire. A murder has been shown to you, over and over, in hopes that you would be able to heed the warning. And my cousin Delacourt, who has never bothered to meet me before, arrives on my doorstep just as two women in my family are sacrificed, and on the eve of his best friend's wedding. It may very well be coincidence – it was Charlotte, after all, who asked him to come to town, and not a design of his own making – but I cannot imagine that we should treat anything as mere coincidence when the consequence might be someone's life." She looked down at her hands folded in her lap. "Enough people have died," she said, thinking particularly of Annie Baker and little Eliza Tate. "And while I don't have your gift, and can only say that I feel strongly about it, *you*, sir, *do* have a gift, and that gift has led you down this road, to the cave, to all the clues my mother left for me and to all the clues the spirits of the dead have left for you. We are meant to be here, sir, in this place and in this time, so that we might solve this mystery as quickly as possible."

Jennings heard her out in silence, then, when she had finished, he reached out and gently touched her face with the fingers of one hand. "I never discount people's strong feelings," he said. "And your words make sense. If we make haste, the worse that happens is that we look a trifle foolish – a situation I have often faced and do not fear now. If we are wrong in our theories, then it's best to find out sooner rather than later." He sat back and drained his mug of ale. "We will journey on to Northampton after the rain lets up, and find your cousin Isabelle and, hopefully, Ned. Then afterward, we will go on to the lake house without delay."

Elizabeth's expression told him that she did not agree with his suggestion. "I believe, sir," she said quietly. "That such a plan would not be hasty enough."

He tilted his head quizzically. "What would you rather we do?" he asked.

"I know I may simply be exaggerating the matter because it is my own father," Elizabeth acknowledged. "But at the cave, you saw Cedric kill Ned, and now Cedric is with my father and Charlotte. If he is truly the murderer of his own friend, then I think we should go to the lake house straightaway."

"Of course," Jennings nodded. "That was my first inclination. We can return this direction in a day or two, or we can send a letter to Miss Isabelle. She may dismiss it out of hand, but at least the knowledge would then be in her possession to do with as she will."

Elizabeth shook her head. "She will certainly dismiss it out of hand," she said. "And perhaps not even read it all the way to the end. Why, indeed, would she doubt her own betrothed over the decidedly odd notions of a cousin she can barely abide? No, if we mean to offer her any help – if she is in fact in danger – then we must journey there ourselves. If *her* Ned is the *real* Ned, then we may be able to prevent his murder, if we arrive immediately."

"My love," Jennings interjected in some confusion. "We cannot go both places first."

"Of course we can," Elizabeth said placidly. "I will go on to Northampton, and you will go to the lake house. I will speak with Isabelle and, if possible, Ned, and force them to hear me out, even if they believe me to be mad. And *you* will be at the lake house in a trice – why, you could reach there tonight on horseback! – and you can confront Cousin Cedric and protect my father and Charlotte. If I don't join you on the morrow, you'll know that I've stumbled onto the truth."

Jennings struggled to absorb Elizabeth's words. "You wish to go on *alone?*" he asked her. "You believe that I would allow you to journey alone into what might be a very dangerous situation?" She opened her mouth to speak, but he interrupted her. "And if I do not see you tomorrow at your father's house, then I will know you have found the 'truth' – in other words, I will know that you've confronted a monster and that he has prevented your leaving. In what desperate imagining did you think I would be amenable to such a notion?"

She smiled softly. "You are as anxious to discover the truth as I am," she pointed out. "And you are as concerned as I that this 'monster' who has preyed upon my family for six generations is about to cause more harm. I am a married lady now, you know," she added archly. "It is perfectly respectable for me to travel to my Cousin Isabelle's alone. I will feel much better knowing that you are on your way to protect my father, and I will join you there as soon as I can determine what has happened to Ned."

Jennings sat for a long moment without speaking. He knew on the surface that she was correct, both in her sense of urgency and in her plan, but he was reluctant – no, in truth, he was terrified! – that something would happen to her. He did not want to let her out of his sight.

"Oh, God," he said at last, his shoulders slumping forward. "I want to keep you in a cage as your father has tried to do." He ran his hands nervously through his hair. "I don't like it," he said. "But I think you are right."

"You are very wise, sir," Elizabeth said gratefully.

He looked at her drily. "I'm sure you may think so," he said. He took her hand in his and stared pointedly at her. "I have a pair of pistols under the seat in the carriage. Be prepared to use them."

She had been trained in her childhood how to use a shotgun, but she had never fired a pistol in her life. The thought of it caused her heart to skip a beat. "Of course," she said.

* * *

An hour later, she found herself entrusted to the care of Perry and the groom and sent on her own toward Northampton.

"Stay with her, Perry," Jennings instructed with uncharacteristic intensity. "Circumstances are even stranger than usual, as I'm sure I don't have to tell you, and I am compelled to go east. You must see her safely to Miss Fetherston's and you must stay with her there as best you are able. Whenever she gives the slightest hint of wishing to leave, you must bring her as quickly as you can either to her father's lake house or to Brightwood. Do you understand?"

Perry, accustomed to his master's unorthodox behaviour, neither batted an eye at the request nor bothered to ask any questions. "I'll guard her with my life, sir," he assured him. "You're certain of your route, sir?"

Jennings nodded. "It is not that far from London," he said. "I should be able to reach it in a few hours."

"It's sure to be above five hours, sir," Perry said. "But I believe there are any number of stops on the way to change horses." He glanced up at the sky. "I fear it may rain again, sir, sooner rather than later."

"I'll be fine," Jennings said. He turned to Elizabeth, who had climbed into the carriage and now sat waiting with an air of slight impatience. "I'm still not entirely sure this is necessary," he said, frowning.

198

She smiled and held her hand out to him. "Enough of my family have suffered, Christopher," she reminded him. "I cannot allow another to do so, if I can prevent it at all." She grinned then. "Even if it *is* Isabelle!"

He chuckled, but swiftly grew serious again. "I vowed, my love, never to let anything happen to you again," he said, his face drawn with worry.

She squeezed his hand. "That was an admirable vow, sir," she told him gently. "But I think it was not within your power to make."

He gazed at her soberly for a long moment, then leaned into the carriage and kissed her. "Take care, my love." He pulled away from the carriage abruptly and swung up onto the horse that Perry had been holding for him. "Stay with her Perry," he instructed again. "I would be greatly unhappy if anything happened to her."

"Don't worry, sir," Perry said. "We'll stay close by her."

Jennings nodded rather tersely, and spun the horse around, urging it onto the road and heading away from the inn at a brisk pace.

Elizabeth watched him for a moment, but then turned and addressed the driver. "We must make haste, Perry," she said. "Let us find Northampton as soon as possible."

"Aye, ma'am," Perry said, and climbed quickly onto the box. He soon had the carriage on the road to Northampton, and in little more than an hour, they had reached the carefully manicured grounds of the Fetherston estate. As they approached the house – at a much more sedate pace than Elizabeth had demanded on the journey – servants appeared as though they had been waiting for the carriage's arrival, and spoke with Perry and the groom.

After a moment, Perry, having climbed down from the box,

pulled open the door to the carriage. "Fetherston Manor, ma'am," he announced, and held his hand out for her to take as she stepped out onto the gravel drive. "I told them you were Miss Fetherston's cousin, and one of 'em's gone to fetch Mrs. Fetherston."

"Excellent," Elizabeth said, straightening her skirts and tucking back wisps of hair. "Hopefully they won't think I'm entirely barmy."

"I'm sure they won't, ma'am," Perry offered.

A moment later, Elizabeth was welcomed inside, first by an obsequious porter and then by Mrs. Fetherston herself, who seemed at first glance to be an imposing woman of stout figure and elegant dress. This air of arrogant grandeur was immediately dispelled, however, as soon as Mrs. Fetherston laid eyes on her young cousin.

"Elizabeth Carlisle!" she cried in apparent jubilation, and greeted her guest with a warm embrace. "Oh, I beg your pardon – Mrs. Jennings!" She beamed at Elizabeth and held her at arm's length, and subjected her to a thorough but benevolent scrutiny. "I daresay you do not remember me at all!" she said. "But I knew you when you were a little girl – you must have been three or four, I think. You were the sweetest thing, and so like your mother! – I recognized you at once, my dear, for you are entirely her, as though she herself stood before me!" She turned, wrapping her arm around Elizabeth's shoulders and walking with her into the house. "I sent Isabelle to see you – I thought it would do you both good to know each other – but I confess I could not bring myself to return to your father's house! He was so much changed after your mother died, and he became – I hate to say it, but it is the truth! – he became completely insupportable! Hatcher, do bring us some tea in the pink sitting room, and some biscuits; Mrs. Jennings must be famished! –

did you come here all the way from London today, my dear? What a long journey!"

She brought Elizabeth into a small sitting room and, after making sure that Elizabeth was comfortably ensconced on the sofa, sat herself in a chair across from her and clapped her hands together. "I am so glad you have come!" she said.

"I should have sent some sort of warning," Elizabeth said with an apologetic smile. "But Mr. Jennings and I had thought to journey into the country, and took it into our heads to come see Isabelle – she sent word some days ago of her upcoming wedding, and I thought it might be pleasant to see her and wish her very happy. And so we drove north without having planned it much at all. I hope I am not importuning you."

"Not at all!" Mrs. Fetherston assured her. She could not be more different from her haughty and dismissive daughter; her demeanour was exceptionally affable and welcoming. "I have wanted any time these fifteen years to invite you here, but your father would never agree to it. And I had thought to write to you, but after a few attempts, your father communicated his disapprobation in no uncertain terms – he did not want to be reminded of his late wife by members of her family, or so he said – and I was in fact quite surprised when he invited Isabelle to come to visit you." Her smile dimmed. "Please forgive me, my dear," she said. "I had thought that when you were older, I would begin writing you again, and then, somehow, time got away from me, and I had not reached out to you in so very long." She grinned again. "But I was informed of your marriage to Mr. Christopher Jennings; what an excellent match, my dear! You are all that is fortunate! And I daresay he is more pleasant to deal with than your father!"

"He is a very agreeable man, ma'am," Elizabeth answered. "I am indeed fortunate. And I *do* remember you. You were very kind to me, and I remember receiving a letter from you. I was very little, and I do not think I particularly recalled it before this moment, but now, having met you again, I cannot understand why I would ever have forgotten!"

Mrs. Fetherston looked decidedly pleased to be remembered in such a way. "I am so glad, my dear! When I sent Isabelle to you, it was with a message from me, but I doubt she delivered it." She pursed her lips. "My daughter – I love her prodigiously – is not like her mama at all! She is very concerned with the appearance of things, and the maintaining of social distances, and the proper configuration of people into their respective categories. She is rather like your father in that regard! – except that she is always quite pleasant, especially to me, and indeed how can I fault her perception of the world when so many others share her view?" She shook her head. "It's all a pack of silliness, if you ask me, and I am glad at least not to have to live in London any longer, and to be surrounded by a lot of silly people."

Elizabeth laughed. "I quite agree with you," she said, her eyes twinkling merrily. Hatcher, the deferential porter, appeared then with a tray of tea and cucumber sandwiches, and placed the tray on the small table beside Elizabeth. She thanked him and gratefully took a cup of tea from him. "It *has* been rather a long journey today," she acknowledged. "But I felt some urgency to come and see Isabelle." She sipped the tea. "Is she at home, ma'am?"

"She is not, I'm afraid," Mrs. Fetherston replied, sipping her tea.

202

"She and Tillman – Polly Tillman, her old governess – have been invited by Ned's friend Cedric to come into the country and spend some days at your father's lake house."

Elizabeth nearly choked on her tea. "Indeed?" she asked, struggling to keep her voice lighthearted. "I did not realize she was so close to Cousin Cedric."

Mrs. Fetherston looked at her quizzically. "Cousin?" she repeated. "Do you know Mr. Delacourt?"

"Yes," Elizabeth answered. "He is my father's cousin, and will inherit his estate."

"Oh, of course!" Mrs. Fetherston exclaimed. "I knew that! I cannot imagine how I came to forget it!" She laughed. "What a singular coincidence!"

"It certainly is," Elizabeth agreed, forcing a chuckle. "I suppose," she added, speaking carefully. "That Mr. Fitzhugh has also gone to the lake house?"

"Well, as to that," Mrs. Fetherston said. "I believe he has been there some time, with Mr. Delacourt. Their tale was that they are hunting, but I cannot imagine so at this time of year. I believe Cedric wanted to abscond with his friend for some merriment before the wedding, and they both have been gone for over a fortnight now." She leaned forward. "Confidentially," she went on in dramatic tones. "I think Ned hopes to convince Isabelle to elope. He has no taste for the grand occasion Isabelle has planned. I suppose I do not care for it overmuch myself! – except that the expense has already been laid out for it, so it might as well take place!" She noticed that Elizabeth's expression had become thoughtful. "Are you all right, my dear?" she asked. "Has something disturbed you?"

Elizabeth gazed at Mrs. Fetherston, and mulled over her choices. Finally, arriving at the only decision she felt she could make, she placed her tea cup on the table, squared her shoulders, and began somberly, "Mrs. Fetherston, I daresay you will find me quite mad, but I cannot leave without apprising you of my concerns. I believe that either Ned or Cedric or both are planning to do Isabelle – and perhaps my father – a harm. I have no basis for it except a recurring dream, and a strong feeling on the matter – the feeling, in fact, that urged me here so precipitously. But I believe I must make all haste to the lake house, and attempt to prevent anything untoward."

Mrs. Fetherston sat in surprise, blinking a few times before finding her voice. "A dream?" she asked at last, setting her own teacup on the table beside Elizabeth's. She shook her head. "I have known Ned these many years," she said. "I have never known him to be anything but affable and kind." She frowned slightly. "But my mother often had dreams," she revealed. "And your mother too." She grew serious, remembering her friend. "She foretold her own death." She sat in silence for a long moment, then raised her eyes to Elizabeth's. "So I don't discount dreams," she announced. "Especially in our family. But I cannot understand how it would be Ned. He has been an excellent man – even more so now that the wedding approaches – and indeed why would he harm Isabelle? He seems decidedly besotted with her, and in any event would have nothing to gain by harming her *now*, before the wedding. But Cedric now," she added, waggling her finger in Elizabeth's direction. "I have never heard anything but good of him, but I allow he stands to gain a great deal if anything should happen to your father. But my dear, what are we saying? Is this some sort of farrago, that we would imagine such nefarious intentions on the parts of these two men about whom no one has ever breathed a negative word?"

"Indeed, ma'am," Elizabeth said quietly. "I very much liked Cousin Cedric myself, when I made his acquaintance." She raised one eyebrow and added pointedly, "I made his acquaintance only a few days ago, ma'am. And he said at that time that he could not stay long with my father and stepmother, for he was wanted in Northampton, where he was going to fetch Ned."

Mrs. Fetherston digested this, her expression becoming increasingly crestfallen. "So one of them is lying," she said. "And it seems Ned is the likelier culprit, since he's been gone for two weeks on the pretext of visiting Mr. Delacourt." She pondered this revelation for a moment, then sighed, and said briskly, "I will send Brothers at once to collect my daughter and Tillman. I never discount dreams, however saddened I am by their tidings." She smiled warmly. "Whatever is the truth, it will be brought to light now," she said. "In the meantime, I would be delighted if you stayed here; I will have Symons prepare a room for you." Her hand reached out to ring a bell that stood on the table, but Elizabeth put her hand out as well.

"I cannot stay," she said. "I would love nothing more, for I have truly enjoyed renewing our acquaintance. But I told Mr. Jennings that I would proceed post-haste to the lake house as soon as I had spoken to Isabelle, and if I don't arrive soon, he will assume that I have encountered some trouble here." She put a hand to her breast. "It's true enough that Ned would lose a great deal if he harmed Isabelle before the wedding," she went on. "My concern for her may simply be that, having lost trust for Cedric and Ned, I don't want to leave her alone with either of them. But I cannot deny my strong feelings in this matter, and I believe for more than one reason, therefore, that I must leave as soon as possible for the lake house."

Mrs. Fetherston impulsively took Elizabeth's hand in both of hers. "Mr. Jennings," she said. "He doesn't dismiss your feelings as a pack of silly notions?" When Elizabeth managed a small smile and shook her head, Mrs. Fetherston continued cheerfully, "Good man! Mr. Fetherston has a terrible habit of saying I'm filled with silly notions, and I heartily dislike it." She sighed again, and rang the bell. "I will still send Brothers to fetch Isabelle," she said. She squeezed Elizabeth's hand. "And when all this has been sorted out, I do hope that you will return to Fetherston Manor," she said. "I too have prodigiously enjoyed seeing you!"

Elizabeth felt tears sting her eyelids. "I would be very happy to visit here, ma'am," she said. "I would have been here long since if my father had told me you wished it. But I am dreadfully sorry to have brought you such strange and distressing news."

"Never mind about that!" Mrs. Fetherston said brightly. "I have missed Mama's dreams and notions, which always proved to be very interesting." She scowled suddenly. "And if Mr. Edmond Fitzhugh has revealed himself to be a cad or charlatan, then I can only say that I am greatly indebted to you!"

Hatcher appeared in the doorway.

"Hatcher, Brothers must be dispatched immediately to the Carlisles' lake house," Mrs. Fetherston informed him. "He must retrieve Miss Fetherston and Tillman over any objections and bring them back here on the morrow. You must also change the horses on Mrs. Jennings' carriage, and give her driver whatever provisions he requires. Then find Mr. Fetherston – I believe he went riding toward

Lord Shelton's estate – and tell him I have an urgent matter to discuss with him. That is all."

"Right away, ma'am," Hatcher replied, bowing and then swiftly retreating.

Mrs. Fetherston turned to Elizabeth. "I will have Cook send you with a bit of cold beef, my dear," she said. "You have a long journey ahead of you."

* * *

Jennings stopped to change horses at an inn not five miles from the lake house. The sun had only just gone down, but the sky had been dark for some hours, and spots of rain fell on him as he stood impatiently waiting for the fresh horse. Rumbles of thunder sounded as a girl from the inn approached him.

"Here you are, sir," she said, handing him a pint of ale. "You're most welcome to come inside, and have a bit of supper."

He took the ale and downed half of it before answering. "I would, my dear," he told her. "But I'm in a great hurry." He glanced at the sky. "Hopefully I won't be too wet by the time I get there."

"How far do you have to go, sir?" the girl asked, also looking anxiously at the lowering clouds. "The storm won't wait more than half an hour, I wager."

Jennings drained the mug and gave it back to her with a few coins that he hastily pulled from his pocket. "If it waits that long," he said. "It'll be good enough."

Unfortunately, the rain only waited another ten minutes, and by the time Jennings arrived at the lake, he was soaked through by what quickly became a driving rain. He approached the house, seeing in the all-too-frequent bursts of lightning a cozy and respectable cottage situated on a slight hill overlooking the water. The cottage was surrounded by trees, and a lengthy set of steps led from it down to a long pier. On any other day, the scene would have been quite pretty, but tonight the water was choppy, crashing noisily up against the pier and the rocky shore, and the trees whipped angrily to and fro in the wind. Two broad patches of yellow, barely visible through the rain, suggested windows, but for the most part, the cottage was dark, and Jennings advanced cautiously, not entirely sure he had found the correct house.

He rode up to the stable and dismounted; no one emerged to greet him, but he had hardly expected it, given the late hour and the storm. With fingers grown numb and stiff from the cold, he managed after some effort to open the door to the stable and to bring himself and the poor drenched horse inside.

"Hello!" he called. "Is anyone here?"

He did not receive an answer. After a moment, he found a stall for his horse, promising it with a few gentle strokes on the neck that he would return very soon to look after it. "I've got rather an urgent mission," he explained. "But you have done more than your duty, and I shall set you up as soon as I can." He made sure the horse had water and hay, before turning once more toward the door.

It was then that he saw three men – or rather, a man and two teenage boys – lying alarmingly still in a nearby stall. They had fallen off of stools that had been set up around a barrel; half-empty mugs of wine sat on top of the barrel, and a plate of biscuits and ham. Bending over the men, Jennings shook each by the shoulder, but none of them made the slightest movement or sound. He saw no sign of struggle, or any kind of wound, and he looked around him completely perplexed. What on earth had afflicted them? He was relieved to discover that all three men were breathing, but not even vigorous shaking and shouting made a dent in their absolute unconsciousness.

Jennings picked up one of the mugs and sniffed its contents. It smelled bitter, and not quite like proper wine. He could only assume that these men had been drugged.

He looked out the open door toward the cottage; when the lightning flashed again, he saw the door to the kitchens. He could not tell whether the suspicious situation in the stable had merely put him on his guard, or if perhaps he was receiving a more otherworldly message, but as he walked toward the house he was filled with great foreboding, and moved as carefully as though he expected at every step to be attacked by unseen enemies.

When he entered the kitchen, he found nothing out of order. A large fire crackled in the fireplace, and he stood gratefully beside it, letting the warmth settle into his shivering limbs. From the looks of things, a hearty supper had been prepared and eaten, but no one had as yet tidied up. He saw the entrance to a little alcove, tucked into the wall on the far side of the fireplace; he could make out a small table there, and realized that this must be where the servants ate their own meals.

"Hello?" he said, his voice barely above a whisper. Something told him it was best to stay hidden, but something else, just as strongly, told him that he needed to find people here, and that he needed to act quickly to avoid calamity. "Is anyone here?" He stepped into the alcove, and saw then that four people were seated around the small table. "I beg your pardon," he began, only to realize that these four, like the men in the stable, were slumped unconscious in their seats. Two of them, a man and a young woman, were leaning against one another and against the wall behind them. Across from them, an older woman sat with her head on the table, and beside her, a girl had slid down in her chair, nearly to the floor.

Everyone's been drugged, Jennings guessed.

He moved as silently as he could through the kitchen and into the dining room. The room was empty, although lamps and candles burned here, and Jennings could make out the faint murmur of conversation elsewhere in the house. He detected the voices of a man and a woman, but, because of the noise of the wind and rain, he was unable to make out what they were saying.

He entered the front hall, and was surprised to find the front door open. Even though the entry was protected by a wide porch, rain had blown into the house, and a puddle was slowly forming. Lightning briefly illuminated the entry, and Jennings saw two large shapes stretched out across the floor; he imagined at first that animals – perhaps dogs – had come into the house to shelter from the storm. But why then had they not greeted him, or taken any notice of him at all? He crept toward them, realizing after only a few steps that they were human.

Another flash of lightning revealed the shapes to be Charlotte and Sir James Carlisle.

Drugged too, no doubt, Jennings thought. He crouched down beside Charlotte and gently took her hand. *They must have been trying to leave when they succumbed to it.* Mrs. Carlisle's hand felt unnaturally cold in his, and, with a sudden sense of alarm, he bent down and tried to detect signs of breathing. None appeared, and, when he pressed his fingers against her wrist, and then to her neck, he could find no pulse. He fell to his knees and put his ear to her chest; he pled with her silently to wake up, but to no avail, and he was obliged finally to accept the grim truth.

She was dead.

Hoping that Elizabeth's father might still be alive, Jennings turned to Sir James, but the older man's eyes were opened wide and stared sightlessly into the storm.

As fast as he had ridden, Jennings had arrived too late.

CHAPTER SEVENTEEN

Perry was ill inclined to proceed at what he called the breakneck speed his mistress had requested. The groom seconded his decision to travel at a more seemly pace, and, in light of the muddy roads and the threat of continued rain, Elizabeth eventually agreed as well.

"But we must make all possible haste, Perry," she reminded him. "As quickly as the horses will safely take us." She glanced up at the dark clouds. "We are scarcely three hours behind Mr. Jennings, and I daresay he will not be in a *monstrous* hurry, since he does not know about Ned and Isabelle. We may be able to overtake him."

Perry handed her up into the carriage. "We may indeed, ma'am," he said. He looked askance at her. "You are set, ma'am, on reaching the lake house tonight? It will be well past dark."

Elizabeth nodded. "Time is of the essence, Perry," she said firmly. "I do not yet know who it is that has been duplicitous, but it is clearly someone, and I believe that since the lie was about the lake house, my father and stepmother – and Isabelle too – may be in harm's way, even this very moment."

Perry could hardly gainsay her, since he had seen his master more than once take unusual actions that proved later to be the best course. But it concerned him that they would be travelling after dark, and he was glad beyond measure that they had thought to bring the blunderbuss. "As you wish, ma'am," he said with an air of worried resignation. "I'll take us quick as I can." With this half-hearted assertion, he climbed up onto the box and steered the carriage onto the road.

* * *

Jennings stood, unable to do more for a moment than stare nonplussed at the lifeless forms of Sir James and his wife. He had no reason to berate himself – he had made all haste in coming here – but he could not help feeling, as he had when he found Elizabeth in the park, that he should somehow have been able to go faster or to arrive sooner. How long ago had the Carlisles been killed? He had stopped nearly two hours in Luton to escape hail and lightning; if he had braved it instead, would he have made his destination in time to save them? The knowledge that his horse would surely have foundered had he forced it to endure such a pummeling was of little consolation.

She was so sure her father was in danger, he thought. *She cared about him, even after all.*

The murmuring voices had stopped when he entered the front hallway, and he realized now that someone stood behind him, even before she spoke.

"You are Mr. Jennings, no doubt!" she said brightly. "I have heard so much about you!"

Jennings turned to face the woman. She was petite, not quite as tall as Elizabeth, but her golden curls were piled high on her head, giving her the illusion of height. She was extremely slender, and her skin was so pale that she seemed to glow in the dimness of the hallway. Behind her, the door to the study was open, casting the orange light of a roaring fire into the hall. She looked briefly over her shoulder into the study, then turned back to Jennings with a welcoming smile.

"I hope you will join us, Mr. Jennings," she said. "We've been waiting for you." Her smile became rather sardonic. "And for your lovely bride, of course."

Jennings raised an eyebrow. "I am distressed," he said, his voice as cold as ice, "to think we would have any place in such a matter." He gave a small nod toward the Carlisles. "Were we expected to allow this? Or to be your next victims?"

The woman stood with her hands clasped in front of her. "It was unfortunate," she said, her regret seeming almost genuine. "But unavoidable." She frowned. "Mrs. Carlisle would not drink *any* wine!" she complained. "It was really most perverse of her, and quite vexing!" She glanced down at Charlotte's body. "And since she could not be got out of the way, we were obliged, I'm afraid, to remove her entirely." She beamed at him. "But now you are here, everything will soon be set to rights – well, for us, anyway."

"Will I not also need to be 'removed entirely'?" Jennings asked. He glanced toward the study; he had heard a man's voice earlier, but its owner had not as yet come into the hall. "Especially since Mrs. Jennings is not with me?"

The woman revealed some surprise at this news. "Why ever not?" she asked. "What would possess you to come here by yourself?" She frowned again. "You weren't *invited*."

"Neither was Lizzie," Jennings noted coolly. "Yet you expected her."

"Because she has been tracking the rings," the woman explained. "No doubt because of clues given her by *you*, sir. Your gifts are rather well-known in certain circles, despite your circumspection about them. When I stopped in London and learned you had travelled north, I knew that, if you had not yet deduced

214

enough to lead you here, you soon would." She tittered. "You *do* have an excellent property, sir! I'm sure I shall enjoy it very much!"

"How did you know she was tracking the rings?" Jennings asked. "We told no one."

"Lizzie's been casting about for weeks, sir!" the woman said. "First to our cousin Marcus Tate, and then to me. Poor Marcus," she added with a disingenuous pout. "His little Eliza taken so suddenly, when it really ought to have been Lizzie. She must feel just *terrible* about it!"

"You must be Cousin Isabelle," Jennings said drily.

"Why, yes!" she answered proudly. "Your gifts are indeed prodigious!"

Jennings' expression was impassive. "I recognized your shallow heartlessness," he said. She bridled at this, but said nothing, stepping back involuntarily as he moved toward her. "You've taken Eliza," he went on. "And Annie Baker. What use is Lizzie to you now? And – I believe I already asked – what use am *I*? Do I not simply await some sort of execution, either by you or your winged henchman?" He remained in absolute control of himself, but his anger was evident. "Why do you stand here *chatting* with me as though I cared a fig for anything you had to say?"

Isabelle pulled herself up as tall as possible. "There's no need to be *rude*!" she announced haughtily. "I can't help it if he picked *me* over all the others! I certainly can't help it if others don't quite measure up!" Her eyes shifted briefly to the floor. "Or if they are meant for other fates." She turned and peered once more into the study, and broke into a delighted grin. "Do come, Mr. Jennings!" she cried, reaching out to take his arm as though he were a dear friend.

Leaning toward him, she whispered conspiratorially, "There's nothing for it, after all. No point in struggling."

Jennings hoped fervently that Miss Fetherston was wrong about that, but he saw no immediate value in trying to escape. Isabelle was hardly able to overpower both Charlotte and Sir James; clearly the man whose voice he had heard was her accomplice, and was likely the one in charge of the beast and of the dark magic that had shielded the cave – without more knowledge, Jennings did not see by what method he could either stop or flee such a formidable opponent, and if he died in the attempt, he would not be in any position to help Elizabeth when she arrived.

And he could feel, as strongly as any message he had received through the slate, that she was indeed on her way.

He was pulled into the study by Miss Fetherston, who looked at him triumphantly before bringing his attention to the other occupant of the room.

It was Cedric Delacourt.

* * *

Elizabeth waited impatiently in the carriage for a change of horses. They had made good time, but she could see that they had just missed a great storm, and the roads ahead did not look promising at all. She leaned out of the carriage window.

"Are we very far, Perry?" she called.

Perry had been talking with the ostlers; he left them with a nod of his head and came to the carriage window. "We're barely an hour behind 'im, ma'am."

She was surprised. "We're overtaking him?" she asked incredulously. "In the *carriage*?"

He nodded again. "He was obliged to stop here for some time, ma'am," he said. "There was a downpour of hail, and a good bit of lightning. Horse wouldn't go through it." He glanced at the muddy road and at the stormy evening sky; his expression suggested that he thought the horse was in the right of it.

"If we can overtake him, we should try to do so," Elizabeth said. At her urging, they left Luton at a smart pace, but after only a few miles, the roads became almost impassible from mud, and Perry slowed the horses down to what seemed to Elizabeth to be a disastrously leisurely crawl. Knowing there were still above twenty miles to cover, she scowled at the sun that already hung very low in the sky. At this rate they would be lucky to arrive at the lake house before dawn, and, if the rain took up again, which it seemed very likely to do, Perry would no doubt put his foot down on the matter, and demand that he not be expected to risk the safety of either the horses or his mistress.

"I could walk faster than this," she grumbled, but knew in her heart that, however pressing the matter may feel to her, Perry was doing his level best to accommodate what was in truth a very silly directive. Why, the only reason they had reached Northampton so early in the day was that she and Jennings both enjoyed getting a preposterously early start on long journeys, and had left Brightwood at the first notion of daylight. Jennings liked to travel fast, as well, and Elizabeth realized with a pang of guilt that, if she were overtaking him, then she was probably pushing the horses.

Feeling rather like a murderess at the thought of hurting animals

– who had been dragging her all over the countryside, no less! – Elizabeth leaned toward the carriage window with the intention of telling Perry to stop at the next village for an actual rest and some supper. But as her hand reached out, the carriage lurched hard to one side, and began to slide rather than roll along the muddy road. Elizabeth found herself flung first against the seat, and then onto the ceiling, as the carriage tilted off the edge of the road and tumbled ten feet down to a ravine.

* * *

Cedric stood beside the fireplace, his hand resting on the edge of a small table upon which sat a number of thick candles, grouped around an ornate dagger that lay on a white cloth. The furniture had been pushed away from the center of the room, and the rug rolled up and shoved to the side; on the wood floor thus revealed were two enormous concentric circles, drawn in white chalk and studded with runes and cryptic words.

Jennings took in the scene at a glance, and gazed dispassionately at Cedric. "You have covered your tracks quite well, sir. My compliments."

Cedric's smile was as sincere and warm as it had always been. "I know you jest, cousin," he said amiably. "But I must say that I *have* done quite a bang-up job of it, for such a *very* long time." He ran his fingers along the hilt of the dagger. "I must say too," he acknowledged. "That you are truly a capital fellow! If I were ever in a jam, I would call upon you, without question!"

Jennings realized that Cedric's appearance was shifting, so that at times he looked like himself, while at others his face seemed to belong to another, or even to several others. "So the magic in the cave," he said thoughtfully. "It was as I saw it in my vision: you have taken over more than Ned's name and fortune. You have taken over his appearance as well." He frowned, his eyes struggling to pin down Cedric's true face. "Somehow."

Cedric grinned even more broadly. "You had a vision of *me*?" he asked, apparently delighted by the notion. "With Neddy? That was a difficult one, I allow. I liked Ned very well, and I will miss him desperately! But you are quite right, Jennings, quite right; I have put a great deal of effort into protecting the cave. It is a sacred place – an anchor, if you will." He raised an eyebrow and added in a conspiratorial voice, "It is the best possible place to transfer their essence to my own. Without that, my ruse would be discovered in a trice, I fear." He noticed that Jennings was squinting at him, and blinking his eyes in irritation. "Oh, of course!" he said. "Your 'gift'! It is allowing you to see me as I really am." He stepped away from the table and stood with his shoulders squared. After a moment, his appearance solidified, and he looked now even more like the portrait of Elizabeth's ancestor than before. "This is my true countenance," he said. "I had been able to shield myself from your … talents … while the enchantment remained on the cave. But when you entered it and broke the spell, I suddenly found myself at quite a loss to maintain any sort of disguise whatsoever. And so I knew, you see, that someone had uncovered my secret, and I assumed it must be you and dear Elizabeth. Of course, since I could not keep any face but my own for more than a few minutes at a time, I was obliged to speed things up a bit from my original plan." He glanced toward the entryway where Sir James and Charlotte Carlisle lay, and his smile dimmed considerably. "Poor Charlotte would not take a drink with me – for no good reason! – although, now that I think on it, she had been looking at me strangely all afternoon, and so I imagine she was very suspicious of my unsteady appearance. I considered sending her on some sort of outing with Isabelle, but the rain prevented it." He sighed. "I was forced, in the end, to eliminate her in a most unseemly fashion!"

Isabelle moved to stand closer to Cedric. "It cannot signify, can it?" she asked him. "You could not have her anyway."

Cedric took Isabelle's hand and brought it to his lips. "I still *liked* her, my pet!" he explained. "I do not enjoy killing people. Especially when their deaths can do me no good."

Behind them, a gust of wind blew the front door against the wall of the entryway, and leaves skittered across the floor, accompanied by the splash of heavy rain. Isabelle jumped, startled, and then laughed at her own nervousness. "She was trying to flee, you know," she told Jennings. "As though anything she did would stop what will happen." She scoffed at the notion.

"And what *will* happen?" Jennings asked. "Why do any of this?" He tilted his head to one side and eyed Cedric Delacourt with undisguised contempt. "It is you, is it not, who unleashed the monster that killed Ann Baker?" He frowned darkly. "And Eliza Tate? Did you contrive to eliminate her as well?" He stepped further into the study. "Why have you visited this dark legacy upon Lizzie's family?"

"Not *her* family!" Isabelle interrupted angrily. "*My* family! She's barely part of it at all! Her only value is in dying!" She folded her arms in front of her petulantly. "Which she should have done

220

months ago," she grumbled. "Annie Baker would have come here most willingly, and all would have been done with no one the wiser! Now we must wait for Lizzie, who does not seem to want to come at all!"

"I'm sure Lizzie will apologize for inconveniencing you so selfishly," Jennings said sardonically. "But I'm confused; I was under the impression that each generation paid a price of *two* women." He turned to Mr. Delacourt. "Why are you waiting for Lizzie, when you've already taken Annie and Eliza?"

Cedric smiled, not quite as warmly as before. "Two females every nineteen years," he said. "I've been following the cycles of the moon – *earning* my prize – for one hundred and fourteen years." He sighed again, and his eyes gleamed in the firelight. "It's been so long," he went on, his voice filled with emotion. "Taking new identities, bequeathing my fortunes to my new selves by increasingly circuitous means, spending decades waiting for this magical immortality to be made permanent." He gazed at Isabelle for a moment. "And to be able to share it now with my beautiful bride." His attention returned to Jennings. "Six generations," he explained. "Twelve females all together. But the requirement, of course, was thirteen. Cousin Elizabeth will be the final offering."

Isabelle sniffed and rolled her eyes. "If she ever comes!" she said. "Since Mr. Jennings has seen fit to come here without her!"

"You're very impatient," Jennings noted drily. "You have waited over a hundred years; why is tonight so important?"

"*I* haven't," Isabelle protested. "I'm only twenty-two!" Her pout dissolved into unabashed joy. "And now I shall be twenty-two forever!" she announced triumphantly. "Because Jon – I mean, 'Ned'

– has picked *me* to be the eternal matriarch!"

"So you *are* Jonathan Fitzhugh," Jennings said to Delacourt. "Your portrait hangs in Sir James' house; Lizzie recognized you." He glanced down at the chalk circles. "But I still don't understand why you're in such a hurry."

"It is, in part, your own fault, Jennings," Mr. Delacourt said with incongruous amiability. "You broke the spell at the cave – my anchor, as I said – and I was not able to achieve any consistent disguise. But in truth I have been rather surprised, all these years, that it has never been breached by some curious lad or fearless fox. So I cannot be too upset with you about it, I suppose, since the spell has certainly given its all." He squinted at Jennings. "Your gifts, too, may have had a hand in it," he realized. "Which were not of your design, after all, but were truly visited upon you. So you see," he said, splaying his hands out in a helpless gesture. "It is really unfair to be irritated with you about it. But it was undeniably most inopportune." He sighed and toyed again with the dagger on the little table. "Mostly, though," he continued. "This final sacrifice must be completed before the next full moon, so we have barely a fortnight to do it. And since I have been compelled to remove Mrs. Carlisle, I have very little time indeed to perform the ritual before people begin asking a lot of pesky questions." He looked around him a bit wistfully. "I suppose fire would be best," he decided. "It is a pity to lose the lake house – it's so delightfully located! – but no one will suspect anything, I would imagine."

"Who would suspect anything anyway?" Isabelle said scornfully. "Who's going to miss Charlotte Carlisle? She isn't *anybody*!" She smiled archly. "*My* family deserve this reward!" she informed Jennings with an air of absolute superiority. "We've upheld the bargain all these years! Amassing a *huge* fortune through advantageous marriages, offering up our own people as payment – *we're* the ones who matter!" She rolled her eyes again. "And *I* have certainly put up with all the Lizzies of the world for far too long!"

Jennings decided he had heard more than enough. "'Bargain'!" he repeated derisively. "In exchange for what?"

Isabelle looked sincerely surprised at the question. "In exchange for immortality!" she said, as though she were explaining a rudimentary fact to an imbecile. She indicated her betrothed with a toss of her head. "*He* is the holder of great power!" she went on, her eyes lighting up. "And *we* were chosen to share in it. For generations, we have known that from our ranks would come the woman who gains immortality at his side. We'll control a fortune beyond imagining! Our children will join us, until our family sways the whole world!"

Jennings snorted. "You fool!" he snapped. "Why would someone with so much power need anyone? Why would someone who is immortal require heirs? His practiced method of taking over other men's lives does not sound like the sort of habit he will be likely to give up. He will no doubt continue killing men and taking their fortunes, their homes and lands, their wives and families; he has no use for you or for your family beyond your willingness to sacrifice your own kind for *his* ends. I will be greatly surprised if he marries you at all, and if he does, it will be for the fortune which, once secured to him, will render your personal contribution completely unnecessary. He will dispose of you just as he has the others, and take over the lives of your father, your uncles, *me* ... without a thought for you or your family, or for any bargain into which you have entered so passively and so naively!"

Isabelle's outrage left her momentarily speechless. She turned to Mr. Delacourt for support, who told her soothingly, "You needn't listen to him, my dear. It is he who is largely unnecessary." He put one arm around her shoulders and hugged her to him. "I will transfer his essence to myself, and then we will have his fortune as well, and all of Brightwood, just as I promised."

She looked slightly mollified. "I *did* like Brightwood," she said. She looked up at him quizzically. "Will *I* be able to alter my appearance as you have done? Will people imagine that I am Lizzie?"

"I am quite sure you will be able to, my dear," Cedric assured her. "A spell is a spell." He looked apologetically at Jennings. "I *am* sorry, old boy," he said. "But Charlotte is not the proper bloodline for the sacrifice, you see; it must be Lizzie. And of course, especially now that you are a witness to these events, you cannot be allowed to leave here." He seemed truly remorseful. "You and I could have been great friends, I believe," he said. "Pity." His attention drifted into the wind-swept hallway. "You must believe Lizzie to be on her way here," he guessed. "Else why would you not flee, since you have had every opportunity? You hope to afford her protection by standing between her and me. But it's no use, I'm afraid, no use at all." He smiled lovingly down at Isabelle. "I wonder how far away she is?"

* * *

"Mrs. Jennings!" Perry wrenched open the door of the carriage, which had survived its tumble largely unscathed save for a broken

224

wheel. The door swung up, and Perry peered down into the depths of the carriage.

"I am quite all right," Elizabeth replied. "Only a bit shaken up." She came unsteadily to her feet, struggling to right herself in the tilted carriage. "Do you mind helping me, Perry?" she asked, raising her arms up to him.

"Good God, ma'am!" Perry exclaimed in relief. "When I saw how it rolled, I was fearful to find you!" He took her arms and pulled her as gently as he could from the carriage; there was little purchase on her side, but she did her best to help him, and soon she had climbed down onto the muddy ground. "Are you quite sure you're all right, ma'am?" Perry asked anxiously. "It must've tossed you about somethin' awful!"

Elizabeth managed a reassuring smile. "I am all intact, Perry, I assure you," she told him. "I have certainly been through worse." She looked around her. "Where is Tom, Perry? Has he been hurt?"

"Aye, ma'am," Perry replied. He gestured a little way down the road, where the groom sat holding one arm cradled in the other. "He's broken his arm, ma'am. But it could've been a lot worse, as far as he got thrown."

"Heavens!" Elizabeth cried. "He looks as pale as death!" She hurried to the young man and crouched down beside him. "I'm so sorry!" she said, tears in her eyes. "This is all my fault!"

"No, ma'am," Tom said. "Things happen. We were hardly movin' at all, in truth, and I'm quite surprised it slipped."

"The wretched mud!" Elizabeth said. "And all because I wanted to push through tonight!" She inspected his arm gingerly. "Does it hurt dreadfully?"

"As to that, ma'am," he replied. "It barely hurts at all unless I try to put weight on it. It'll be right as rain in a few weeks, don't you worry about it at all." He seemed more concerned about Elizabeth than with his own injury, and asked her solicitously, "Are *you* all right, ma'am?"

She nodded. "A bit bruised," she said. "But I'll be 'right as rain' as well in a day or two."

"I'll ride back to Luton," Perry said. "The horses broke free of the carriage when it twisted over; they're a bit spooked, but none the worse that I can tell. I'll take them back and hire another carriage, and it'll be here for you before you can wink an eye. We'll be tucked up at the inn before ten o'clock, I wager!"

Elizabeth was instantly besieged by a feeling of dread. *I can't go back to Luton*, she thought. *I must reach the lake house.* "I cannot explain it, Perry," she said. "But I believe – most strongly – that something bad will happen if I do not reach my father tonight. I cannot return to Luton."

Perry could see her sincere distress; whether or not he shared her belief, he knew that she would act upon it with or without his help, and he had experienced too much in Mr. Jennings' employ to be dismissive of 'bad feelings'. "We can press on tonight, ma'am," he said, surprised himself to hear the words come out of his mouth. "But the horses can't take all of us, and I think it would be unwise to leave Tom here by himself. So I'll ride to Luton, and hire a carriage, and you and Tom can wait here with the blunderbuss. I'll return as quick as I can, and then we'll go on to the lake house." He sighed gustily and eyed the muddy road. "If there's a carriage or wagon or aught to be had, I fancy we might reach the lake house sometime after

226

midnight. I can't make no promises, but we can try."

"That will be excellent," Elizabeth said. She stood and held her hand out to Perry, who took it in some confusion. "I know what I ask," she added. "I know that Mr. Jennings would not countenance such urgency." She glanced guiltily at Tom. "None of this would have happened if I had not gone alone to Northampton, or if I had not decided to reach the lake house today. But it seemed to be a very sound plan at lunch-time, for many very good reasons, and although I had thought earlier to stop for the night, my heart tells me now that I must get to the lake house as soon as possible, even if I must walk there." Great drops of rain began to fall as she spoke, and a low rumble of thunder punctuated her words. Her dread became overpowering, settling in her chest like a cold, angry fist; she could hear her blood pounding in her ears. "Mr. Jennings' pistols are under the seat," she said. "Unless they have been thrown clear of the carriage altogether. You must take them, Perry; you should not be unarmed on such a dark road."

Perry had known about the pistols but had forgotten. He welcomed her reminder with relief, and made his way quickly to the overturned carriage. The sooner he got back to Luton the better, especially now that it was beginning to rain. After a few moments, during which he contorted himself through the canted opening of the carriage, he called over his shoulder, "They're here, ma'am! Safe and sound."

"Perry!" Tom cried out, and Perry turned in time to see Elizabeth, her skirts gathered up in a most undignified manner, sitting astride one of the horses. In one arm she carried the blunderbuss, while the other kept a practiced hold on the reins.

227

"Mrs. Jennings!" Perry shouted. Carrying Mr. Jennings' pistol case, he ran up the hill to the road. "Ma'am, what are you thinking!"

She spun the horse around. "I'm truly sorry, Perry!" she told him over her shoulder. "But I can't ask you and Tom to do anything more for me than you already have. I'll send someone for you straightaway, I promise!" She took off then at a near gallop, skillfully keeping the horse on the driest parts of the road.

Perry stood looking after her, struggling to comprehend what his mistress had just done. He debated riding after her, but he could not leave Tom alone and relatively helpless. Finally, his shoulders slumping in dejected resignation, he squatted down beside Tom. "The master won't like that one bit," he said.

Tom shrugged and gave Perry a half-smile. "He might be well pleased about it," he said. "If Miz Jennings is right, and he's in some kind of trouble."

Perry raised his eyebrows. "I had not thought of that," he admitted. "But then ... do we hope he's fine, or do we hope he's not fine?"

Tom let out a bark of laughter. As the droplets of rain became more of a steady shower, he gestured with his good arm toward the carriage. "I think she had a parasol. It's better'n nothin', I suppose."

"Aye," Perry agreed, coming to his feet and heading back to the carriage. "And then we'll put you on the other horse, and walk us back to Luton. If we're gonna be stuck in the rain, it might as well be on the way to somewhere."

Tom laughed again. "Can you imagine it?" he asked. "Me, bein' escorted into Luton, carryin' my *parasol*!"

Jennings gazed with pity on Isabelle Fetherston. "You know, he promised Annie Baker a lot of things as well," he said. "You should take care, I imagine."

Before Isabelle could retort, Mr. Delacourt said smoothly, "Annie Baker was a sacrifice, Jennings. She was never intended to be anything else." He stepped into the chalk circle. "Since I cannot take you unawares," he went on. "I shall be obliged to let my pet do the honours. I prefer to do such things at the cave, but this will certainly suffice, as long as I have your blood." He spread his arms out from his body, and lifted his face to the ceiling. Behind him, the fire built to a roaring crescendo, and the white lines of the circle began to glow faintly. Isabelle, watching with wide eyes, moved away from the circle, until she stood with her back against the far wall of the study.

Jennings felt a stab of fear in his chest, as well as the familiar sensation of otherworldly presence. Whatever Cedric Delacourt was doing, it clearly had nothing to do with this mortal earth, and Jennings waited with a mixture of apprehension and fascination.

He did not have to wait long.

Coalescing in the fireplace as though drawn from the stone itself, a great beast appeared in the flames. It was the beast Jennings had seen in visions – the one that attacked Elizabeth and murdered Ann Baker. It looked like no earthly creature, but its body had the form of a man, while its head resembled that of a wolf. Its massive arms rippled with muscle and sinew, and its yellow eyes shone even brighter than the fire in which it stood. It stepped over the hearth and into the room, trailing burning cinders behind it that fell sizzling to the floor, and its wings as it spread them wide spanned the whole room from wall to wall. Miss Fetherston cried out in spite of herself, and shrank away from the towering monster.

The beast, pinning Jennings with a piercing stare, emitted a long, shrill shriek and advanced toward him.

CHAPTER EIGHTEEN

The creature's fangs were barely a foot away from Jennings.

"Get down!" a familiar – and most welcome – voice said behind him, and Jennings crouched abruptly.

The resounding blast of the blunderbuss shook the air, and the head of the creature exploded into sickly-green blood and torn flesh. The creature froze for a moment, its wings stiffening, then it slumped to the floor. Its skin began immediately to sizzle and smoke, and, after a very few seconds, to dissolve into ash. Soon nothing was left but bones and entrails, and then even these began to collapse in upon themselves, disintegrating until only charred stains and patches of yellow slime remained.

Isabelle cried out in disgust and alarm; she ran to Cedric, who held her rather mechanically, and stared at his dead "pet" with an expression of surprise and disappointment.

"That was not very kind of you, Cousin," he complained, turning to Elizabeth.

She stood in the doorway, the smoking blunderbuss clutched in her hands. The rain had soaked her clear through, so that water dripped from her hair and her clothes onto the floor. She was covered in mud. She held the blunderbuss with the ease and confidence of someone who was quite accustomed to the use of firearms, and Delacourt noted this with a rueful twist of his lips.

"I had forgotten your proficiency, Lizzie," he said. "I should never have allowed you to learn it."

Elizabeth frowned at him. "What are you talking about?" she asked, her voice angry and peremptory. She glanced at Jennings, who had risen and now stood beside her. "Are you all right, Christopher? I arrived as soon as I could."

"Never better, my love," Jennings responded. "You are here earlier than I expected."

"I have been here several minutes," she revealed. She glared at Cedric. "Listening to *you* explain all the ways that you have burdened and tormented my family!" Her eyes narrowed. "My mother!" She squared her shoulders and waved the blunderbuss in a menacing manner toward him. "And I believe, Cousin, having heard your tale, that your life has extended far enough!" She moved forward, stepping into the chalk circle as Cedric backed out of it.

He reached behind him to the little table where the dagger still sat; he gripped it in a steady hand and brought it between him and Elizabeth. The firelight glinted off its steel blade as he turned it to and fro. "On the contrary, dearest Lizzie," he said affably. "It is *your* life that has gone on too long." He became suddenly serious, and his eyes turned dark and cold. "It is your destiny, Cousin, to be given in sacrifice. There is really nothing you can do about it." He advanced, crossing into the chalk circle.

Elizabeth, her eyes never leaving Delacourt's, swung the blunderbuss with all her strength, delivering a shocking blow to the side of Cedric's head and dropping him to his knees.

Miss Fetherston screamed and rushed Elizabeth, pushing her out of the circle and across the study. Elizabeth swung the blunderbuss again; it poked sharply into Isabelle's gut, causing her to double over in pain. Elizabeth took this brief opportunity to hit her again, slamming the butt of the gun into the juncture between Isabelle's shoulder and her neck. Isabelle cried out and fell to the ground, but, as Elizabeth turned her attention once more to Cedric, who struggled dizzily to regain his footing, Isabelle scurried to the fireplace and wrenched a poker from its stand.

"Get away from him!" she shouted, her face contorted with rage, and, raising the poker over her head, she charged Elizabeth a second time.

Jennings lunged forward, hoping to stop the swinging poker, but Miss Fetherston saw him coming and quickly brought the poker down on his outstretched arms. He stumbled backward, and Isabelle swung the poker at Elizabeth, who parried it with the blunderbuss.

The two women spun around, Isabelle trying repeatedly to move the poker past the blunderbuss and Elizabeth countering her efforts.

By now, Cedric had come to his feet. Blood trickled from the side of his head, and he stood hunched over, still too dazed for proper balance. He had managed to keep the dagger in his hand; as Isabelle and Elizabeth danced into the chalk circle, he summoned what equilibrium he could, and stabbed out at Elizabeth.

"No!" Jennings cried, leaping forward too late to stop Delacourt's attack. The knife met flesh, sinking to its hilt into Isabelle's heart.

Elizabeth fell back, horrified. "No!" she croaked. "Isabelle!"

Isabelle stared at Elizabeth in absolute confusion. Blood spread out across her bodice, and she slumped against Delacourt. "Jonathan?" she said weakly, gazing up at him. "What – what have you done?"

Delacourt pulled her to him, and gazed back at her with a look of resigned pity. "So sorry, my dear," he said gently. "It was truly meant for Lizzie." He lowered her to the floor, into the middle of the chalk circle, and lovingly brushed her hair away from her face. "No matter," he went on with a slight shrug. "There's thirteen."

Isabelle's eyes revealed all the disbelief and heartbreak that she no longer had the strength to vocalize; she coughed, blood spraying out from her lips onto her white cheeks, and her fingers clutched at the collar of Cedric's shirt. She pulled him close to her as though she would speak, but her throat could only sputter and click. In a moment, she was dead.

Cedric sighed and stood up. "How vexing," he announced. "Now the joining of the fortunes will be more ... protracted." He looked from Isabelle to the crumpled form of Charlotte Carlisle that lay in the entryway. "And I've lost Charlotte too," he added in long-suffering tones. "Such a waste."

"'Lost' her?" Elizabeth protested. "You've murdered her!"

Cedric blinked at her. "But I *liked* her!" he explained. "I had *planned* to keep her!" He frowned down at Isabelle, whose sightless eyes stared back at him. "Her ... exuberance ... has always been a welcome departure from Isabelle's simpering affections." He sighed again. "Well, it doesn't really signify," he said. "I shall simply turn to one of the other Misses Fetherston in my 'grief'." He laughed. "Would it not be amusing if one of Isabelle's sisters married Ned and the other married Sir James? Or better yet, Cedric! ... I have long thought that it was time for Sir James to die."

Elizabeth scowled in bewilderment. "What are you talking about?" she said harshly. "Where is my father?"

Jennings put a hand on his wife's shoulder. "Did you not see, my love?" he asked gently. "His is the other body in the hall."

She glanced at him for a second before bringing her attention back to Cedric; shaking the blunderbuss to remind her cousin – and herself – that she would be more than capable of caving in his skull with it, she said, "There's only Charlotte in the hall."

Jennings whipped around and peered into the hall. Charlotte Carlisle still lay there, but Sir James' body was indeed gone. Jennings had seen the body himself – it did not seem possible that Sir James could still have been alive, but if he was, why would he make no sound upon waking? Why would he sneak away without involving himself in the happenings in the study?

Cedric saw Jennings' thorough confusion and laughed again, a far more sinister sound now than before. "You are wondering, dear boy, where Sir James has got off to," he said. "Why, he was only *playing* dead, you know!" He grinned at Jennings and then at Elizabeth. "Well," he went on. "That is to say, *I* was only playing dead. Sir James – the real Sir James – has been dead for eighteen years." He tilted his head to one side. "Your father who went so often into the country without you, dear Lizzie, was also Cedric Delacourt, and, most recently, Ned Fitzhugh, whose business in London has kept him from home more often than not. And all of them, of course, are … me!"

Elizabeth, attempting to digest what Delacourt was saying, could do no more than stand frozen and dismayed, shaking her head wordlessly and blinking away sudden tears. "This cannot be," she whispered at last, her heart pounding in her chest. "It cannot be."

"It's impossible," Jennings murmured. He could barely comprehend what he was hearing. "All this while," he said. "You've been keeping Lizzie close to you."

"Oh, not by choice, I assure you," Cedric said. He bent down and pulled Isabelle out of the circle, then began taking off his coat. "But I wanted Sir James' fortune, so I took it. And because of his standing, any number of women were eager to be chosen, even if he was a dreadful curmudgeon." He tossed his coat unceremoniously onto the floor outside the circle. "His was a most difficult role to play. He is – was – a very unpleasant sort of man, and, unfortunately, the spell does not work as well if I make too many changes to the original man's character." He untied his cravat. "I did my best to stay away from Lizzie, in fact," he said, smiling warmly at her as though this information should comfort her. "I did not want to become too close to her, for quite often children can see through magic. It helped that she was so young when I arrived." He removed his shirt, and stood now bare to the waist; around him, the chalk runes had begun to glow with white light.

Elizabeth, goaded from her mental shock by the glowing circle, stepped back. Beside her, Jennings felt his chest tighten in a way that was at once familiar and suddenly far more severe – something even more dire than Cedric's monster was about to make an appearance. His breathing became jagged, and he was obliged to steady himself by leaning against the wall, his hand tugging his collar away from his throat.

"You might well be concerned, Jennings," Cedric said, observing him. "Isabelle was the final sacrifice." He crouched down in the circle and ran his fingers through the puddle of Miss Fetherston's blood. "My long wait is now at an end." He lifted his hand and drew a symbol in blood across his chest. "I have at last paid my part of the bargain; I will live forever." He positioned himself in the exact center of the circle and spread his arms out wide.

"Good God!" Elizabeth breathed, stepping further back as the runes became intensely bright, and the fire turned so wild that it threatened to break free of the fireplace and engulf the room.

"My blood will seal the bargain!" Cedric shouted over the roar of flames. He jabbed the tip of the dagger into the flesh above his heart, and, as his own blood welled up, he himself began to glow. His eyes lit up in exultation; he dropped the dagger, and it clattered onto the floor. "I will be immortal!" he cried. "Generations will be mine to command!" His blood ran down his chest in a thick, red-black thread.

Behind Cedric, a figure appeared in the fireplace. It was not so huge as the winged creature had been, but it was somehow more frightening. It bore the shape and size of a man, but the skin was as glossy and red as painted leather, and the face was twisted into a fearsome grimace. It stood naked and hairless, its features blended as if it were molded out of living clay, and its eyes were dark pits that seemed to swirl with the black æther of the abyss.

"His blood can't touch the floor," Jennings gasped, staggering forward. The demon figure saw him and lifted its hand, squeezing its fingers into a fist. Jennings' chest seized with gripping pain that brought him to his knees.

Cedric watched him fall, and a sneer curled his lips. "You cannot stop me now!" he proclaimed. "I will have what is mine!" He laughed in delight as the light that surrounded him pulled him a few inches off the ground. "I will have it all," he informed the Jennings. "And people like you will be helpless before me!"

"Or not," Elizabeth replied, grabbing the blunderbuss once more by its muzzle and swinging it into Cedric Delacourt.

He flew backward, tumbling out of the circle and slamming

against the fireplace mantel. "No!" he bellowed, but his anger turned instantly to triumph. "You're too late, Cousin!" he said.

Elizabeth looked down to see four drops of blood at the inside edge of the glowing circle of runes; even as she had pushed Cedric away, his blood had dripped onto the floor.

The fire exploded out of the fireplace and began to creep up the study walls. The figure stepped over the hearth and into the room just as the beast had done, but, unlike the beast, this demon stood in silence, turning neither one way nor the other, and favouring the Jennings with not even a single glance. It waited on the hearthstone, its eyes – if they could be called such – riveted on Delacourt.

Delacourt pushed himself away from the mantel and strode back into the circle. In a flash, his hand was around Elizabeth's neck, and the pressure of his fingers caused her vision to go black. She feared she was going to faint, and her pulse beat so loudly in her ears that she could barely hear Cedric's words. "Your husband's gifts have proven a curse," he said, his voice sounding to her as though it came from a long distance. "He is sensitive to my demon's hand, and is rendered quite unable to move, or even to breathe. In a moment I will command my demon to kill him." He smiled down at her. "But you have been such a bother to me, Lizzie, that I believe I will kill you myself." He brought her face close to his, and she could feel his breath. "I will kill you both and take his fortune, and I will blame all this ..." He waved his free hand expansively to indicate the whole house. "... on you. You, Lizzie, have poisoned the whole household, and murdered your father and stepmother, and your cousin, and you've run off with Isabelle's Ned, never to be heard from again." He clucked his tongue. "How dreadful of you, Lizzie! How ... uncivil."

He came so close to her that their cheeks touched, and his words hissed in her ear. "And I, Christopher Jennings, was helpless to do anything! You poisoned me too, of course, and even though I managed to escape, there was no one for *miles* to come to my aid." He chuckled. "Thank you, Cousin, for finally being useful to me."

… *come to my aid,* his words echoed in her brain. *Come to my aid. Come to my aid.* The words triggered a memory – something important. Something important. *Come to my aid. Come to …*

The words of her mother's letter flooded her mind. *"If ever you find yourself in harm's way, call upon me, … and I will render you what aid I can."*

She let the blunderbuss slip from her fingers and began fumbling frantically for the pocket of her cloak. *Please let it be there!* she prayed. *Don't let it have fallen out in the carriage.* Cedric's grip on her throat had tightened, and everything was swimming before her eyes. With some difficulty, she wriggled her fingers into her pocket and touched the drawstrings of her reticule. *Thank God!* But even as she tugged at the opening of the reticule, she felt her legs give way beneath her. Her eyes rolled back in her head, and she went limp.

Cedric gazed at her for a few seconds, before releasing her and allowing her to drop to the floor. He raised one eyebrow in surprise at how easily she had been dispatched – after causing so much trouble! – and then turned to Jennings, who still knelt with his hand to his throat, the skin of his mouth and fingers a frightening shade of blue.

"You don't look so well, old boy," Cedric said amiably, bending over and clapping Jennings on the shoulder. He glanced at Elizabeth. "I suppose you're not too happy about that," he said. "But never worry! You'll be with her soon enough!" He shoved Jennings roughly to the ground, and kicked him in the stomach. "You even arrived before her," he said pityingly. "And you're still too late. How maddening for you! Or perhaps comforting," he added musingly. "You would never have been able to save her, you see. It was never really within your power to do so, despite your talents."

Jennings, desperate for air, stared helplessly at Elizabeth. He had failed her, again. He was tempted to give up his struggle to breathe, and to let himself slip into death, but the thought that she might yet somehow be alive would not allow him to do so.

Yes, there! He saw her move. *Ungh!* He received a second, fiercer kick in the stomach from Delacourt. Involuntarily, he doubled up and shifted backward, but before Delacourt could bring his attention back to Elizabeth, Jennings summoned every ounce of strength that he possessed, and hurled himself at Delacourt's legs.

Cedric was thrown off balance and toppled over, landing with a loud thump at the feet of his own demon. The demon did not move, but looked on Cedric with apparent curiosity.

"What are you waiting for?" Cedric growled, glaring up at it. "Kill him!"

The demon's head pivoted slightly to the side, and it watched Jennings for a few seconds before striding toward him and picking him up by the collar. Jennings, nearly insensible from lack of oxygen, and assailed by the notion that his heart was not beating as it properly should, hung like a ragdoll in the demon's powerful grasp and hoped simply that his actions had bought Elizabeth enough time to get away.

Elizabeth, having feigned unconsciousness to escape Cedric's throttling, took full advantage of her husband's distraction; no one noticed as she wrangled her reticule out of her pocket and pulled open the drawstrings.

Mother, she thought. *Please be able to hear me.*

She drew the peridot ring out of the reticule.

"Mother," she whispered. "I am very much in harm's way."

She slid the ring onto her finger.

CHAPTER NINETEEN

At first nothing happened, but something told Elizabeth that her mother's ring was more than an heirloom. The weight of it on her finger felt different somehow, and it tingled on her skin. It tingled, and then it burned, and she saw that it was glowing with silver-white light.

"Mother," she breathed, staring at the ring. "It's real."

Words entered her head, and then her ears; a soft voice was speaking to her. "Call upon me," it said. "I will render what aid I can."

"Mother," Elizabeth said again, and struggled to sit up.

The fire blazed higher, and turned bright blue. Sparks shot out of the fireplace and skidded across the floor, followed by a score or more yellow lights that floated up out of the flames one by one. The demon turned its attention to these lights; its grip on Jennings' throat relaxed. Jennings seized this opportunity to wrench himself away, and to drag a great gulp of air into his lungs.

"Elizabeth!" he cried, his voice hoarse. He stumbled toward her.

She held up her hand, pointing to the lights. "Look!" Her eyes were wide with wonder. "Look at all of them!"

Jennings turned, and what he saw left him dumbfounded. The yellow lights had become more substantial, taking on the shape of people. He felt their presence in his heart – the customary sensation in his chest, compounded a hundred times – and he fell back, winded.

Each light was a spirit. Each face was little more than vague wisps of features and shadows, but Jennings recognized them as though he had always known them – they were the spirits who had spoken to him through the slate. As he watched, a dozen more lights burst out of the fire, and they too transformed into the people he had only ever encountered with his emotions.

The cluster of lights converged on the demon, surrounding it and resolving into translucent beings. For its part, the demon stood as still as a statue, its face impassive, its eyes scanning the circle of ghosts around it. It seemed to be waiting for something.

The ghosts closed in until their shoulders touched; in a moment, they had formed a solid glowing band that obscured the demon from the Jennings' sight.

Delacourt had wasted precious moments goggling at the lights. He stood now, and stumbled backward. "What is this?" he asked, not knowing if the spirits belonged to his demon or not. "What is happening?"

The demon peered at Delacourt over the heads of the ghosts. In a rasping voice that put a dagger of fear and revulsion into Elizabeth's heart, it answered its master: "They will try to prevent me."

Delacourt stared bewildered at it. "Well, prevent *them*!" he commanded, frowning.

The demon looked away from Delacourt and again surveyed the ghosts. It gave no response to Cedric, but its hands lifted, almost as though it were prepared to surrender. The fire changed from blue to red, and surged so high that the flames touched the ceiling. The air around the demon shimmered, and Jennings perceived that the ghosts girded themselves against some sort of attack.

By now Elizabeth had come to her feet, and was standing beside Jennings. "What are they?" she murmured, her hand reaching out for

Jennings'. "They are not demons?"

"No," Jennings replied, shaking his head without looking at Elizabeth. His attention was fixed on the glowing circle, and on the demon inside it. "They are the spirits who spoke through the slate."

"Of course," Elizabeth said, nodding in sudden understanding. She squeezed Jennings' hand. "They have come in answer to the ring." They had come at her mother's request.

Around the demon's upraised hands, the atmosphere became altered, distorted, rippling as though seen through warped glass. The ghost-circle tightened, and the human shapes dissolved into a dense fog with hints of limbs and heads dotted throughout. The yellow light intensified, but the demon was somehow disrupting the inner borders of the circle, and Jennings could sense the spirits' struggles to stay in formation.

The fire raged blue again.

A woman stood on the hearth; she was as transparent and amorphous as the other spirits, but where they shone yellow, she radiated white. Her eyes blazed, and she glared at the demon for a brief second before launching herself toward it.

Its hands lifted to stop her, but she drove it back. The strange trembling of the air ceased, and from every point of contact between the spirit and the demon, black and red sparks flew out in all directions. The ghost-circle grew stronger; its yellow light began to pulse bright gold. The demon seemed unwilling or unable to break through the circle; it jerked away from the spirits' touch as though burned by it.

Delacourt had observed this display with incredulity, but now, realizing that he would likely be obliged to handle matters on his

244

own, he turned on Elizabeth. He noted the glowing ring on her finger, and frowned at it curiously.

"This is your doing," he said, his expression hovering between amusement and irritation. "Your mother has tainted my ring! I cannot imagine how." He stalked toward Elizabeth, who quickly stepped backward, covering her mother's ring with her other hand.

"You?" she cried. "*You* cannot imagine how? You have used magical forces for a hundred years, but you cannot imagine that *good* people might do the same?" Her retreat from Cedric ended when she bumped into the study wall. "All the spirits Christopher has helped – they will stop you!"

Delacourt considered her words. "What I cannot imagine," he said. "Is how your mother's abilities escaped my attention. I could easily have chosen her instead. But perhaps she would only have defied me." He smiled condescendingly. "The two of you are very much alike, after all." He stood inches from her, and brought his face so close to hers that his nose was almost touching her. "But her little army can't truly hurt my demon, and even if it could, I don't really need *him* to get rid of *you*."

Jennings appeared behind Delacourt, and slammed the butt of the blunderbuss into the side of Cedric's head. Cedric dropped to the floor.

"And *I* don't need spirits," Jennings said. "To get rid of *you*."

Cedric's head was bleeding, but he looked up at Jennings with a taunting grin. "I will heal from all your hurts, Jennings," he said, staggering to his feet. "But you will not recover so easily." He lunged forward and grabbed the blunderbuss; the two men stumbled across the study, fighting for control of the gun.

Beside them, the demon still stood in the center of the ghost-circle. The white spirit had disappeared, but the other spirits remained, linked arm-in-arm and shoring up all their strength to keep the demon contained. It spun one way and then the other, its hands lifted to attack, but despite any weakness it may have perceived or attempted to create, it was unable to breach the barrier. Time and again, it charged the circle, only to be thrown back into the center.

Elizabeth gaped first at the circle of spirits, and then at her husband wrestling with Delacourt. The demon was immortal; how would these spirits of the dead be able to hurt it? They more likely would only manage to confine it for a while, and if they did succeed in driving it back to the netherworld, there was surely no way for them – or for anyone – to keep it there. As long as Cedric Delacourt held sway over this demon, it would no doubt stay in this world, performing all the wretched deeds that Delacourt carved out for it.

Elizabeth glared at Delacourt in fury. All that she had suffered had been at his hands! But how could he be stopped? He was much stronger than she, and, as he himself had noted, his injuries would heal in a trice. What sort of weapon could possibly affect such a man? – especially now that Jennings was locked in combat with him, any sustained attack on Cedric would also be an attack on her husband.

"Mother," she called out. "Please! I don't know what to do!"

The white spirit, who had a moment before abandoned her assault on the demon, reappeared now inside the chalk circle; she rose up through the floor to stand floating and translucent, surrounded by the ring of glowing runes. "Elizabeth," she said, her words more like a thought in Elizabeth's head than an actual voice. The spirit reached out for her.

246

"Mother," Elizabeth murmured, and stepped forward. Her feet crossed the runes, and she felt the spirit's arms closing around her. There was a strong smell of roses, and a warmth that Elizabeth had never felt, as though her very soul were being pulled into a loving embrace.

"Elizabeth," the spirit – her mother's spirit – said again. "Our efforts will falter." She put her ghostly hands on either side of Elizabeth's face. "Our strength is built on the foundation of Jonathan's magic, and this rune-spell will wane any moment. Lizzie, you must take your birthright."

Elizabeth frowned in confusion. "What do you mean? What am I meant to do?"

Her mother smiled. "My sweet girl," she said. "You can take Isabelle's place, and command the demon."

Elizabeth's eyes opened wide. Of course, she thought. She stared unblinking at her mother's ghost, then slowly, as though she were in a dream, she bent down and picked up the dagger that Cedric had dropped. Across from her, she saw Delacourt and Jennings still grappling with one another; beside her, the light of the ghost-circle had all but vanished, and only the very slightest remnants of the spirits remained. Their linked arms were fast becoming invisible mist, and the demon's attempts to break the circle were meeting with less and less resistance.

Elizabeth looked once more at her mother. Her mother nodded, and Elizabeth found herself nodding back. She was rather terrified at what she was about to do, but there was nothing for it – it was this course of action or, she feared, all would be lost. She raised the dagger in one shaking hand and, after a pause during which she clenched the dagger tightly, she brought the blade down into the palm of her other hand, driving its point through her flesh. The pain shocked her; she cried out, and jerked the dagger back.

Her blood welled up from the wound and dripped onto the floor.

The runes glowed brightly once more, and the fireplace exploded into aggressive flames. The fire that had spread to the mantel and walls now surged with lightning speed, until half of the study was engulfed. Smoke began to fill the room, and both Cedric and Jennings, taken by surprise, fell away from one another and stumbled quickly back from the fire.

Elizabeth wasted no time on incredulity. "Demon!" she shouted. "Heed me!"

The demon turned to her, its expression quizzical and – although its visage was too strange to be sure – somewhat amused. It stopped rushing the ghost-circle, and the spirits themselves released their grip on each other. The circle broke, and the demon was allowed to walk toward Elizabeth.

"Lizzie!" Jennings cried, but Elizabeth did not answer. Instead she squared her shoulders, and, bringing every conceivable shred of bravery to bear, she faced the demon.

What should she do? she wondered. What sort of birthright had she taken on? What had been her mother's plan? It was too late now to ask her, for the demon stood scarcely two feet away, clearly awaiting instructions. What on earth was she supposed to tell it to do?

Well, she thought. *What do I want it to do?*

She held her bleeding hand out to the demon, who gazed at it for a few seconds before extending its own. Its skin was somehow both scratchy and clammy at the same time, and it was with more revulsion than she had ever felt that Elizabeth took the demon's hand in hers, and pressed her blood into its palm.

"I release you from your bargain with my family," she said.

"No!" Cedric screamed, lunging forward in panic. Jennings grabbed at him, dragging him to his knees.

Both Elizabeth and the demon noted Cedric coldly. "Demon," Elizabeth said, turning her attention once more to the creature whose clawed hand still rested almost amiably in her own. "Take this man who has contracted with you, to whatever judgment he faces. Release the souls of my family, and do not return to this world, or torment any of us any further. In this way, our bargain will be forever ended."

The demon tilted its head to the side. Its voice emerged from its mouth as rancid vapours might escape from a festering grave. "As you wish," it said, and its eyes glinted with what Elizabeth could only describe as humour.

"No!" Cedric bellowed again. He kicked away from Jennings and clambered to his feet, but his knees suddenly failed him, and he fell again. It soon became clear that he was labouring, not only to stand, but even to breathe, and his countenance changed rapidly from outrage to anxiety to dread. "What –?" he gasped, sinking down onto his elbows. "What's happening?"

"Our bargain," the demon announced in a gravelly monotone. "Was thirteen deaths in exchange for immortality for you and your bride, for the duration of our bargain."

"I gave them!" Cedric protested. His skin was turning colours; his breath wheezed in and out with increasing difficulty. "I gave all thirteen!"

"And I gave immortality," the demon replied impassively. "For the duration of our bargain – one hundred fourteen years."

Cedric collapsed entirely. "No," he murmured, his words inaudible over the roar of the fire. "That's not ... not ..." His movements ceased, and his skin grew instantly mottled grey. It wrinkled into blackening parchment that cracked and broke; powder escaped from each fissure, followed by an oozing yellow slime that formed a dank puddle underneath his shrinking corpse.

"Our bargain is ended," the demon said, and let go of Elizabeth's hand. It turned then without any other word or glance, walked unscathed through the spreading flames, and disappeared into the red bowels of the fireplace.

The mist that comprised all that was left of the spirits coalesced around the Jennings. Elizabeth's mother, her form nearly dissolved, manifested just enough to smile at her daughter. "You must leave," she said. "The house will be consumed by both fire and magic. The rain cannot save it."

As if to punctuate her words, the fire raced across the ceiling of the study and dripped down onto the books and furniture. The smoke was now so thick that it burned Elizabeth's eyes and lungs.

"We have to go, Lizzie," Jennings said, putting his arms around his wife.

Coughing, the Jennings hurried from the study and into the kitchen. There they found the servants slowly rousing from their induced sleep. "We have to go!" Jennings told them, and Elizabeth bustled from one of them to the other, pushing them out of their chairs and toward the back door. They were groggy and disoriented, but they had recovered enough to stagger with the Jennings out into the yard.

"What's happening?" a girl asked in consternation. "Where's Miss Isabelle?"

Elizabeth shook her head. "I'm sorry," she said. "Isabelle is already lost."

Behind her, the lake house had transformed into a mountain of fire. As Elizabeth's mother had warned, the driving rain had no effect on the conflagration; whatever magic Cedric Delacourt had commanded had been funneled into the frame of the house, and into this final cleansing act.

The Jennings and the servants rushed to the far side of the stables, and watched in horror and fascination as the lake house turned into ash.

* * *

Despite the steady rain that fell through the night, the fire raged for hours, until nothing was left but the chimneys. It smoldered for many more hours after that, and it was afternoon before the bodies of Charlotte Carlisle, Miss Isabelle Fetherston, and Sir James could be brought out.

The servants and many others from the nearby village discussed amongst themselves that both the fire and the smoke possessed a strange colour and odour, as though fueled by something well outside the usual. They also noted that the body especially of Sir James had been reduced nearly to charred bones, so that he was completely unrecognizable; the two ladies were far less assaulted by the flames, and some who had known Sir James and his acidic personality saw this discrepancy as an indication of his character being suitably

251

brought to task by a higher power.

Of Cedric Delacourt and Edmond Fitzhugh there was no sign. Only Delacourt's and Sir James' rigs were on the property, leading people to speculate that Delacourt had run off with Ned in Ned's carriage, but no one, for all their conversations over the next few days, could offer a reasonable motive for such an amiable man as Delacourt to be capable of murder. If it was Sir James' fortune he was after, then he was the most foolish of men, for now any attempt on his part to claim his inheritance would result in his arrest. People were equally shocked at Fitzhugh's role, for his reputation was solid and good, and the notion that he had had anything to do with this horrid business was seen as almost incomprehensible. But there it was: both men were gone without a trace, and the servants were only too happy to describe Delacourt's strange behaviour earlier in the evening.

"He insisted that we drink with him," the cook explained with a cluck of her tongue. "All of us, even the men in the stable. He said it was part of a grand celebration, and he would not rest until we had taken wine. I had wanted to make a supper for our guests – Mr. Fitzhugh and Sir James were expected at any moment – but Mr. Delacourt would have none of it, and I felt helpless to remonstrate with him." She clucked her tongue again. "I don't remember at all after that until Mrs. Jennings roused me and took me from the house." For this she was most grateful to Mrs. Jennings, and had nothing but praise for her.

Indeed, everyone spoke of Mrs. Jennings with a respect bordering on reverence. Word of her alleged premonition had spread quickly, and it was clear from her mad dash from Northampton that she had done everything within her power to avert calamity. The injuries Delacourt had given her were evident upon her, yet she comported herself with a graceful equanimity that was rightly perceived as the epitome of strength of character. In truth, she had been more concerned for Mr. Jennings' injuries, and for the health and safety of the servants. She said little to anyone, other than to thank them for condoling with her on her grievous loss, and to answer their flabbergasted questions as to Delacourt's possible motive with the simple suggestion that her cousin seemed to have fallen onto the path of dark magic and had viewed the murders as some sort of sacrifice to a dire power.

Such a thing was unheard of, and intriguing enough to keep people talking; soon, gossip had created an image of Delacourt and Fitzhugh that was, surprisingly, very close to the truth that the Jennings had felt it prudent to keep to themselves.

The Jennings put up at the inn down the road from the lake house, or rather from the eerie skeleton of the lake house, and stayed there some days recovering from – as the locals came to call it – the Tragedy. Elizabeth decided wisely to sell the lake house property, and to see the servants safely employed elsewhere. She could not imagine ever wanting to visit the place again.

Her letter to Mrs. Fetherston had filled her with dread; she was sure that Isabelle's mother would blame her for being unable to save her daughter. But in the end, Mrs. Fetherston travelled to the lake house herself, and shared her grief with Elizabeth, whom she regarded with deep gratitude for being, as she said, "the only one of Isabelle's acquaintance who cared enough for her to risk life and limb in such a way, and to put personal differences aside to try to save her."

The two women spent a week together, and Mrs. Fetherston helped Elizabeth contact those who would need to deal with Sir James' estate. "For I cannot want it, ma'am," Elizabeth said emphatically. "I will take some portraits from it, I believe, and I will make sure the servants are well looked after, but I am certain that nothing is in that house that I would care to have." She had, after some consideration, revealed to Mrs. Fetherston the whole truth of Delacourt's identity, and it was therefore with real understanding that Mrs. Fetherston pulled Elizabeth into her arms, and told her that all would be handled however she wished, and that she need never be obliged even to walk past that part of town again.

"But you must promise to be my family, Lizzie," she said, smiling through tears. "Especially now that I understand why Sir James became so cold, I regret abandoning you all those years ago."

"How could you possibly know what he was?" Elizabeth asked her. "Even I did not know, and I lived in the same house with him all my life." She returned Mrs. Fetherston's embrace. "And I am most gratified and fortunate to call you family, ma'am," she averred. "I only wish …" A tear ran down her cheek, and she brushed it away. "I wish I could have saved Isabelle, ma'am! *I* was his target, not she!"

"You saved your whole family, Lizzie," Mrs. Fetherston told her gently. "Your actions removed a curse from us that had been so insidious in its evil that we did not even notice our sacrifices to it." She too wiped away tears. "Of course I wish Isabelle was here. But it was Delacourt who killed her." She took Elizabeth's face in her hands and looked pointedly at her. "Don't forget that, my pet. It was he."

Elizabeth had difficulty heeding these words, but, after some days, she finally allowed that she had done her very best, and had been as resourceful as anyone could ask. It was true enough that she had ended the curse – no more women would be lost for the sake of one selfish man, or for any other reason. For the first time in over a hundred years, her family was safe.

And, at the end of it all, she had been given the opportunity to see her mother, to feel her mother's arms around her and to see the love in her eyes. She had seen and heard a woman who, until that moment, had only been a character in Elizabeth's imagination; who else could make such a claim? She could only count herself fortunate, and to see such an extraordinary occurrence as a sign of divine approbation. Both Jennings and Mrs. Fetherston concurred wholeheartedly with her in this, but it was not until she spoke with Perry that she relinquished her need to feel somehow culpable in Delacourt's crimes.

Perry had been beside himself that he had not brought her to the lake house soon enough to save her father and stepmother; he allowed that the rain and mud were not under his control, and that he was obliged after the crash to focus on Tom, whose injuries needed to be tended to, but he still chided himself that he had not found a better road. Elizabeth would have none of this, and told him in no uncertain terms that he was in no way to blame for anything. "For you know, Perry," she told him somberly. "No matter how strongly I believed that something bad would happen, I cannot think that any of us, not even Mr. Jennings, would have been able to predict such a disastrous outcome as that which awaited us at the lake house." She impulsively reached out and patted his arm. "I am, in fact, monstrously relieved that Tom was not more badly hurt, and that you looked after him and made sure he was well. He will be all mended in a month! – and I had feared that my decision to journey in the rain had gotten him killed!"

She spent some time with Perry, relating to him her immense gratitude for all that he had done, and by the end of the conversation, he seemed somewhat more willing to place blame solely on Mr. Delacourt. It was then that Elizabeth realized that, if she believed her own words to Perry, then she must follow them as well.

"Delacourt is the villain here," she reminded herself, and was even able to appreciate that she had been spared from a great evil, not because of luck or even because of others' fortitude, but because she herself had vanquished it.

She made her way to the little garden behind the inn. Jennings awaited her there; he was sitting on a low stone wall that separated the garden from the road. When he saw Elizabeth, he smiled broadly and held his hand out to her. "I thought you might find your way here, my love," he said. "It is a beautiful morning."

"Indeed it is!" she said, smiling back at him. She took his hand and sat beside him on the wall. "I have just spoken with Perry," she told him. "He was most concerned that somehow he had done something untoward. I hope I have dissuaded him from such a notion."

Jennings chuckled. "It was all I could do," he said. "To convince him that I was not upset with him. Between the unusual haste, the storm, the crash, Tom's broken arm, and your running off on horseback in the middle of the night, poor Perry was sure I was going to execute him!" He shook his head. "But, as I told him more than once, he did exactly as he was supposed to do, and I would not have had it any other way." He looked at her, his eyes twinkling. "I do not like to think what might have happened to me if you had not arrived when you did."

She still smiled, but her eyes were serious. "I was only following your example," she said. "I would have died weeks ago if not for you. You have saved me in every conceivable way."

He raised her hand to his lips. "*I* was saved," he argued. "From a wretched life without you." He grinned, and added, "I am in awe of you, you know. I daresay you could move the course of a river if you put your mind to it, and so I told Perry, when he suggested he should have tried harder to stop you."

Elizabeth, embarrassed by this praise, did not know what to say to it, and sat instead in silence for a moment, her hand cheerfully ensconced in her husband's.

"I wonder," she said at last. "What sort of man my real father was."

"I am sure he would have loved you more than anything," Jennings said.

"I have met my mother," Elizabeth said. "Who has been gone these nineteen years. Perhaps somehow I will meet my father as well." She leaned her head on Jennings' shoulder. "After all that has happened, I begin to feel that anything is possible."

Jennings gazed down at her, and squeezed her hand. "I believe that more every day, my love." He kissed the top of her head. "More every day."

Made in the USA
Middletown, DE
14 October 2021